ALIEN TRIBUTE

A SCI FI WARRIOR ROMANCE

LEE SAVINO
GOLDEN ANGEL

ALIEN TRIBUTE

<Swipe right for abduction>

Who knew that reading sexy alien romances could lead to abduction?

Or that aliens could cure my cancer? Not me. But here I am, the captive bride-to-be for an alien warrior, just like the heroine in the book I was reading in my hospital bed on Earth.

Except the surly warrior who's supposed to claim me **doesn't want a mate.**

Disclaimer: The authors are not responsible for any actual alien abductions that may result as a consequence of your purchase of this book.

PROLOGUE

Pareena

BEEP. *Beep. Beep.* I never thought the hum of hospital machines would become the soundtrack to my life. But the sound, along with the rattle of breath in my chest, tells me I'm alive. The sound is sweet because I won't hear it for much longer.

Hospitals are never quiet. A never-ending stream of doctors, nurses, and food service workers, coming in, checking charts, dropping off food trays and picking them up. The doctors frown. The nurses murmur "how ya doing, honey" and force smiles as they plump my pillows and check my vitals. The food service people don't comment as they pick up the food trays with most of my meal uneaten. I can only manage a few bites a day, another sign that I can measure the rest of my life in minutes and hours versus weeks and years.

I used to be so busy. Used to be one of the white-coat workers hustling past patients' doors. I used to hate being late, hate waiting, hate making small talk. I had so much time, I had the luxury of complaining that I had none.

Now my seconds are measured by the drip, drip, drip of my IV. I have nothing to do but doze or watch silly sitcoms on the tiny TV suspended in the corner of my room. Both early and late to my death, I'm happy to wait. I have nothing left to do but die.

My fingers crawl to the edge of the bed and find the smooth surface of my new best friend—a glossy black e-reader. I don't know who left it on my hospital bed but it's full of stories I'd never let myself read before. The ones I'd avoided at the library—the ones with strong-jawed, shirtless guys on the cover, with bulging muscles, and another bulge straining the front of their tight pants. I was always tempted to read them, but too embarrassed. I was such an elitist coward. I missed so much.

The Tribute rises from the Jabolian pod. Her body is lithe and strong, all the scars from her past are gone. Her skin glows and her hair falls in shining waves past her waist.

Now that's a fantasy. I haven't had hair in a long time. The chemo took everything, including my eyebrows.

Her Tsenturion master stands on the receiving deck to greet her. His suit molds his strong frame, a glittering grey color that reflects his impatience. As his female tribute approaches, the suit glimmers with a silvery sheen. By the time she has walked the long path to stand before him, the silver has turned to gold.

She is a worthy Tribute.

I finish the story and sigh. Becoming a Tsenturion bride sounds great right about now. Fix all my imperfections and heal my disease. Replace the cancer cells with healthy ones.

Throw in a pair of eyebrows, and it'd be worth getting abducted.

I click back to the beginning of the story, ready to read it again, but as I swipe to the first chapter, the e-reader blinks a few times. A new screen appears.

Initiate questioning phase.

New words form onscreen: *Are you Doctor Pareena Singh?*

I jolt awake and glance around the empty hospital room. How did the device learn my name?

The e-reader gives a little chirp as if reminding me to answer the question. *Are you Doctor Pareena Singh?*

I tap "Affirm Identity" and type in my full name and title as prompted. I haven't referred to myself by my title since I stopped working as a psychologist, after the first round of chemo failed. The staff around here don't know I have my doctorate.

It feels good to be recognized. I turn the e-reader over, checking for signs that someone has tampered with it. Whoever sent it to me must have programmed it with my name.

Another question appears on screen. *Do you have children?*

What the hell? That's invasive. I should throw the thing aside in protest. Instead, I hit "No" in a huff. I must be really bored.

Another question pops on the screen. It keeps chirping, so I keep answering.

Over an hour later, I lay back on the pillows, exhausted. I've answered over a hundred questions. They just kept coming—asking about my family, my career, even whether or not I had a cat. It reminded me of a dating site one of my friends got me to join—answer all the questions and they'd match you with your true love. After my diagnosis, I stopped dating. I didn't want to find my true love only to tell him I had a few years to live.

I close my eyes for a moment until the device beeps impatiently. New words swim across the screen.

<Swipe right for abduction>

That's new. The text blinks at me, green.

<Swipe right for abduction>

This has got to be the weirdest computer game ever invented.

<Swipe right for abduction>

Well, what can it hurt? I touch the screen with a finger, pressing lightly to steady it. My hands are bony with veins standing out. They look like they belong to a much older woman.

<Doctor Pareena Singh> My name scrolls across the screen once again. <Swipe right for abduction>

What the hell. I'm stuck in this hospital bed, dying of Stage IV cancer. My e-reader wants me to swipe right to play a stupid game?

I have nothing to lose.

I place a trembling finger on the screen. The e-reader gives an encouraging chirp as I slowly slide my finger to the right. The screen starts to glow.

Is something happening to my eyes now? The doctors didn't say anything about my eyes possibly being affected, but I'm not sure that means anything. They don't tell me a lot of things these days if they don't think I need to know.

I can't tear my eyes away to find the call button for the nurse though... it's like the screen is fracturing into rainbows, filling my vision... and it's beautiful. Something tugs at me, pulling at my body.

Am I finally dying? Is this the light that I'm supposed to go toward?

I open my mouth to call for help—I'm not ready!—but there's no air and suddenly it feels like there are tight bands around my chest, pulling me towards the light. Tears slide down my cheeks in despair. I'd hoped to come to accept my death but now I have no choice.

Rings of light burst ahead of me as the darkness closes in. Pain, which thankfully feels distant because of the morphine, swirls as I shatter apart.

My last thought is mournful.

I'm not ready.

1

P areena

I DON'T HURT.

That is my first thought. A thought filled with as much awe as relief, because I didn't expect to wake up at all. My momentary joy at waking is tempered by the knowledge that my time is almost up. At some point I need to move past the stage of depression and into acceptance that my life is ending, because it's obviously coming sooner rather than later.

"Greetings, Pareena Singh."

The unfamiliar voice and formal greeting make me sigh. Great, another doctor. I open my eyes to see who I get to deal with now. Then I frown, because I must be dreaming. Not only am I no longer in my hospital room and the man in front of me looks *wrong* somehow, like he's CGI and not a real person, but I'm seeing everything through heavy eyelashes. That's happened in my dreams sometimes, where I think my hair has returned. I reach up and, sure enough, there's thick, soft hair covering my entire head.

Tears spark in my eyes as I pull it forward to see the thick, glossy strands. They feel so real. *Look* so real. This is probably the most vivid dream I've ever had. Hm. I wonder if I'm in a coma. Do people in comas dream? Technically I have my doctorate, but becoming a psychologist didn't make me an expert on people in comas.

"Pareena Singh, why are you leaking?"

"Leaking?" I ask, looking up at the not-man. He gestures at my face, his movement awkward, as if he's not used to using his hand. I reach up to touch my cheeks and feel the wetness of tears as they overflow from my eyes. I hadn't even realized I was crying. "These are tears. I'm just... sad. I miss my hair so much and this feels so real."

"It is real," he says seriously. And then he starts telling me the most fantastical things I've ever heard. His name is Frllil and he's a Jabol Luminary, in charge of finding females for an alien race—and, of course, human females are the only compatible beings.

The last trilogy I read, the Tsenturion Masters trilogy, is, according to him, based on reality and I've been selected as a Tsenturion Tribute. I've been cured of my cancer and my body has been not only restored to prime health, but actually enhanced so that I will never have to worry about cancer—or any other illnesses—ever again, and my life expectancy has been expanded exponentially. That I will be trained, 'primed,' and then presented to my new master.

For a coma dream, it's pretty detailed. I haven't ever really thought of myself as the imaginative sort, but being trapped in a hospital room with no visitors for weeks on end has apparently sparked something in my brain. The desperation to get out of my situation, perhaps, or some kind of delusional wish fulfillment.

To be truthful, I'm not really into self-examination right now.

Yes, I know that some part of my brain has conjured this outlandish scenario, that I'm pretty much out of my gourd. But I can't stop touching my hair.

Is this real? Or has this been happening inside my head?

Of course it is happening inside your head, Harry, but why on earth should that mean it is not real?

For a crazy old man, sometimes Dumbledore did make sense. Does it matter that this isn't real? It feels real. My hair, which my fingers are continuously running through, feels real. The lack of pain feels real. Why not enjoy this dream while I can? Eventually, I will wake up and be thrust back into the awful reality of my current existence... or maybe I'll never wake up at all. Neither option is appealing. Even my subconscious thinks so, or else I wouldn't be dreaming about alien abduction.

For the first time in my life, I decide to follow the advice I gave so many of my patients and just go with the flow, for as long as it lasts.

"Okay," I say. "I'm a Tribute... so now what?"

Frllil is watching me with an air of anxious wariness, and I'm kind of getting used to his odd appearance, but it's still creepy when he smiles widely. It's so close to approximating a real, human smile, but the fact that it's so close somehow makes it more unsettling rather than less. It's the Uncanny Valley effect, but knowing that doesn't make it less strange.

"I must say, you're taking this a lot better than the last Tribute," he says, sounding very relieved.

Other Tributes—very interesting. Although, I suppose it

only makes sense that my brain has included other humans in this dream. I'm very tired of being alone, after all. My subconscious apparently doesn't want me alone in any manner, even in a dream. I'm not sad about it.

"Is there any way to escape?" I ask, because it seems like he expects me to.

Frllil shakes his head. His expression doesn't change—he isn't sorry. If anything, he looks pleased. "There is no way for you to access the wormhole you came through, and a return trip would be inadvisable, even with the improvements I've made to your physical form."

I shrug. "Then resistance is futile. So, what comes next?"

"Now we begin your training."

Bogdan

BLACK SPACE STRETCHES BEFORE ME. I grip the sides of the command chair, willing my expression blank. But nothing hides my mood. My suit is as dark as the empty quadrant.

"Scan complete," Science officer Kalexston reports. "No signs of the enemy."

I glare at him for announcing the obvious. He ducks his head to study his screens. "Shall I scan again?"

"No. Officer Zakhar, take us on a patrol pass."

"Yes, Commander," Zakhar snaps to attention.

I am failing everyone counting on me.

Again.

The feeling is far too familiar, but it never becomes easier to bear.

High Commander Gavrill, the leader of our entire fleet

—which makes him the leader of our entire race, since we are all that is left of it—put his faith in me to lead our warriors in his stead while he is distracted by his Tribute. I also failed at convincing him and the others that we aren't ready for Tributes. In my defense, I had not really thought the Jabol would be able to procure acceptable substitutes for Tsenturion females.

But they found a planet, currently accessible only through an unstable wormhole, on which there are many suitable females.

The thought strikes fear in my heart, although it is unlikely that the Vgotha would be able to mount an attack on that planet. While they know about the High Commander's Tribute, they do not know the location of the wormhole or the planet. Even we do not know it, only the Jabol involved in procuring them do. It is safer that way.

The bridge door slides open and a tall warrior marches towards me. I rise.

"Arkdhem, reporting for duty," the third in command salutes with a fist to his chest. He is a hand taller than me, but I am broader, with more muscle. Sometimes he wears extra battle spurs about his shoulders to make him seem bigger, but I know his true size.

"Commander," I glance at my screen. "You are not due for duty until later."

"I volunteered for a double shift." Most see Arkdhem as a pleasant, jovial sort. I know better. There's a reason he has risen so high in the ranks.

"Where is High Commander Gavrill?" I question, even though I can guess.

"With his Tribute. He and Dawn are celebrating ten semicycles since her abduction and return."

In the corner of my eye, Kalexston's suit lightens to a

happy blush. A color that should never reveal itself on a warrior. "Has it been ten already?" he exclaims. "Truly a cause for celebration."

"Will they accept gifts?" Zakhar asks. His suit is light red. Another idiot.

"I don't know, but a visit would not be amiss. Perhaps at mealtime," Arkdhem says. The rest of the bridge breaks out in exclamations of intent to visit the Tribute and express their congratulations.

My fists clench at my sides. Fools, all of them.

"Perhaps if you have so much time to waste, you all should pull double duties," I bark, and the discussion quiets to a murmur. Arkdhem raises a brow at me. He knows better than to smile. I would beat his face off.

My fellow warriors are excited by the news of Tributes. They want more of them to come *now*, before we've even eradicated the Vgotha threat. Fortunately, the procurement process is both long and difficult. Made even more so by the High Commander's Tribute, Dawn. She insisted the protocol for selecting the tributes be adjusted, so that the women of Earth are given as much of a choice as can be provided to them. A choice which she feels was denied to her, although she is happy enough under the circumstances.

All the while, we are not given a choice about whether or not we even want Tributes on the ship with us. The Jabol provided Tribute Dawn to the High Commander on their timeline, not ours. Already she's proven to be a liability. We had one of the Vgotha ships within our sights when she was kidnapped. She managed to escape in one of their small pods, but then insisted it be released back into space so we could follow it. She said the pod—and the Vgotha ship she'd been taken to—were actually sentient, and allowed her to escape.

The pod disappeared, leaving us none-the-wiser about where the Vgotha have vanished to this time or why their 'sentient' ship might have assisted her.

The High Commander was too relieved to have her back and fully bonded to him to be able to focus on the Vgotha's disappearance. That duty has fallen to me, as his second-in-command, and I am *failing*.

I do not understand how they could have disappeared so completely.

We've been hunting the Vgotha for tsencycles and what Tribute Dawn described is technology like they've never had before. Where did it come from? When did they upgrade their ships? Who would have helped them?

So many questions and more. Over a thousand Tsenturion warriors depending on me. The High Commander relying on me.

When I reach my quarters, my suit retracts automatically. I rub my head, wishing I could remain on duty forever, and never sleep. Never remove my helmet.

There are times when I find myself wishing I had resigned my commission earlier. That I hadn't taken that last trip. Because then I would have been on Tsentur when the Vgotha destroyed it. I have no death wish, but the burden of living has become endless and with the addition of Tribute Dawn we have both hope for the future and an even higher burden.

She is another innocent life, another responsibility to bear. Adding more Tributes to our population will only increase the onus of keeping our small fleet safe from attack. Before, if the Vgotha had killed us, our mission of vengeance would have ceased, but we are all willing volunteers to the cause. We are all Tsenturion warriors, ready to lay down our lives in battle. The Tributes will be neither.

I march to my private console and scroll to a view of the solar system nearby, directing the unit to scan it for Vgotha signatures. A small gesture but at least it's something. I cannot sit in my quarters and do nothing.

I do not like to think about what would have happened if Tribute Dawn had not escaped from the Vgotha's clutches. The pain the High Commander would have felt... I know it too well. It is not a pain I would wish upon anyone. The only one who has a semblance of understanding is Medik, but his grief is so far beyond my own that I cannot fathom how he has remained sane. In some ways, he has taken all the remaining warriors under his wing and become our communal mentor, a replacement for our lost parents, but I have not been able to agree with him when it comes to the Tributes.

He sees them as our future's hope, but the truth is, they are just another thing we could lose.

2

Pareena

I HATE FRLLIL.

I hate my training.

I definitely hate my 'Bride Trainer.'

I hate my brain.

If this is some kind of subconscious attempt to prepare myself for death... well, it's almost working. Because after days of training, which apparently means a *lot* of sexual arousal but no actual culmination, I am ready to do something drastic. Unfortunately, being a Tribute also means that I no longer have any control over my own body. It was far more fun reading about it than it is experiencing it, even in a dream. Whenever Frllil's not looking, I claw at the Bride Trainer he's put on me.

The Bride Trainer is a belt that goes around my waist and down between my legs, covering my pussy completely and splitting my buttocks like a thong. It's surprisingly comfortable when it's not driving me mad. When I stroke it, it feels like regular cloth but trying to break through it... well, I might as well be trying to tear apart steel. It's pliable, fitting to my shape exactly. Too exactly. I can't even wedge a finger between the thing and my pussy.

Frllil says its nanotechnology. The damn thing even cleans itself and me, after opening *just* enough for me to go to the bathroom but not enough for me to ever touch myself.

Supposedly my Tsenturion warrior will be able to control it with his mind, which is when it will finally be removed so that he can claim me. Which sounds hot, in theory, but it's not in reality. Well, in my dream-reality. Mostly it's so frustrating that I'm beginning to feel murderous.

It's *my* dream, I should be able to get it off and play with myself if I want to. The sexual frustration feels very real.

The fact that I haven't been successful makes me wonder if this is maybe an internal metaphor for my cancer. Just another instance in which I have a complete lack of control over a situation's outcome.

How very frustrating.

According to Frllil, this is exactly what being 'primed' is supposed to do. I'm plenty primed. I'm so primed that I couldn't possibly *get* more primed. I'm ready to climb the walls I'm so primed.

Frllil promises that I'll be able to climax when I'm finally given to my Tsenturion Master.

Bogdan.

A large part of my 'training' involves staring at photos of the alien male while being aroused by the vibrations through my training belt. Alien, but attractive. I'm pretty sure I'd be aroused even without the belt. Square shoulders, square jaw, he looks like a battering ram come to life. Alien, but attractive. Golden skin. Actual metallic golden skin. Not much of it is visible underneath the armor that covers his entire body though.

The armor changes color according to their mood, supposedly, but in every vid and photo Frllil has shown me of Bogdan, his armor remains resolutely black. I do catch flashes of color from the others around him, although I never see their faces. They're unimportant apparently; it is only Bogdan who matters, Bogdan who is going to be my world.

Right now, as long as I get off, that doesn't sound like too bad of a deal. Lurking in the back of my mind is the fear that I'll never get off again, that at some point this dream will end when I die... perhaps when I'm taken off of life support. I have such a weird imagination. I've accepted the fact that yes, I *am* dying, or already have. This is one long hallucination of the book I was reading. Pure deathbed fantasy. How do I know? I have eyebrows again and they look amazing.

But did I have to imagine so much orgasm denial?

Then again, I can't deny that it's working. Staring at the hot alien my mind has conjured up is a welcome distraction from my reality.

Who can worry about death when a vibrator is tormenting them while they're staring at what looks like six and a half, maybe seven, feet of pure muscle?

No wonder the Jabols hired the Tsenturions to be their muscle. The Tsenturions are so buff, when the time came for evolution to hand out muscle to the Jabols there was none left. Frllil is just an amorphous blob that can form into any shape at will. While he tries to hold his humanoid shape, he often 'ripples' in a way that makes my stomach churn. He changes more rapidly when he's excited.

Why my subconscious has conjured up such a strange being, I'm not sure but there must be some reason for it.

"Pareena, you will pay attention," Frllil chirps. He points at yet another vid of Bogdan. My pussy clenches and I want to scream because I already know it's going nowhere.

"Dr. Singh," I mutter, frustrated beyond belief with both him and the training.

The Jabol quivers around the edges of his form. "Explain."

"My name is Pareena Singh, and when I earned my PhD, 'doctor' became my title. You're pissing me off, so you don't get to use my first name anymore." Normally I'm not such a hard ass but my pussy is throbbing, and I want to cum!

Frllil gives a little trill. He's such a pill. He needs to chill.

Great, now I'm rhyming. I recognize the distraction technique and wish it worked a little better.

"I am using your first name to engender goodwill. I was instructed to do this by one of your species."

"The state I'm in, you're not engendering anything. And what do you mean, 'one of my species?'"

"Another hu-man," Frllil's pronunciation of the word is still odd, no matter how I've tried to help him. "Dawn Cahill. She was the first Tribute, you are the second. She instructed me in the proper way to address Tributes. After a certain period of time, we have become familiar and it is correct to use only your first name."

Well that explains why he finally stopped calling me 'Pareena Singh', but it doesn't help my frustration in any way. He's sexually torturing me, and I'm not even attracted to him.

I narrow my eyes at him, because I think he actually

sounds a little petulant. Frllil is so often completely unemotional, but apparently the name thing is important to him in some way.

"Yeah? Well I'm going to start calling you He-Who-Must-Not-Be-Named if you don't help me out." The noise he makes is definitely unhappy and I hide my smile. "But you can use my first name if you get this thing off me." I rap my Trainer hard, but I can't even feel it through the tech.

"Your Trainer can only be removed by your Tsenturion Master," Frllil sounds both reproachful and frustrated at repeating himself again. Well, join the club. "I have explained this."

"Pretty sure I'm going to die first," I mutter. Because I'm well past 'primed' and yet there's no sexy alien in sight.

"You are not dying, Pareena. Your system was in a state of shut down when you first came through the *direth* wormhole, but your health functions have been restored." As usual, Frllil takes my statement completely at its word.

"I know, I know," I rub my face, feeling my eyebrows and then run my hands back up through my hair, luxuriating in the silky strands sliding through my fingers. While I want to scream at him, there's no point. This is all a coma dream, right? So I'd just be yelling at myself. And I already know from my days of training that Frllil is easily confused by my emotions. He's pure logic. Thanks, whatever part of my brain conjured him up. "I'm just really, really, really ready to meet Bogdan."

Meeting Bogdan, aka, getting my orgasm.

"Your Master," Frllil reminds me sternly.

"My Master." I sigh but try to be agreeable. I'm no stranger to BDSM. I visited a munch or two and went to a few parties as a submissive. I'm not surprised by this aspect of my dream.

Orgasm control and denial can be a big part of BDSM. I didn't think it was one of my fantasies, but it must be for my brain to have dug it up. The only other option is that all of this is real, which, of course, is impossible.

Therefore, some part of me must have been interested in it. A really, really stupid part of me that didn't think through how awful being teased and denied an orgasm for days would be.

Or maybe I've already died and gone to hell.

My hand drifts upwards to my hair, stroking the long strands. My hair has become a comfort object. And I can't imagine that I would have my hair in hell. No, if anything, the return of my hair confirms that this is a formulation from my imagination.

~

Bogdan

I AM NOT surprised when my presence is requested on the bridge even though I am off duty. It is a normal enough occurrence.

I *am* surprised when I walk through the door to find the High Commander there, an actual smile on his face, and his Tribute by his side, on her collar and leash. The long dress she is clothed in would not be out of place on a Tsenturion bride. To our collective surprise, somehow the pair fully bonded in the manner of our people and her dress shows off the mating mark she now bears.

I thought for sure they would not be leaving the High Commander's quarters during this time of rest they are taking. If it weren't for the gold color of the High Commander's armor and his expression, I would be alarmed, assuming his unexpected presence indicated another unexpected Vgotha encounter.

That cannot be the case, though, and I do not know what else could have lured him and Tribute Dawn from his chambers.

"Commander." I come to a halt in front of him, my fist clenched in salute.

Something about the way Tribute Dawn is beaming at me makes me uneasy. While we have reached an understanding in interacting with each other, I have never seen her look so happy to see me. It is unsettling.

The other warriors on the bridge are staring with curiosity and it is obvious they have no knowledge of why the High Commander is present either. Which does not reassure me.

"Bogdan." He greets me with a nod, his suit turning brighter gold with a quick streak of something else through it. Ever since his mating with Tribute Dawn, his control over his emotional indicators has been affected. Or perhaps he just no longer cares. "I am pleased to inform you that your Tribute has been selected and her training is almost complete."

"*What*?!" I'm not the only one to practically shout the word, across the room, Arkdhem is now on his feet, his suit flashing red and orange with rioting emotions, the dominant one being envy, before settling to black. My own suit barely flickers, but I feel the emotions sticking in my chest, behind the wall of ice where I keep them. When the High Commander claimed Tribute Dawn, he'd said I would be next, but I had dismissed his words as a mere threat or perhaps even a jest. The Jabol chose the matches, not him.

"And she's the perfect candidate!" Dawn says clapping

her hands happily while I stare at her. She has been my only ally against the procurement of more Tributes for some time, even though she's been helping Medik, the fleet's doctor, refine the selection program. I always assumed she was undermining it, as she was so outspoken against taking more human women from their home planet. To see her celebration of this shocking news feels like a betrayal. "Not only did she have almost no emotional attachments to Earth, but she was dying. We saved her life by taking her!"

This time my suit does flicker, too quickly for anyone to see the color, which is well enough. I cannot identify the emotion that stabbed through me so quickly and viscerally. But I am not unaffected at hearing that the woman would have died without the intervention of the Jabol.

Still... why must she be *my* Tribute?

"Why him?" Arkdhem nearly shouts the question. Although his armor is now a controlled black, his fists are clenched by his sides, and I do not think I imagine the frustration seething in his eyes. He is one of the biggest supporters of the program. "He doesn't even want a Tribute! He is not fit for one. Why not one of us?" He gestures to the rest of the bridge, but it is clear he really means himself.

I draw myself up. While I might not desire a Tribute, I will not let Arkdhem impugn my worthiness either. I have my pride.

"A Tribute for you?" I ask. My disdain does not need to be broadcast by my armor, as it is clear in my voice. "As what, a reward for allowing the High Commander's Tribute be captured?"

Red streaks through the black of his armor, shaded with the bright yellow of his shame. He takes a step toward me, the promise of violence in his eyes. If he wishes to fight, I will not deny him. In fact, I find myself eager to take out my own frustration on him.

"Bogdan! Arkdhem!" The Commander barks out our names and Arkdhem comes to a halt, still glaring at me. I turn back to the Commander and Tribute Dawn, ignoring the other warrior. My move can be construed one of two ways—either that I trust him not to attack when the Commander is watching, or that I do not consider him a threat, and therefore do not care that my back is to him. I don't care which way he takes it, but I hope it's the second.

Tribute Dawn gives Arkdhem a sympathetic look before focusing on me. The expression on her face is far less friendly now. This does not bother me as I do not wish to be friends. I wish to be left alone.

I stare at High Commander Gavrill rather than meet her gaze, knowing that I am not as immune to her pout as I wish. However, I will never reveal my weakness, and that is the difference between Arkdhem and me.

"The Jabol matched Tribute Pareena Singh with Bogdan," the Commander says, sweeping his gaze around the bridge as if daring anyone to contradict him. "It is a near perfect personality match, according to them." His eyes meet mine. Any hope that the Tribute might be bestowed upon a different warrior dies with his words. "You will prepare for your Tribute and fulfill your duty. Her file has been sent to you. I recommend that you read the provided manuals."

Because he knows that I am one of the few Tsenturions who hasn't touched the manuals. When the Commander and Tribute Dawn had bonded in the Tsenturion manner and it was announced that more Tributes were to come, I was the only one not to request the manuals.

I can feel the weighty stares of the rest of the crew, feel their collective wish that they were the ones receiving a

Tribute. Arkdhem's envy I do not mind, but I do not want the others to think I am wasting a gift many of them long for. I know how to do my duty.

I will not allow her to distract me from the rest of my duties. I will learn from the manuals and I will train her as quickly and efficiently as possible so that she is well behaved and out of the way until the Vgotha threat is taken care of. And perhaps when the Vgotha are gone, I will no longer ache with loss and I will be able to set down this heavy burden of justice, and truly bond with my Tribute.

Until then, at least I will receive some enjoyment from watching Arkdhem writhe with jealousy.

"Of course, High Commander," I say formally, with another salute.

3

Bogdan

ACCEPTING the congratulations of my fellow warriors, all of whom now look at me with the hope that they will one day be in my position, rankles. I leave the bridge with as much dignity as I can and return to my quarters.

While part of me wants to dwell and seethe, I do not have much time. As with Tribute Dawn, the Jabol did not inform us of my Tribute until she was nearly ready for me. Like us, they do not accept failure lightly, so they do not announce they have something until they are sure that they do. Which means Frllil is very certain that Tribute Pareena is ready.

Ready for me.

Something tightens my throat, an emotion I'm not willing to acknowledge, much less put a name to.

I will not be weak.

I will not fail.

Accessing her file, I push away everything that threatens my composure and make myself focus on my new assignment. That's all she is. I read about her life, finding myself strangely fascinated. She is a strong female. I cannot regret that her life is saved by becoming a Tribute. Perhaps her strength is why the Jabol decided we are a near perfect match. I am strong for my kin and she has been strong for hers as well as for herself.

She will need such strength.

I am relieved as I read through the file. Nothing about Pareena reminds me of *her*.

There is still time before my sleep cycle, so I begin to read the courtship manuals. High Commander Gavrill claimed that human courtship rituals are not so different from our own, but I will be thoroughly versed by the time my Tribute arrives. If they are similar enough, then she should be no trouble, but where they differ, I already know I will rely more on Tsenturion rituals.

She is to be a Tsenturion tribute, after all; her old life will be over and gone.

We will have that in common, at least.

"How are you, Bogdan? Are you prepared for the arrival of your Tribute?" The sneering question comes from Arkdhem a few daycycles later when we are at a meal, his tone implying that I am neglecting my duty. I glare at him. The only joy I have is knowing he wants a Tribute beyond anything, and he must wait. As I study him, his suit darkens slightly, a sign of the envy he was attempting to keep hidden.

Foolish male.

The lack of control over his emotions proves he is not ready for one. While he might want one more than I, I doubt his ability to master a Tribute. Especially having witnessed how he lets Tribute Dawn do what she pleases when he is her escort.

"I have nothing to prepare. My quarters are adequate. She is the one who must be prepared for me." The courtship manuals have reassured me of my role in the relationship. I will establish dominance and gain her submission and loyalty, and she will be the perfect Tribute, serving me in every way. The manuals describe how human females are capable of more emotional relationship and bonding, but I see no need to enter into a deep connection with my Tribute unless it is necessary for breeding. Even breeding feels a betrayal, but the chance to continue our race cannot be denied.

Arkdhem stares at me, anger flickering through his armor. For a moment, I tense, expecting a blow. He and I have fought before, but not recently. Arkdhem prefers to hide behind his jokes and smiles, while plotting his true intent. He is a smooth edge, while I am rough. No doubt a Tribute would prefer him to me, but it would likely be to her detriment.

"The Jabol are generous," I say. I do not need to taunt him outright. My words are enough to invoke his ire. "They have sent me copious footage of her training. I haven't had the time to view them yet, but perhaps you would review them and see for yourself how prepared she is for me?"

Arkdhem's suit darkens further. "Is that an order?"

I would not actually trust *any* warrior with intimate viewings of my future mate. Even as I think the words without inflection, pain flickers through me. I will not consider Tribute Pareena a mate, not a real one. Even so, she should not be subject to another male's gaze, especially of her special training to accept me as master. To share the recordings would be discourteous.

I ignore the part of me that feels possessiveness at the idea of Arkdhem viewing her training. I am merely possessive about her because it is my duty. It has nothing to do with her. I don't even know her.

Arkdhem meets my gaze with his own blank one. In the next moment, he smiles, and I realize I have been silent too long, withholding my answer. "It would be my pleasure to assist you with your Tribute in any way you wish. Is the footage stored on your personal console? I will access it, if you give me the code."

"No," I bite out. "That won't be necessary. No one need see the Tribute but me. I will do my duty by reviewing them myself."

Looking suspiciously like he wants to laugh, Arkdhem salutes me again and takes my spot on the bridge.

Drakk. I told myself I wouldn't care about my Tribute, but I have already broken this vow. If my suit turns any darker, it'll become a black hole.

MY MOOD DOES NOT CHANGE as I march to my quarters. On the lift from the bridge, Officer Borodem falls into step with me. As soon as the door closes, he turns. "If I may offer my congratulations, Commander, on procuring a Tribute—"

"You may not," I cut him off, as I have begun doing when congratulations are offered. The other warriors need to see a Tribute for what she is—not a prize or a reward, but another thing to protect, a living burden aboard our ship. "It is my duty."

"It is not merely a duty," the fool exclaims. Spines rise on my suit and he reconsiders. "Would that we all had such a duty." He moves away from me, finally recognizing my need for solitude.

I close my eyes and remind myself that most of my fellow warriors had no expectations for the last Mating Festival. They lost their families and friends in the Great Tragedy, as did we all, but they had not begun to make plans beyond the next mission.

My next mission had been to make a family. To be with *her*. And then it was all gone. *She* was gone, along with our plans, our future, our world. But I went on.

They know this, but they do not understand.

They do not realize what it feels like to have to replace the one I could not save.

Pareena

PRESENTATION DAY IS HERE. Finally. Frllil is more jiggly than normal. A sign of his nervousness? Why he should be nervous, I don't know. I'm the one having a coma dream which involves being thrust into the unknown. Despite all the training I've done, I feel completely unprepared.

That this entire sequence of events is a clear metaphor for death that my brain has conjured up does not escape me.

I'm gonna miss his weird face. Is it because I'm actually going to miss him or because I'm worried that the next step in this sequence of events is actually my death? Orgasm is known as the 'little death' after all. If I wasn't dying, I could have a field day writing a paper about all of this... if I could concentrate.

I'm a bit more distracted than usual. I had no idea I had so many fantasies about orgasm denial. I followed a few femdenial accounts on the Tumblr account I use for porn, but it wasn't my main kink. Nothing to warrant days of edging. I'm starting to think the Cruciatus Curse would be easier to bear.

I'm not quite ready to face Avada Kedavra yet though.

I really don't want to leave Frllil.

But what if I'm not about to die? What if I'm actually just continuing the dream, which was heavily affected by the books I was reading before I fell into this coma? In which case, what's about to happen might be really fantastic. I sincerely hope it's the latter. I want to see Bogdan and run my hands all over him and have fantastic sex and orgasms before I die.

Or maybe I'm already dead. Frllil was purgatory and now I'm headed to heaven.

I'm not Catholic, or Christian, or even Hindu like my parents, in fact I always considered myself an atheist, but the analogy is too on point to ignore.

Either way, it will all be over soon. I smooth the front of my gown nervously. This is the most attractive I've looked since I started chemo. My hair spills over my shoulders in shining waves, the nearly see-through dress clings to my curves, the dark red color setting off my coloring nicely. I feel pretty. Feminine. And I still get a thrill of happiness whenever I touch my hair.

"Now remember the process of the ceremony," Frllil flutters beside me, pushing me into the pod even as he tries to dish out last minute instructions. "Your role—"

"Is to leave the pod and walk down the row of warriors to my Master. Then Dumbledore places the Sorting Hat on my head, and I think *Ravenclaw* really hard—"

"What?" Frllil's platform zooms in front of me. His whole mass quivers in upset. Jabol, I've discovered, don't exactly have a sense of humor. And despite using books as a lure for women, they don't really understand fiction either. Trying to explain Harry Potter to him went over as well as him trying to explain how nanotechnology worked to me.

"Relax." I sigh. "It was a joke. I walk up to my Master and he'll begin the process of bonding our nanotech." Which Frllil hasn't really explained what that means other than we will 'touch' in a ceremonial manner and the bond will initiate.

"This is very important, Pareena Singh." Back to first and last names. I stifle a groan. "You must—"

"I know. I'm ready. I'll miss you, though," I say honestly. In a weird way, despite the training, we did bond. I'd say we're both Ravenclaws. We both want all the information and facts we can get our hands on. "You did a great job of easing the transition." I know that's the compliment he'll appreciate the most.

"Thank you, Tribute Pareena." Frllil puffs up happily. "It has been a pleasure to train you. I believe the process was much easier this time, in large part due to your attitude." This is not the first time he's referenced how difficult the previous Tribute was, and I can't help but be amused. Apparently, even in my head, I feel the need to excel in an imaginary comparison. Extending a tendril, Frllil waves as I step into the pod and lie down. The door swishes shut, cutting off the view of him on his platform.

I can feel the subtle hum of vibrations shift. The pod is

moving. Supposedly it will only take minutes for me to reach my destination.

But minutes can feel like hours when you aren't sure what's going to happen next. Am I going to reach the next step I read about? Or is this my end?

I got this. I can do this.

Lots of positive self-talk. That was something I always advised my clients to use. Affirmations can be incredibly useful in developing a positive mental attitude.

Whatever happens next, I can handle it.

I almost start to believe it until the pod's vibrations change again. My jaw clenches shut in reaction as fear blooms in my chest. I'm here. Wherever here is. Before I can completely psych myself out, the pod opens to a large atrium. From the curved lines of the walls, I can only assume I'm in the belly of one of the big Tsenturion ships. Probably the Command Ship, a part of my brain supplies, since that's where Bogdan is supposed to be stationed.

Ranks of Tsenturions in full battle armor line my view, staring at me, waiting for me to make my next move. Right.

I can do this.

Pushing back my fear I step out of the pod and they snap to attention. Turning my head back and forth, I look over them. At the back of their ranks is a small raised platform with a gangplank leading up to it. It's exactly what Frllil described the ceremony would look like. Maybe that's the reason for the orgasm denial. If I wasn't desperate to climax, I'm not sure I'd have the courage to take that next step. Not with all these massive, intimidating males staring at me.

As if responding to my thoughts, the Bride Trainer whirs to life, like it's encouraging me to get moving. So, I take that first step. And then another.

The closer I get, the more my Bride Trainer vibrates. My

body flushes, my knees trembling with need. I move faster, like an arrow seeking out my target.

There are five figures on the gangplank. Three are giant warriors in glittering armor. Frllil schooled me on the armor colors. Two of the warriors wear a neutral navy. The one in the middle is in shiny black. Could it be—

The Bride Trainer hits max power and I almost misstep. Fisting the folds of my dress, I force myself to walk slower, even though every nerve ending in my pussy is screaming at me to pick up the pace. Falling on my face wouldn't be a good first impression. Not that the Trainer is making it easy for me. I can feel the hot blush in my cheeks as the silky material of my dress rubs against my nipples and the heat between my legs becomes unbearable.

I stare up at my new master, his features much clearer now that I'm nearly to him.

Bogdan looks the same as he did in the training videos. Seven feet of pure muscle. Suit armor black as night. A lighter color flashes over the dark surface as I watch, too fast for me to register. Under his helmet, his jaw is set as he stares into the distance. Another alien warrior nudges him, and Bogdan glowers at the other warrior before transferring his foreboding gaze to me.

His expression is far from happy. In all the footage I watched of him, he is never smiling. I thought it was because he's an intense type of person, the type who becomes annoyed when you try to make small talk at work. He's been on duty for a millennia ever since his planet was destroyed. That's a ton of trauma right there. How do you deal with your entire species getting wiped out? Have these guys really dealt with their feelings about—

No. I mentally smack myself. Rule number one of sexual

fantasies: do *not* psychoanalyze the imaginary aliens. Not what I'm here for. I'm here for an orgasm.

I'm too aroused to think clearly anyway. And I can't take my eyes off Bogdan. Master. My new Master. All of this is so formal. High protocol. I never got into the pomp and ceremony of BDSM before. Guess this is my chance to try it.

Thanks, brain.

I raise my chin and meet Bogdan's gaze. His face is blank. I'm almost to the gangplank, close enough to see when he looks me up and down. Nothing, not even a flicker of interest. Does he not like what he sees?

My hands automatically go to my hair, stroking a long strand that's settled over my shoulder for comfort. It's like a security blanket. *This isn't real. It's your fantasy. Of course, he likes what he sees, otherwise why would your subconscious have created him? You control this, if you want him to smile then make him smile!*

The warrior beside him nudges him again and he moves to the head of the gangplank, glowering in no particular direction.

And wow does he have a major glower, the kind that makes me want to drop to my knees to avoid it. All right then. I've fantasized about a strict dominant Master who will fulfill all my sexy fantasies, and my subconscious delivered. I can deal with this.

I hope he lets me orgasm soon. I mean, I hope I let me orgasm soon. This whole thing feels so real it's becoming more and more difficult to remember it's not, especially when things don't go to the way I want them to.

I climb the gangplank and stop in front of the giant warrior. With a smooth sweep of my arms, I spread my gown and dip my knees like I've practiced. It's not quite like a curtsy on Earth, at least not like one I've ever seen. My feet are together, and my knees bend forward. The Tsenturion version of a curtsy I suppose. Three, two, one, then I straighten but keep my gaze on the ground as the Bride Trainer's vibrations swell between my legs.

My part is done. I sway a little. *Just don't pass out.* I'm so close to orgasming I can almost taste it.

Bogdan hasn't moved, but I can feel his gaze on me. I lean towards him. My salvation. The Giver of Orgasms. At least, I really hope he is.

The tallest of the group steps forward and Bodgan salutes him.

"Commander Bogdan, as High Commander of the Tsenturion fleet, I present your Tribute."

I startle as the ranks behind me break out into a shouted chant. The huge room rings as over a thousand hands hit their armored chests in salute. The tall warrior—the High Commander—nods and steps back, reaching down to draw a small figure forward with a flutter of colorful robes.

There's a human on the deck with us. Blonde and draped in a flowy gown like mine, she's wearing a small smile. When I glance at her, she winks.

This must be Dawn, the first Tribute. Huh. She doesn't look like she could possibly have given Frllil as much trouble as he claimed. The attitude he described is not immediately obvious either. I smile back at her a little, feeling relieved not to be the only human and female. What must it have been like for her to be all alone?

She wasn't, remember? You're imagining yourself a human companion so that you *won't be all alone.*

I'm having so much trouble letting go and enjoying the fantasy that I can't help but wonder if part of me is worried that this is all real. Which sounds insane, but it's true.

Bogdan beckons me forward. His face is still blank, but

his eyes burn, moving over my form, pausing on my lips, my breasts and further down before sweeping back up to my face. It really does feel so real. I try to relax into it.

Because this is it. The moment I've been waiting for.

My knees wobble, strangely weak. I studied the pictures of him, but I didn't expect the presence he'd have in the flesh. His face is as hard and chiseled as the armor he wears. His broad shoulders block out the sight of the ship. Up close, his armor is clearly molded to his skin. The amount of muscles clearly delineated on his body are inhuman. Obviously.

He reaches for me, something in his hand. Maybe some kind of tech to help with the nanotech bonding? Silently, I curse Frllil for not being more descriptive, but I step forward, ready to embrace him, when he lifts my hair. That feels nice. Then something clicks, a cool metal presses around my throat, and I freeze.

Did he just collar me?!

Frllil definitely didn't mention anything about that! Maybe I should have expected it because serious BDSM relationships often involve a collar, and I think I do remember something about it from the books I was reading, but I thought we'd at least get to know each other a little first. Not just wham, bam, collared ma'am.

The collar is smooth yet soft under my fingers. Not metal but not fabric either—or if it is, it's something I haven't encountered. I can't figure out how it latches, although my fingers frantically search for one.

Bogdan holds up the end of a long, glittering leash which now connects us and gives the lead a warning tug. "It is forbidden for anyone to touch your collar but me." I drop my hands but he's still glowering at me. He tugs the leash again, and the way it jerks on my throat makes me want to reach out and smack him. "The correct response is 'Yes, Master'."

I grind my teeth. *Do not curse at the giant alien.* If my subconscious was directing this scenario from my reading material, I definitely did not want to go there. "Yes, Master."

Despite my annoyance, my pussy throbs at the words. He turns back to the High Commander.

"The Tribute is acceptable." Without warning he's moving forward, past the warriors and human, tugging me in his wake. Wait a second... where's my ceremonial touch? Aren't we supposed to kiss, or hug, or at least hold hands or something? I feel bereft and more than a little lost at the suddenness of our departure. I wouldn't have thought being collared was going to be the outer limit of our interaction.

Dawn gives a little wave as we pass her by, and I see that she's also collared and on a leash. At least I'm not the only one. She looks happy though, even content, standing at the High Commander's side.

"Good luck," she mouths before Bogdan tugs the leash again and I hurry to keep up, almost stumbling through the door into the hallway and letting the low light swallow me.

Still no orgasm in sight. Drat.

4

Bogdan

I MARCH down the hall to my quarters, leading my Tribute, doing my best to ignore her beauty and the way her tech already tugs at my consciousness. I am far too aware of the training belt around her waist and what it reveals about her state of arousal. Her nanotech responded to me as soon as I touched her, integrating with my own. It is not the full Tsenturion bond, but it feels so close to what I imagined the bond would feel like that I am disturbed.

Because of Tribute Dawn, I know the full bond is possible, but she and the High Commander did not immediately have such a strong connection. I am acutely aware of my own Tribute, which rouses both my temper and my protective instincts. Especially when she tries to dawdle in the hall, looking around rather than following me closely.

After a few tugs on the leash when she tries to slow, she

seems to realize I will not be indulging her, and she matches my quick pace. Good. I knew from her file that she was intelligent.

Leaving the Ceremony so abruptly will cause questions, but I had no desire to examine my new Tribute in front of my Commander or the warriors. I have followed the bare minimum of protocol and everyone will have to be content with that. It is bad enough that she has been matched to me and that the tech bond is so strong so quickly. I do not trust myself to contain my emotions and therefore I need to sequester us.

The door to my quarters slides open and I march inside, relief washing over me now that we are in the safety of my own quarters, away from prying eyes.

"Stay," I order her. The beautiful female just stares at me silently and I turn away, needing a moment to myself, to adjust to my new reality.

My head throbs. I retract my helmet so I can rub my scalp, trying to soothe away some of the pain. Behind me, my Tribute sucks in a breath. I don't know why. I tell myself I don't care.

Pretending to ignore her, I drift to my console. The screen reflects her image, still watching me curiously from the center of the room.

She is even more attractive in the flesh than she was on the vids. Tawny skin, shining dark hair, big brown eyes. But much smaller than I expected. Somehow, she looked larger, more sturdy in the pics and vids. In the flesh it is clear she is fragile, delicate, and far too breakable, even with the changes the Jabol have made to her body. What were the Jabol thinking, abducting human women to be our mates? The top of her head does not even reach my shoulder and I must be three times her weight. I could crush her by lying atop her. How does the High Commander manage it?

"*Drakk*," I mutter the curse under my breath. Already I am overwhelmed by this new duty and I have barely begun.

"What's that, Master?" My Tribute's voice is low and sultry, tugging at my senses with feminine allure, yet her tone is hardly subservient. I know from the manuals from her world that I must begin as I mean to go on.

I turn and fix her with a foreboding glare. "I did not give you permission to speak."

She raises her chin, dark eyes flashing with emotion that I can feel a small spark of. She is annoyed by my response, and strangely unafraid. Small as she is, she is full of fire. The hard look in her eyes says she is strong... but her skin is so soft and fragile. She is an interesting dichotomy and I feel a reluctant admiration for her already.

From death she was rescued through the wormhole and delivered to the Jabol for training, and now she is here as my Tribute, yet she stands tall and proud. Still, her fire must be tempered. For one so small, she is foolish to think she can stand against me, even were I not a warrior.

Perhaps her intelligence was overstated.

Crossing the room, I loom over her. She doesn't shrink away. Either she is very brave or very foolhardy. I cannot help but feel some admiration for her courage, regardless, but I also know I must take control of her.

I take hold of her nape, gently but firmly, feeling the coolness of the collar against the warmth of her skin. She gasps at my touch, her lips parting, a reaction I approve of. Her nipples bead at the front of her filmy dress and I can almost feel her arousal. Or perhaps I can actually feel it, through the nanotech.

She is well primed.

A thousand tsencycles and I am mated. Just not to the one I should have been, because that is how long she has been gone. Loss stabs my chest, thwarting my own arousal.

No, not mate. Tribute. She is human. A prize for my stellar service, and a vessel to continue our race. As lovely as she is, I will not forget my warrior responsibilities nor my mission to destroy our enemies. No matter how soft her skin or enticing her scent, I will not be distracted from my vengeance upon the Vgotha.

My Tribute is my duty, nothing more.

Perhaps one day... but certainly not now.

And it is my duty to train her properly.

"Remove this," I growl and pluck at her gown. I release her neck and she sways backwards, her breath coming faster. She blinks, but obeys without protest, her movements graceful and slow. Something about the look on her face is almost trance-like. I cannot tell what she is thinking, but the nanotech informs me that her arousal has increased.

My seela stir as her body is bared to me, my own arousal growing as she steps out of the gown and straightens. I clench my fists to keep my suit from lightening. Her hair falls about her narrow face, brushing the tops of her breasts, which are full, rounded, the perfect size to fit in my palms. Her nipples are upturned, begging me to stroke them.

She actually smiles at me, tilting her head to the side, her body shifting to an even more seductive stance. My seela react immediately and my cock pulses, thickening with interest.

"You prefer me naked?" She flutters her eyelashes at me, her voice sultry. I do not understand why she moves her eyes in such a manner, but I have to admit, there is something oddly appealing about it.

"Inside my quarters, yes."

"Our quarters," she corrects me, throwing me off balance.

"What?" I did not mean to ask the question, but she surprised me so much that I did so before I could stop myself. Asking a question is not weakness, I decide. I need to know how my Tribute thinks if I'm going to properly train her.

"Our quarters." Her smile widens, confusing me. "Because I live here now, correct?"

"I... that..." Technically she is correct, but she makes it sound as though we will be equals within these rooms, which is not at all correct. I cross my arms over my chest, giving her a hard look. "You will be staying here with me. These are *my* quarters and you are *my* Tribute."

I emphasize *my*. She belongs to me and she is staying in my quarters. Both are mine. I can tell I have not established proper dominance with my stumble over answering her question though, because her smile just widens. I will establish my mastery over her now and then there will be no more question in her mind about whose quarters these are or who she belongs to.

I issue a neural command and a platform rises from the floor at the foot of the bed. I stop it at the perfect height for her to kneel upon it with her upper body braced by the bed. "Get on all fours. I wish to inspect you."

My Tribute blinks. It is her turn to be thrown off balance, to my satisfaction. "Right now?"

"Are you disobeying me?" If she is, I will be happy to demonstrate the consequences of doing so. My lower body throbs at the thought. Sometimes, one can take pleasure in duty.

"No..."

"No?" I point at the platform. "Then obey."

"No, it's not..." The seductive stance she had adopted has fallen away and she looks uncomfortable. I find her no less attractive this way, in fact I rather enjoy seeing her look a little more unsure. "I just need to... powder my nose."

An errant lock of hair has fallen over her cheek. Moving closer to her, I brush it back, my fingers lingering on her soft skin as I frown. She sighs and leans into my touch and the tightness in my chest eases.

"Why do you wish to powder your nose?" I caress her cheek and then run my fingers over her nose, not understanding her request but not wishing to be cruel if it is something important. She closes her eyes and my tech tells me that her arousal is increasing, her pussy growing slick and ready for me. Her responsiveness makes me want to draw her into my arms and sink back onto the bed, to learn all the ways to make her sigh and moan. I could spend cycles with her, exploring her body.

I stiffen, uncomfortable with the direction of my thoughts.

But I am meant to train her, to master her, and ultimately to protect her. To do the first two, I must explore her form. Thoroughly. I relax. This is my duty. And I will be recalled to the bridge when it is time to return to my regular duties.

"I meant that I need to use the little Tribute's room," she explains, but I do not understand the explanation and I frown down at her in further confusion. She sighs. "The bathroom. I need to pee."

Ah. I do not understand why she did not just say so, but Tribute Dawn sometimes says strange things as well. Humans do not always speak the way Tsenturions do and it is another reminder of the differences between us.

I release her and step back. "Go then. You have five minicycles. Then you will return, and your inspection and training will commence."

With a shaky nod, no longer looking so sure of herself, she sways in the direction of the bathing room. The rounded curve of her bottom is very appealing, and I am looking forward to seeing the secondary entrance all the manuals make much of. I can feel it through the nanotech, but I want to see it before I do anything to it.

∾

Pareena

HOLY HELL. What have I gotten myself into? This fantasy is out of control.

I thought I could keep it together right up until he wanted to inspect me. The thought of getting on all fours for him to look me over, touch me... for some reason I balked. Even though I'm desperate for an orgasm, this is all happening so fast.

It's not real.

But it feels so real. If it didn't, it would be so much easier to just let myself go. I stare at my reflection in the mirrored surface of the wall. This helps me remember that it's not real. Because if this were real, I'd see a body eaten away by cancer, with my ribs showing through, skin dulled, and hair gone. Instead, my hair falls around my full curves, my skin glows with health, and my eyes are bright with energy.

Exactly as I wish I was.

Which means I need to get back to my fantasy and enjoy myself. I could wake up at any moment and be thrust back to cruel reality... or I could never wake up at all and this dream could just abruptly end.

It does not do to dwell on dreams and forget to live.

Dumbledore almost had it right. When there is nothing left to life and you're given the opportunity to live in the Mirror of Erised, you don't say no. I'm going to grab onto this particular dream with both hands and savor the ride. *Carpe diem* and all that. It's definitely what I would counsel a patient to do.

The giant warrior is waiting for me when I return to the bedroom. His suit has retracted from his torso, leaving only the lower half of his body covered, and his golden skin glitters in the low light. His muscles are ridiculously huge. If I hugged him, I'd barely get my arms around the barrel of his chest. The expression on his face remains as foreboding as ever. Why I find that such a turn on, I have no idea, but my alien master is as stern as any of the doms in my fantasies. Maybe sterner.

My pussy pulses against the training belt. I can't wait for him to take it off and touch me. There's no sense in feeling shame or embarrassment about an inspection, because this isn't real, right?

Bogdan points to the platform a few feet off the ground.

"Up." His command is said in a voice so deep it sends tremors through me.

I make myself move forward, well aware of how naked and vulnerable I am. Not real. Happening in my head. *Just enjoy the fantasy, Pareena!*

Taking a deep breath, I place my knee on the platform and push up with my other foot. With my knees spread wide to help keep my balance, I bend forward and rest my elbows on the bed. It is soft, but doesn't have too much give, and my breasts sway beneath me, my hair falling like a curtain on either side of my body and providing me with a tiny bit of coverage.

My ass and pussy are completely displayed by the position though, and for the first time I'm grateful for the training belt. Imaginary alien sex fantasy or not, my emotions feel very real.

"I will inspect you now. If you disobey me at any point, I will punish you."

The temptation to disobey is strong... exactly what would punishment entail? But considering that everything feels so very real, maybe I don't really want to know what my brain would come up with.

"We will proceed according to manuals."

"Manuals?" I echo the word without thinking and then cringe. "Sorry, Master, I didn't mean to speak out of turn."

I feel a little silly saying it, calling him Master out loud in a manner that isn't joking, but it feels oddly right too. Probably because I had always wished I could find a Dom who would become my Master. So my brain provided. *Thanks, brain.*

"The courtship manuals, like the one you were reading before you chose to come here."

"You mean the book I was reading about Tsenturions?" Aka the whole reason my brain must have latched onto this particular fantasy for my dream.

"Those books were modeled after your courtship manuals, I am told." Fingers touch beneath my chin and lift my head up, directing my gaze to a small stack of books at his bedside. Yikes. I recognize those titles, those authors. *Zylonn's Human Bride* by Sue Lyndon. *His Human Slave* by Renee Rose. A Berserker book by Lee Savino.

"These are your manuals?" My voice goes a little high and my ass clenches automatically. I downloaded these after getting into the stories already on the e-reader I now know Frllil sent me. Books with lots of sexy discipline. Drat. Where are the slow burn romances when you need them?

"They were collected from Earth. The Jabol tell us they are very popular."

"Yeah... as entertainment, not instruction books."

Bogdan gives me a patronizing look. "The Jabol sent devices to monitor your responses as you studied the manuals. The stories primed you for your role as Tribute."

That made almost too much sense.

"That's a huge invasion of privacy," I mumble and duck my head. Or at least it would be, if this wasn't in my head. If I wasn't imagining this, I would be livid. Even knowing it's not, I feel indignant at the idea of aliens studying my kinky preferences for their own sordid reasons.

Bogdan releases my chin, letting my head drop back down. "Your responses were why you were chosen as a Tribute. This is the life you sought. Now that you are here, you will submit to me in all things."

I squeeze my legs together to hide my wetness. Fine. I was chosen. My brain has pulled from all my favorite books to put together my fantasy.

"Okay." I lick my lips and turn my head to look up at him. "What's my safeword?"

He gets the same blank expression as he did when I told him I needed to powder my nose. Apparently, that's what he looks like when I confuse him.

"I do not understand. You are safe here with me. You may use words, unless I forbid your speech."

"I mean, a word I can say to make the play stop."

"This is not play." He fists a hand in my hair and tips my head back, much less gentle now, and my body responds immediately. A whimper falls from my lips and I am quivering all over at his touch. Yes, please, more hair-pulling. "You are not in control. You will submit to my desires. I am your Master."

I'm panting now, my arousal back up to a full ten. I've been a bit back and forth, but now I'm finding it easier to get into the right mindset to just enjoy myself. Guess my fantasies of no control are coming true. In the safest way possible, but hey, might as well enjoy it.

"Consensual non-con. Okay. I can be down for some edge play." As long as I get my orgasm.

Bogdan's face goes blank, his grip gentling, and he turns to look at the books again. "I will do more research."

He releases my hair, starting to step away, and I panic.

"No, please, Master," I blurt, afraid he's going to walk off and start reading, leaving me here to burn. "Please. I will be good. Use me as you wish." I flush at my wanton words but push back my embarrassment. Especially because it works. He looks down at me, contemplation in his dark eyes.

"You will obey my every command."

"Yes, Master," I agree breathlessly. Yes! Let's get this party started!

"I will inspect you. If you are a good, obedient girl, I may permit your climax."

I press my lips together. Yes please, that's what I'm talking about!

He digs his hands into my hair again, rubbing my head like he's petting a cat. I love it, though. I almost want him to stroke my hair forever, except my pussy is pulsing like a second heartbeat, trying to get his attention. *Me, me, me!*

Bogdan takes his sweet time sliding a hand down my back, over my shoulders to encircle my arms. His hands are so big he can easily shackle my wrists. He crouches to explore my chest and belly, tracing my breasts with a single finger. I close my eyes and moan at the teasing sensation. When he rises and cups my breasts in both hands I hum happily. My nipples press against his palms, his fingers deftly massaging my soft flesh and I feel like I am literally turning to putty in his hands.

When he moves away, I almost protest, except that I feel the Bride Trainer moving against my swollen pussy and I realize it's receding. Yes! Tracing his hands over my back, he slides them down my sides to my ass and I sense him crouching down behind me, his hands on my ass cheeks, holding them apart as he inspects my pussy. At this point, he could breathe on my clit and I'd cum. Shivers spread through my body, little champagne bubbles, like I'm a bottle, corked, shaken and ready to explode.

Gripping either butt cheek, he pushes them even further apart and I realize it's not just my pussy he's interested in. I feel him staring at my little hole. I squirm a little and he grips me tighter. I wait for him to touch or lick me or something, but there's just a light brush of his fingers over my crinkled hole and then he moves on and I moan with disappointment.

The light touches return. He leaves almost no part of me unhandled. Not even my ears or toes, which he spends some time inspecting. He touches me everywhere—except my pussy. Almost like he's avoiding the one part of me I want him to touch the most.

When he returns to my breasts, I almost scream with the building sexual frustration. His fingers brush my nipples and I arch my back, sighing with pleasure.

"You find this pleasing?" He asks, pinching each nub lightly and I hum.

"Yes. More please, Master. You can pinch harder." Please do.

"I wish to understand your responses."

"I respond to you."

He steps away, his fingers falling from my nipples and leaving me aching, throbbing, and starting to get a little worried that I am really never going to come.

"Did I do something wrong?"

"You have forgotten to call me Master. Again."

Oops. "Forgive me, Master."

"You will learn your place. Perhaps now is time to test your response to punishment." He turns and a panel of the wall beeps and slides aside. Behind it is a closet of some sort. It takes a moment for my eyes to adjust and I gasp at the assortment of punishment implements hanging in neat rows. Floggers, paddles, long and thin reeds that will leave painful lines on my skin, straps made out of an assortment of materials and in a variety of lengths. A sadist's dream. A sub's nightmare. A masochist's hidden fantasy.

"These are Enforcers. I trust I will not need them often. I was out of practice, but I have been re-training myself to wield them, in order to discipline my Tribute when necessary." The matter-of-fact way he announces this makes the words seem all the more sinister. It doesn't matter though, all of it turns me on even more. I'm torn now—do I want him to punish me or fuck me? "We will start with the least severe and move to the one designed to impart the most pain." Apparently, they are lined up by severity because he picks up a softer looking flogger first, then one with knots at the end, and keeps up picking out 'enforcers' until he reaches a thin whippy-looking cane.

"You're going to use all of those on me?" I squeak out the words, unsure if I'm more excited, turned on, or terrified. His gaze whips toward me and I gulp. Shoot, I forgot again. "Master?"

"Obviously you are in need of a reminder of your place. This will be a demonstration of what you can expect if you continue to forget it. You are my Tribute and you will call me Master and obey my orders. I will have your submission and claim you in the manner of both of our peoples." He pauses, as if waiting for me to answer. I'm too busy taking in the wall of pain and I'm not really sure there was a question in there until he speaks again. "Well, Tribute? What do you have to say?"

I lick my lips. What else can I say? "Yes, please, Master."

5

B ogdan

MY TRIBUTE STARES at the wall of my Enforcers, dark eyes wide and full of interest. Her tongue darts out. My *seela* quiver, the thin tendrils around my cock very interested in the female in front of me. The tightness of my armor is almost painful against my arousal. I can feel a longing to join with her, to sink into her with my cock so that my *seela* may latch onto her soft skin and begin the exchange of biological information. According to the manuals, humans do not have *seela*, they have something called 'pubic hair' instead, but the High Commander has told me that his Tribute enjoys the difference between us.

The manuals also indicated that human females sometimes enjoy pain, that they are aroused by their punishments. Although, the females also seem more reluctant to be disciplined in the manuals, whereas my Tribute is almost eager. Perhaps that is an effect of the priming. The nanotech tells me she is as painfully aroused as I am, perhaps more so.

First, I must punish her though, so that she will know her place. I will prove myself a good, if demanding, Master and she will acknowledge my dominance over her. Then and only then, will I give her the pleasure she craves.

. With a thought, I send an order to the platform. It shifts, rising to display her hindquarters even more than before. The middle section morphs and curves under her to take her weight off her knees. She ends up tipped forward with her head down and the perfect globes of her rear on display.

"You are nicely primed for your Master." The glistening folds of her womanhood are a wondrous sight. I cannot help but reach forward to touch her, to put my fingertip to her wetness, just to feel it.

She strains back towards me. "Master, please—"

I move my hand away from her pussy and spank her right flank, hard enough to leave a dark print on her tanned skin. "No. You will accept your discipline and if you please me, you will climax. Not a microcycle before."

My words are stern, but I find myself restraining a smile at her breathy sigh and minute tremors in her shapely legs. Her eagerness pleases me, calling to instincts deep inside my psyche. I stroke and tease her nether parts a minicycle longer. More fluid leaks from her lovely folds. I find myself probing and peering into her juicy slit, my lips parted and tongue ready to taste her. But I pull back at the last moment.

In due time, I remind myself. Discipline first.

"With proper training, you will be the perfect Tribute. Ready and willing to serve my needs." I mutter to myself, but she murmurs back anyway.

"Yes, Master."

My cock stiffens at her soft, submissive tone, my prime seela arching above in readiness. My lesser seela waft around my shaft as if searching for my Tribute. The tiny suckers open and close against the inside of my armor. It is all I can do to keep the armor on my lower body up, to keep them from tasting and fastening onto my Tribute's skin, pulling her close and holding her still for my cock's invasion. The thought makes me lightheaded.

I have chosen my Enforcers but find myself reluctant to start with anything but my bare hand on her warm flesh. My Tribute's skin is so soft. She was made to be touched, and I am happy to oblige. No more than is my duty, but it is my duty.

"We start with manual correction. This will not always be punishment. At times I will order you to present for inspection. I might spank you then, to remind you of your place."

I let my hand crash down on her curvy cheeks, admiring how they bounce and quiver with each light impact. I angle my hand to catch the underside of her bottom, fascinated by the way her flesh moves beneath my hand.

~

Pareena

BOGDAN IS HOLDING nothing back and it hurts so good. I can't remember the last time I was spanked for the sheer pleasure of it, and that is what this feels like. It doesn't feel like a punishment at all—yet. His hand is hard enough that it could certainly get there. But right now, with my arousal at an all-time high and endorphins running through my brain, I'm starting to think I might orgasm just from the spanking.

Cool air wafts over my pussy but does nothing to dampen the heat of my body. If the platform beneath me had not changed to fit along my stomach, I would be trying to sneak a hand down between my legs to touch my throbbing clit.

Instead, all I can do is lay there, ass in the air, moaning as he spanks me, lecturing me all the while.

"You must always submit to me." His voice is deep, commanding, the cadence almost hypnotic, like he's trying to use his hand to imprint his words into my flesh.

Smack!

"Whether it is pleasure or pain—"

Smack!

"I will give you what you need."

Smack!

I cry out as he punctuates his declaration with a flurry of sharply stinging swats, my pussy clenching in reaction. The spanking burns, but the heat is transforming inside me into something more erotic, more pleasant. Especially when he pauses and his hand squeezes each cheek in succession, as if testing how well-punished they are.

"Please, Master..." I manage to gasp out the words, wagging my hips up and down. Suddenly he stops spanking me and I feel two fingers slide into my dripping wet pussy. He has very big fingers, but I am so well-lubricated that he easily penetrates me, pumping them back and forth.

I quiver, gasping, and the pure bliss of having him inside of me is so intoxicating that I actually experience a small orgasm. The hot rush of pleasure does not satisfy the gaping need inside of me, but it smooths the edges of it, makes it bearable, as my pussy spasms around him. Utter gratitude fills me.

I can orgasm!

"More, my Tribute," he commands, his fingers moving again, rubbing over my g-spot and then I feel him touching my clit. "Climax for me." There had been a part of me that was so scared I would never actually get to come, but now I can feel it, inexorable and inevitable, ready to overwhelm me.

The platform under my body is the only thing holding me up as la petite morte engulfs me. It's weeks of waiting, culminating in the most intense orgasm of my life. If this is true death, I am no longer afraid. I am drowning in sensation, in ecstasy, in uninhibited rapture.

Truthfully, I'm almost surprised when the crescendo of my pleasure recedes and I am left panting and spent. My body throbs, from the more painful ache in my spanked cheeks to the satisfied pulsing in my clit. Bogdan's fingers slide out of me and the next thing I know they are in front of my lips.

I'm so shocked, so thrown off balance, by my continued existence and how real the aftermath of my spanking and orgasm feel, how real the scent of my pussy on his fingers smell, that I jerk away rather than opening my mouth. Before I can say anything, Bogdan has already moved his fingers away and is back behind me.

"Perhaps it is time to move on to the real discipline," he says.

"But—" I start to protest and then gasp as his wet fingers push into my asshole. I'm not a virgin there, but it's been a long, long time since that area has been touched by anyone other than a nurse. The burning stretch hurts and feels good all at the same time. My fists clench the sheets and I groan, my muscles trying to clamp down around him.

Bogdan

PENETRATING her secondary entrance seems to have the exact response the manuals indicated it would. I can feel her submitting to me, her body working to accept the abrupt invasion of my fingers and allowing me to do with her small hole whatever I please. The hot, dry channel intrigues me greatly and my cock throbs, my seela straining eagerly toward her. I ignore my own impulses though.

This is about my duty, not my body's sexual needs.

Pulling my fingers from her tight hole, rather than continue to test my willpower, I select an Enforcer. It's a small one, made of organic material much like the wood of her former planet. An oval shape not much larger than her hand. I'll pepper her bottom with rounded marks, layering sting over sting. A flick of my wrist is all I need for a warning. Nothing that will leave a mark for longer than a day or so. I tested the Enforcers on my own flesh first to prepare for my Tribute.

She's breathing easily, her body limp on the platform I've molded to my purposes, satisfied from the orgasms. I wish for a moment she was draped over my lap, bottom upturned over my knee, hair hanging to the floor.

My seela strain under my armor, reaching for her bare skin. Next time. Next time she will be over my lap when I discipline her.

The thought makes me pause, because why should I desire such an intimate change?

But part of my duty is to discipline my tribute as I see fit. If she is over my lap, flesh pressed to mine, I will better determine her responses. The fact that I will enjoy her writhing is not a consideration, I reassure myself.

"I will discipline you now." Her breathing becomes more rapid as I touch the hard surface of my chosen Enforcer to her rear.

I tap the Enforcer over her quivering buttocks, lightly at first and then harder. Her skin is darker than Tribute Dawn's and does not show the same pink, but I can still see the color changing. Her legs kick up helplessly and I pop the implement against the wet skin between her thighs.

With a yelp, she reaches back to try and protect her pussy. I grab her wrist and pull it to the side.

"If you cannot keep your hands down, I will restrain you."

"No, please, Master. I'll be good."

I keep hold of her wrists as I finish with a flurry of sharp smacks that leave her writhing and panting, a sob dragging from her throat, but she does not try to escape my hold. Only when she keeps her word to not fight do I let her go.

I am not done, though. This first discipline must be thorough and set the stage for what she can expect in the future. That each solid thud against her chastised flesh sends a hot gush of arousal through me has nothing to do with it. I select another Enforcer, modeled much like the previous one, but with a larger head, square-shaped. I angle it to catch the crease where her buttocks meet her thighs.

~

Pareena

I AM ON FIRE.

No matter how I try to convince myself that I'm not really feeling this pain, my brain doesn't cooperate. Each hard smack of the wood against my already burning bottom makes me jerk and flail, tears sliding down my cheeks at the blooming pain. Not just at the pain though.

At the release.

At the sheer joy of feeling something.

At the conflicting mix of sensations that sink into my skin, the utter ecstasy of feeling so alive, and the submissive rush that always accompanies a spanking for me. Or, that always used to. I still feel it though. The heady submission, the growing ache, each hard swat sending me higher and higher.

The hard wood smacks against my sit-spots, hurting me perfectly, deliciously, and sending more tears spilling down my cheeks. I am throbbing, burning, stinging all over. Not just on the surface of my skin, but deeper. I crave Bogdan's touch and he does not disappoint.

The spanking pauses and his fingers dip into my pussy. I can feel the excessive wetness from my previous orgasm as he rubs his fingers through my lips, exploring my sensitive slit.

"You are doing well." The praise is sincere, if a bit formal.

"Thank you, Master." I feel dreamy, but also a little hollow. As much as I enjoy his hand now curving over my bottom, the masochistic side of me craves more. I want the pain, the endorphins. I want to fly.

"As you have been so good, I will allow you to choose the next Enforcer."

It takes a moment for his words to penetrate the erotic haze that the spanking has sent me into. As soon as they do, I feel my anticipation surge and my bottom throbs. Nothing too harsh, not after the spanking he's already meted out but... "The belt, please."

I can hear the begging in my voice as I turn to look longingly at one of the implements he'd left hanging on the wall.

"This?" He leaves my side, walking over to touch the long, hanging strip of leather. At least, that's what it looks like to me. The *kurdzu* hide?"

"Yes, I love the belt." I almost sigh with happiness as he picks it up.

∼

Bogdan

I PAUSE on my way back to her, thinking over her words. When I reach her again, I caress her right bottom cheek and then squeeze the soft flesh. The chastised skin is warm to touch. "You have been disciplined before."

"A few times. At a club. And a party." Her words are slightly slurred from the pleasure. So, she has been courted before. But either her previous master abandoned her when she sickened, in which case he was no master at all, or...

"Have you ever belonged to a master?" I squeeze her bottom more firmly and she croons happily as I dig my fingers in. The nanotech tells me that she does feel the pain, but she also feels pleasure along with it. Some part of her enjoys the punishment. Just as the manuals indicated. Truly, they are far more helpful than I could have believed.

"No. But I obviously fantasized about it." She lets out a little laugh, as if she just told a joke. Before I can ask what she means by that, she adds, "The belt was my favorite. Leather feels yummy."

Now it is my turn to chuckle. I do not know what 'yummy' means, but it's clear she means it as a positive thing. "I wonder if you will be able to say the same when I am through."

Unbelievably, she smiles at me through her hair, tilts forward on the modified bench and offers her already darkened bottom. "Do your worst."

I can't stop the swell of pride under my breastplate. My Tribute is strong and courageous. I unwind the strip of hide and crack it beside her head before doubling it over in my hand to give me more control over the long length.

"Breathe," I remind her when I notice she's gone still. From fear? From expectation?

Perhaps this discipline is not as effective as it should be, considering how she seems to be enjoying some of it. But I do know that she feels the effects, thanks to the nanotech. It also just seems to arouse her. In that way, she is very like a Tsenturion female.

The reminder nearly causes me to drop the kurdzu strap.

I shake myself, focusing on the here and now, because even if she is not a Tsenturion female, even if she is not my chosen bride, she is my Tribute and she deserves my full attention when I am disciplining her. When she wiggles her reddened bottom, it is easier to focus on her.

I lay the belt across her rear, admiring the pink edged mark that appears on the sultry curve of her bottom. She cries out but manages to hold her position, her bottom bobbing up and down, the welted stripe standing out against even the rest of her punished flesh.

"More, please," she begs.

I step back and paint thick lines on her backside, enjoying the loud crack of the Enforcer. As I work her over, my own body heats with exertion. My seela are practically screaming, dying for release from the hard shell of my armor. Judging by the slickness between her legs, she is enjoying the discipline, too. Her pleading words fall sloppily from her lips.

With a thought, I could remove my coverings and alter the platform I created to be at the perfect height for my cock. She's so wet, I would slide right inside, my prime seela flowing over the marks on her bottom, soothing and stroking. My lesser seela would suction onto her sensitive labia, delighting in the copious moisture, fastening onto the pinkish skin and splaying her for my invasion. Her inner walls would feel so good kissing along my cock. So soft.

I pause to regain control over myself, panting with the need riding me. But... I can't. I loosen my armor around my shaft and seela, relieving some of the pressure. I have no plans to use her body for my own satisfaction. Not yet. I have seen the change wrought upon the High Commander. How he lost himself in Tribute Dawn after her arrival and how he seems to have forgotten our duty to our lost, our vengeance.

The same will not happen to me.

What is it about these Tributes that they rouse such strong feelings?

Gripping her silky dark hair, I ease her head back and study her face. Her lips are pink and plump, slightly parted. I lean down to nuzzle my nose against her cheek, drinking in her scent, trying to determine what is so appealing about her. A sweet aroma, like the harvest flowers of my home planet. Her delicate jaw fits easily in my hand. Her cheek curves and she angles her head to place a small kiss in the center of my palm before she leans into my touch. I freeze at the freely given affection.

After a minicycle, she blinks and lets her head roll to look up at me. "Did I do something wrong? Master?"

A fist squeezes my insides. I barely find my voice. "No. You are ... perfect."

6

P areena

I LOVE this part after a good scene, my body warm and head high on the endorphins singing through me. The moment after the last strike and before my top opens his pants and rewards me with his dick. My thoughts blur, turning the strong figure of my dominant into an all-powerful god, my submissive posture into one of abject worship. I feel small and safe, tucked into my defined role. At the same time, the chemicals in my bloodstream have me flying, spread over the galaxy in tiny, glittering particles.

Bogdan looms over me, breathing hard. I don't know much about Tsenturion anatomy—yet—but there's a package in his pants I bet is for me.

He smells so good. Maybe it's just the nanites talking, but his scent fills my lungs like I need it, not oxygen, to breathe. If this is what it's like to be fully primed and bonded, it's awesome and scary at once. To need someone so much my skin is screaming for him. My mouth is watering and body aches with a craving to be touched. I'm a Bogdan addict and I need my fix.

"You did well," he tells me. "We will continue your discipline another time. It is not necessary for you to feel all the Enforcers now. In time, you will submit to all of them."

Facing the wall of implements, hearing my Tsenturion master promise to bring me to heel, My pussy throbs at the thought.

"Right now, I will test your response to pleasure."

Yes, please.

The platform rises under my bottom, tipping my front forward even more. I'm splayed embarrassingly, my well-marked hindquarters throbbing, face height for the tall warrior.

What is he—?

Two of his large fingers slide into my heated slit.

"Ooooh," my moan escapes. I wanted his cock but I'm in no position to complain, not tipped forward and strapped down like this.

"So responsive," he murmurs, sounding thoughtful. I strain back as much as I can towards his fingers. I just need a little more stimulation to tip over into orgasm...

He pulls out his finger and smacks my ass with a wet sound. Before I protest, his fingers return to my pussy.

"I wonder," he pulls my left butt cheek aside, opening me to his gaze. I imagine him taking in every inch of me, from my plump pussy to the brown whorl of my anus, and blush so hard my face is as red as my bottom. He probes deeper and my legs quiver. "Is all this lubrication from the pain?"

He swats my ass again, awakening the dulled sting of my punished hindquarters. My pussy juices in response.

"Or is it because you are trained to respond to me?" Large hands grip my bottom, massaging away the sting until the pain is a pleasant hum far away, adding depth to my rising desire. I'm dripping now, inner thighs coated in wetness. I've never been so ready for cock in my life.

"Both, Master," I answer his musings even though I can barely talk. Enough with the philosophizing. Let's get to the good part.

But his fingers explore my ass, brushing the sensitive crinkle. I clench my bottom and he smacks me in unspoken command to relax. When I do, he rubs his thumb over my asshole while his other hand returns to my pussy. It's embarrassing how much I like a finger in my ass. I'm not opposed to ass play but haven't had a dom I trusted enough to progress to this point.

"You are making more lubrication," he remarks, sounding both clinical and intrigued. For some reason that just makes me even hornier. "You enjoy this." It's not a question and he continues to probe my tight hole. "Perhaps some experiments are in order."

Is he going to focus all his attention to my ass? I love the thought of being anal trained, but right now my clit is feeling pretty neglected.

"Please, Master." I'm not above begging.

It's the right thing to say, because his left-hand drops and he returns his full attention to stroking and stimulating my clit and labia. He twists a finger inside me, and another, and when he adds a third, I'm undone. I'm so full, so hot, so *needy* that I almost joyously fall into the pleasure.

My climax slams into me, pleasure and pain and need colliding in my core, grains of gunpowder that had been waiting for a spark. I cry out, mouth open, convulsing on his thick digits which thrust deeper into my pussy. He keeps twisting them, stimulating me further, and my orgasm loops back around, curling through me, one climax turning into two, two turning into four, until I can't even count them anymore.

At some point he moves around to my front, bending to watch my expressions. All the blood has rushed to my face and I'm light-headed. He does something and the platform straightens out, so I'm lying on my front, arms at my side, cheek pressed to the smooth surface. My hair is stuck to my sweaty skin.

Bogdan dips so he's right in my face. The angles and planes of his face are too blunt to be pretty, but the effect is overwhelmingly masculine. I wonder what he'd do if I called him 'hot.' "What does my Tribute say after I've given her pleasure?"

"Thank you, Master." I sigh, and when he offers his wet fingers to my mouth, I clean them without protest.

Bogdan

MY COCK THROBS insistently as my Tribute licks her essence off my fingers. I command the platform to release her and I catch her before she rolls. Her weight is negligible, but she makes a soft and sweet-smelling armful as I carry her to my bed. I pause to order my resting place to grow larger and form a supply of thick blankets. I always sleep on a spare pallet, bare of comfort. Even when I sleep I will be ready to go on alert and race to duty if our ship is attacked.

But such an uncomfortable resting place will not do for my Tribute.

She sighs when I place her on the newly formed plush surface. I brush her hair back from her face—the better to monitor her expressions—and rest a hand on her head. She stills under my touch. Her eyelids fall. Her chest rises and falls peacefully. Pleasure and pain wrung her out in their grip and now she eases into sleep, certain of my protection. I straighten proudly.

And she is the perfect Tribute. I did not overstate my approval. Not only is she sweet and obedient but she responds to discipline beautifully. I wonder if the High Commander's Tribute is the same. But Dawn always seems reluctant to conform to our laws. Not so with my Tribute. She is superior in every way. I would never shame the High Commander by telling him so, though.

I touch her face, admiring the soft curve of her cheek. She turns her head in her sleep, mouth open as if ready to accept anything I would feed her.

I force myself to step back. There will be time to explore all of her responses. For now, she must rest.

Guilt stirs in my chest as I look at her, a female in my bed, the soft emotions she stirs in me, the desire I feel... now that she sleeps and I am more clearheaded, it feels like a betrayal.

My com chirps, distracting me, and relief rushes through me. Immediately, I march to the screen in the corner of my quarters. First, I order the message alerts to mute themselves within the cabin. No need to disturb my sleeping Tribute, unless there is an emergency.

A few taps of my screen show our ship is cruising beside an asteroid belt. Scans show no sign of life, but the Vgotha have hidden in such areas before. I check the time. Third watch. Most days, I would be on duty at this demicycle. The High Commander took me off duty for the next semicycle, allowing plenty of time for me to train my Tribute. But she is sleeping. A quick scan of her vitals tells me she is entering a state of deep rest that she will not exit for some time, if undisturbed. There is time for me to report to the bridge.

The more I ponder it, the better my plan sounds. I will not have to see her, in the place where I always pictured another, and I will show my fellow warriors that it is possible to prioritize our duty over our Tributes.

I tell myself that leaving my rooms does not feel like a retreat.

"COMMANDER BOGDAN." Kalexston's suit flashes with surprise when I enter the bridge. I am not surprised to see him in charge over my usual watch in my absence, as he is technically in command beneath me when I am there. "What are you doing here?"

"It is my watch, correct?" I ignore the assembled warriors and head to the com as if everything is normal and this demicycle is like any other. As if I did not, a few demicycles earlier, receive a Tribute.

The warriors stare at me. In awe, no doubt of how I balance my duty with the responsibility of my Tribute.

"What are the results of the scans of the asteroid belt?" I ask, eyes on the rock-studded space on screen.

"We haven't done anything more than a preliminary one," Kalexston says, but his tone is strange, like he doesn't understand why I am asking. I turn to look at him impatiently.

"Well? What are you waiting for?"

Kalexston exchanges a glance with Miths and I can see the uncertainty in both of their stances. The operations officer clears his throat. "Commander, you are not on duty."

"I am present, so I am on duty."

"I mean... you were relieved of duty so you might tend to your Tribute."

"As I am here, you will assume my Tribute is well tended. Kalexston," I snap, and the warrior straightens to attention. "The scans. Now."

A few minicycles pass with the quiet hum of the energy scans. An asteroid belt on the edge of the galaxy is not something we'd submit to deep level scans, but the Vgotha are out there. We must be vigilant.

A soft hiss behind me warns me the transport has arrived. The warriors on deck rise and salute whoever entered the bridge. I turn more slowly and offer my salute.

"Bogdan," the High Commander presses his fist against his chest in acknowledgement. He doesn't look surprised to see me. That combined with his sudden presence means someone reported my insistence to take command. I resist the urge to look around, to see which warrior betrayed me. "You look well. How is your Tribute?"

"She is sleeping." The listening officers almost sigh, relaxing slightly as if they were worried about my Tribute. I suppress a glower. They should not worry about her. She is my concern. And she is fine.

"Good." The High Commander's suit is a neutral silvery grey, his expression blank. But something lurks in the corner of his mouth—a smile? "I require a meeting. Private quarters."

"With all due respect, we can discuss my duty here, so I do not abandon my post." I have the feeling that if I allow him to lead me from the bridge, I will not be returning this watch.

The High Commander is really smiling now, his amusement clear. "But you are not on duty. The post is not yours. Kalexston—" He motions, and the science officer steps up, ready to take my place.

"But my Tribute sleeps and I am willing to serve my watch." I almost feel as though I am begging, although of course I do not let any of that enter my voice or show on my armor.

"You were relieved of the responsibilities of command for the next semicycle. You have a new Tribute. You belong by her side." The High Commander's smile has dipped now, and he appears more stern than amused.

"She is resting. I have no reason to miss my watch. I do my duty."

"You have a Tribute. Your first duty is to her."

I can't hide the flicker of annoyance that streaks through my suit. "With all due respect, my first duty is to my command."

"No, it is to your Tribute. The entire race rests on your bonding with her."

Color flickers through my suit. Kalexston and Miths stare as if they'd never seen my suit respond to my emotions before. Maybe they haven't.

I clench my fists. My Tribute will not make me weak.

"Come." The High Commander turns, obviously expecting me to follow him. "Let us speak privately in my welcoming chamber."

"Is that an order?"

The High Commander's suit darkens slightly. He is losing his patience with me. "Yes."

He marches off the bridge. After a glare at the watching

warriors, all of them since I do not know which individual reported my presence, I follow him. Murmurs start up as soon as I step off the bridge and I restrain myself from returning and challenging them all to a fight for daring to whisper about me and my Tribute.

To my surprise and displeasure, the Commander doesn't lead me to his ready room, an office close to the bridge, but boards the transport as if to return to his private quarters. I bite back my protest and follow him.

As soon as we step into his private chambers, the High Commander retracts his helmet and armor. I stand stiffly at attention, choosing to remain armored, although I retract my helmet. To remain fully armored would be tantamount to disrespect.

"Make yourself comfortable. I'm going to check on Dawn." He disappears from the welcoming chamber to the inner one reserved for sleeping. I turn away but can still hear the soft, feminine murmur of Tribute Dawn's voice and the High Commander's answering rumble.

When the High Commander returns, he commands the door behind him to close.

"Dawn will not be joining us. She's also resting." The High Commander's voice and demeanor changes when he refers to his Tribute. I have never mentioned it but am inwardly determined to never allow my Tribute to affect me so.

"I thought I told you to make yourself comfortable." The Commander shoots a wry look my way.

I straighten further. "I am comfortable."

"Relax, Bogdan, it wasn't an order." He crosses to the replicator and orders a beverage. "Would you like something?"

"No, thank you." I relax, as ordered, although I do keep my armor on.

Although he is the High Commander, in a personal setting, Gavrill is also my friend. As warriors, we keep to our strict hierarchy when on duty, but in a more personal setting we are able to speak as equals. Although, truthfully, I am often given more leeway even on duty, because of our personal relationship.

Gavrill takes a long drink, studying me.

"Bogdan, when the Jabol told us that Tribute Pareena was a near perfect match to you, Medik and I discussed whether or not we should heed their recommendation. We knew you would be reluctant. But we also knew your responsibility and commitment to a Tribute would be second to none, if you could overcome your reticence. Most of our warriors want a Tribute but wanting is not enough. Tributes need a strong, caring protector, one who treats them as the gift they are."

I hold back a smile. That is more in line with my thoughts. "You do me honor, High Commander. Of course, I will fulfill my role and prove a worthy choice."

He gives me a look and I realize he wasn't finished. "Tributes also need a warrior who will try to understand them and treat them as the individual they are, not just as a vessel for bearing our seed. I wonder if we should've given the Tribute to another. Arkdhem perhaps."

What? No! I nearly jerk to my feet; my armor flashing streaks of red and yellow as I lose control over my emotions. The image of the Tribute tangled in blankets on my sleeping platform flashes through my head. From the top of her dark head to the tips of her toes: she is mine. He gave her to me. He cannot take her away from me now.

When I open my mouth to protest, I notice Gavrill is

smirking at me. "I see you are already possessive of Tribute Pareena. This is a good sign." He swirls the liquid in his cup, looking pleased and smug.

"I fail to understand why you are playing games, Commander," I grit out the words, using his title almost as an insult to show my displeasure with the direction of his conversation.

"No game. I needed to know if you will care for Tribute Pareena. She is precious."

"I understand. The Tributes are our only hope for the continuation of our race. She herself is a good choice. She is strong, brave, and well-behaved. I see her for what she is." I had already noted the differences between her and Dawn. There is no need to reveal to him that I feel I have the superior Tribute. He might take it as an insult. "Already she has submitted to my dominance. I will continue to train her."

The Commander's tone is gentle. "And you will bond with her? You are not fighting it?"

I come to my feet and turn away before I can stop myself, pacing to the wall, pretending to study it. Bonding. The connection with a mate so deep, two become one. We would share one another's sensations, thoughts, even feelings.

I run a hand down my armored chest. To have another being sensing every mood? Experiencing feedback from my emotions? At one point in my life, I was prepared for such a thing. It was all I wanted. Now...

"A bond is not necessary. The Jabol gave us Tribute Dawn without knowing if it was even possible."

"Medik thinks it is. He has been studying our biology and it has changed after Dawn and I fully bonded. Not to mention the mating marks." He pauses as if considering what to say next. "That's another reason we chose you. You were at the end of your tour and ready to attend the Mating

Festival. You had gone through training for the transition. Like Medik, you would have been the first to return planet side." He doesn't continue to explain what went wrong. He doesn't have to.

When our ships returned to our home planet Tsentur, we found nothing but an asteroid field. We'd already known something was wrong when no one answered our coms, but we hadn't expected the entire planet to be gone. As the shock of what happened settled in, the High Commander ordered all members of the crew to battle stations. We all kept busy, under orders to hide and remain alert as we scanned for evidence of what happened. There was nothing we could do but search for the enemy who'd caused the destruction.

The Commander himself had remained on the bridge for over a semi-cycle, retreating to his away room for the barest amount of time to rest. The rest of us ate and slept as little as possible before returning to our posts. The few who broke down were given sick leave, sent to the medical bay and sedated. But many of us, me included, remained on duty as long as we could, so when we returned to our bunks, we fell asleep immediately, too exhausted to dream.

Our military training saved us. There was no time for me to sit in my quarters and grieve. We had an enemy to find and punish.

We've been hunting ever since.

And until now, I hadn't had to dwell on what I'd lost.

The air in the Commander's quarters is thin. Or my suit is too tight. I find I can barely breathe, and I flex my fingers, which have gone strangely numb. Yes, I was to attend the Mating Festival. Everyone knew that.

But I do not speak out of turn. I had told no one that I had already chosen my mate. That I was not looking for one, but that I would be presenting myself to a female for courtship. That she had already told me, before that last trip, that she would wait for me. I had wanted to be sure of her, to have the official acceptance of my interest, before I spoke of her to anyone.

"That was a long time ago." My voice is raw. Strangled by the past, by a memory of a sweet voice and warm smile. A female who was as delicate as she was beautiful, as kind as she was shy, and as enamored with me as I had been with her. I would have done anything for her... and instead, I did nothing. I was not there.

I failed her.

"Bogdan." Gavrill's deep voice breaks through the blackness that has engulfed me.

I turn. My reflection in the mirrored section behind him shows my armor has grown into full battle mode, without my conscious intent, complete with vicious spikes along my shoulders. As if I faced the enemy in these quarters, not my own Commander.

His voice is gentle. "You are my most trusted officer. Number two in the entire Tsenturion fleet. You always do your duty."

"Yes."

"Then I trust you in this. Get to know Pareena. Bond with her. Through the Tribute program we have a chance to reclaim some of what we had."

Never. I want to howl. We will never have another Mating Festival. There will never be a time when young warriors and their brides meet under the blooming night flowers and dance until dawn. And I will never see... *her*... again. This time I am prepared for the pain and I do not lose myself in the memories.

Gavrill claps a hand on my shoulder, avoiding the armored spines. "It's not easy. I know what you lost."

"I did not have a mate." Only a promise. Sometimes, in my dreams, I smell the night flowers.

"But you were closer to getting one than all of us." He regards me solemnly, even though he does not know how very close I was. "And now you have Pareena, the second Tribute of all time. Your loyalty and sense of duty has earned this reward."

"Reward?" I want to smash my fist into his unprotected face. "Would you give one to Medik? Who was mated for twenty deca-cycles and lost his whole family?" Tsenturions mate for life. To replace a mate is to spit upon the bonding ceremony. Many of us suspect that if we had not needed him so much, Medik would have followed his mate and family into death.

"No," the Commander has the good sense to drop his hand. He stays close and does not shift into a defensive stance. He is taller than me, though not as tall as Arkdhem. But I am broader. We would be evenly matched in a fight. "I would not dishonor him that way. But you were never mated. It is this loss that plagues you."

"We all lost." I know he is correct. I never mated. I owe her nothing... except justice. Vengeance. The eradication of those who took her life like she was nothing, like none of us were.

"Other's pain does not detract from your own. Forgive me, old friend. I knew you were grieving but didn't know how much. You feel things more deeply than most. *The prettiest castle has the highest walls*," he quotes an old Tsenturion sage, his eyes sympathetic. Although I have never mentioned her to him, he now sees something that he had not before. Perhaps his bond with Tribute Dawn has made him more sensitive to such things.

The mirror beyond us reflects our contrasting forms. Me in full armor and the High Commander's armor in its resting state. I give the silent order to my suit to retract a little. The spikes slide away and the helmet recedes into my neck.

"I am not pretty," I mutter. "I am a warrior."

"Indeed." Gavrill puts his hand on my shoulder. "And I trust you will do your duty, whatever it may be."

Yes. I will do my duty to my Tribute. I will still avenge our people... and her. Somehow, I will find a way to do both. But my resolve is not reflected back at me; instead I see a hollowness when I look at myself. I am not the only one, either.

"Courage, Bogdan. You are the finest warrior in the fleet. You will not fail in this. Now. Return to your Tribute. Fetch her some food along the way. If she is resting, she will surely wake in need of nourishment. You do not want her to become hangry."

What the drakk is 'hangry'?

7

P areena

I WAKE UP AT A NOISE, aching and yet deliciously satisfied. The soft bedding beneath me feels almost like a cozy little cocoon. So much better than a hospital bed. It might even be better than my bed at home. *Thanks brain!*

Pushing up on one elbow, I turn toward the noise that woke me and blink when I see Bogdan standing in the middle of the room with a tray.

"Master?" I blink, just to see if he disappears, but no... my alien fantasy dream continues. "I fell asleep." Does one sleep in dreams? Apparently, I do. Perhaps there are levels to a coma and sometimes I slip into a deeper one.

I watch as he sets the tray down. Nothing on it looks even remotely familiar but some of it smells appealing and my stomach grumbles.

"You needed rest." He comes toward me, looking at me

strangely. There is something almost wary about his demeanor, which I do not understand at all.

Sitting down on the bed, he looks me over, studying me. The sheets have pooled around my hips, leaving my upper body completely naked. The training belt is back around my lower body, I can feel its snug grip against my hips and pussy, but I don't feel any need to try and cover myself.

Almost tentatively, he reaches out and traces a finger down the center of my nose and then over my cheekbones, like he's trying to map my features. Arousal stirs at his touch, innocent though it is.

My hand creeps over to touch his thigh and my eyes drop down. Pretty sure I just saw something move there, his bulge beginning to grow. Oh yes. Alien fantasy is back online and raring to go.

"Do you need me, Master?" I ask, my voice sultry.

His answers shocks me.

"No."

My mouth drops open, my hand freezing. Wait, what? That's definitely never happened in my fantasies before.

"You must eat." He stands, holding out his hand as if to help me up from the bed. "And then I will bathe you."

As if on cue, my stomach grumbles.

Well, okay. I *feel* hungry. Although I know the hospital is taking care of my physical needs, I wouldn't mind actually eating something. Especially if I'm able to taste it. Frllil never fed me anything except 'nutrient water,' which he said took care of all my needs. I figured that was my brain's interpretation of an IV or maybe a feeding tube.

But hey, the sex feels real and pretty amazing, maybe the food will taste real too. I'm willing to try.

"These are the things Tribute Dawn seems to like the most," Bogdan says as he leads me over to the table. Wow.

Seriously, it all looks super alien. Sitting next to me, Bogdan picks up an orange-y cube that doesn't actually look like food to me and brings it to my lips. "Here. Try this. It is a fruit that she eats almost every meal."

I mean, my brain made it up, how bad can it be?

I open my lips and allow him to feed me.

To my shock, it's good. Fruity, almost like a citrus taste but not like any citrus I've ever eaten. It's like if a lemon was combined with a peach and had the texture of Jello. While I became really tired of Jello in the hospital, the flavor more than makes up for it.

I can taste again.

Looking up at him, I lick my lips. "Yummy. What else?"

Bogdan

Your Tribute is a gift.

I cannot bond with her. I do not want to, and I know that will be enough to keep the bond from forming. It does not appear where it is not welcome. But I can train her to be in tune with me. I can come to know her and become in tune with her.

Perhaps it will be sufficient. The Jabol certainly thought it would be, when they sent Tribute Dawn to us. We should not have to bond to be fully biologically compatible.

The High Commander and Medik will have to accept that as the best I can do. Tribute Pareena and I will not bond but she will still bear my young. If I claim her in this way, they will not reassign her to another warrior. Like Arkdhem.

Having the facsimile of a bond is not a hardship. I do not

mind feeling her joy as she tastes the food I have brought. It seems she likes similar things to Tribute Dawn. Her teeth nipping at the tips of my fingers is both pleasant and arousing. At some point I will have to actually join with her. I do not think that will be a hardship either, yet...

Somehow, I do not feel ready.

The High Commander will not try to take her from me so soon after our discussion though. He does not know what I do or do not do in my own rooms. No one need know that I have not claimed her body yet.

It feels like another betrayal to *her* to even contemplate doing so, but I know I must. If I do not, eventually the High Commander may feel that he has erred in giving her to me and he might try to take her away. To give her to another.

Possessive anger, erupts inside of me. I am being forced along a path that I did not wish to take, far faster than I would go by my own choice.

"Master?" The soft question is accompanied by a hand upon my arm. "I'm finished eating. Are—are you alright?"

I realize I do not know how long I have been sitting there, not feeding my Tribute, while she took care of herself. I inwardly curse myself for not paying attention. I must do my duty.

"Come. I must bathe you." I scoop her up. She yelps in surprise, but grabs hold of my shoulders, pressing her soft body into mine. She has no fear of me, despite my abrupt actions, which I admire.

At my unspoken command, water pours into the massive bathing tank. Colorful soaps add a sweet, floral scent to the water. When I set my Tribute down onto the first ledge, she hisses as the shallow water laps at her waist.

"Are you hurt?" The Jabol chose a race that would match our anatomy, but perhaps immersion in water isn't something she's used to? There were bathing scenes in the manuals though. Hygiene seems important to their courtship rituals, I thought.

"No. Only sore. The water feels good." She scoots down to a lower ledge, immersing herself further. "This tub is huge." She giggles, the happy sound echoing off the hard surface of the bathing chamber. "All I need is some bubbles and I'd be set."

I do not understand what she means by bubbles, but seeing her cavorting in the tub, water sliding over and off of her skin, I feel my arousal rising again. With a mental command, my armor recedes, leaving me with nothing covered but my groin. Allowing my cock and *seela* loose now is too much temptation to bear.

"Come here," I order, and she scoots toward me with a smile. I stroke water droplets off her face when she reaches me, cupping her cheeks with my hands. "Present for inspection."

With my help, she gets on all fours on the highest ledge, where the water is shallow. I run a hand down the curve of her back and note her response. We are both humming in pleasure.

I enjoy touching my Tribute. From the way her breath stutters as my large hands coast over her back and backside, she enjoys my touch too. I reach under her to rub soap into her gently swaying breasts and she closes her eyes. With her head tipped back, I can watch every nuance of her blissful expression.

"You don't have to wash me, Master." Her voice is a low purr.

"You are my Tribute. It is my duty." I gather more soap onto the washing cloth and swirl it over her collarbone. My hand is so large it can cover most of her chest. I could break her, snap her bones easily, and I remind myself to be gentle.

I position her before me, having her tilt her head back to wash her hair. I am thorough, massaging her scalp as she sways on her feet, totally relaxed. I have to pick her up to return her to the top step.

Rinsing my fingers, I touch her face again, tracing the fine features. "You are so small."

"You are very large." Her mouth tips up and I can't help rubbing my finger over the pad of her lower lip. Soft as a petal.

Boldly, she rises to face me, water streaming off her flaw-less skin. Her hand stretches towards my bicep, the curve of my muscle uncovered by armor. She hesitates.

"You may touch me," I allow softly. My skin prickles and I swallow to hide my need.

~

Pareena

I KNEEL in between Bogdan's massive thighs, in a tub that makes me think of when Harry uses the Prefect's bathroom in the fourth book, and I run my fingers over his gold skin. His shiny hide is smooth, hairless, almost poreless. Tougher than my skin, but not as tough as the armor that seems to be a part of him. The black material is the skimpiest I've seen so far. Bogdan's version of letting down his guard, perhaps? His groin and upper thighs are still covered, his muscles bulging as if they'll burst at any moment.

There's an interesting bulge at his crotch. Large enough to make my mouth dry. What does alien peen look like? The books I read on Earth only seemed to have one consistent rule about the alien heroes: Always upgrade the dick.

What's hiding under that suit? Some sort of Bad Dragon worthy dong? Is he hiding it until I'm so consumed with lust when he whips it out, I won't run screaming?

Which brings me to another realization: somehow in the middle of all the orgasms, I kind of missed that he never actually had sex with me.

"What do you want me to do?" I meet his gaze, flirtatiously smiling up at him. Not sure why I'm so eager to take our physical relationship to the next level, when obviously I don't need sex for orgasms, but I am. My eagerness might have something to do with his Mr. Universe level muscles. Or the strong-jawed beauty of his face. He hasn't smiled or shown any pleasant expression, but the longing I feel restrained under his iron self-control is a turn on. He wants me. He just doesn't want to show it.

It's my damn coma dream, I should be able to get a smile out of him if I want it. And I should be able to get laid. *Come on, subconscious. Get with the program.*

He shifts on the edge of the tub and strokes my wet hair back from my face. Catches my chin in strong fingers, holding my face immobile, and looks deep in my eyes. Searching for something? I stare back at him, waiting.

Finally, he lets go. "You will bathe me."

Holy hell. Yes. I grab the washcloth he used on me and dip it into the bowl of soap-like substance. He slides fully into the water with me, so I can easily wash his torso. I enjoy touching his muscles, even though it doesn't really seem like his gleaming skin needs actual washing.

My brow furrows in confusion when I start to move the cloth lower, nearly reaching where his armor *still* covers him, and he catches my arms, stopping me.

"What about—"

"Enough. I will finish bathing you."

Dammit. I was just getting to the good part!

He turns me around and positions me as he wants. I'm bent forward so my arms prop on the top of the tub, I'm sticking my butt right at him. I know what's coming.

He nudges my feet apart and I obey, quivering. *Touch me!*

He spends countless seconds running his hands up and down my legs, pressing on my back to make my bottom arch up further, combing my wet hair to the side.

Come on, come on. Finally, he stands behind me, parting my inner thighs until I'm on display the way he wants, my bottom cheeks parted and nether parts flashing him. He rubs soap into my still sore bum with a touch as light as butterfly wings. His fingers drift over my pussy.

Yes, yes, yes...! I resist the urge to writhe. I don't move, don't breathe, wanting him to give me more.

"So small." He penetrates me with a finger and my body clamps on it. *More, more, more!*

To my dismay he rinses me and moves on. He dips the washcloth between my cheeks, then loses it to spread soap directly on my anus. The little hole tingles, but I don't protest. I want to see where this is going.

"And tight," he pushes a finger into my bottom, and I give a frustrated hum when it slides back out almost immediately. Then he starts squeezing my battered cheeks—a sensation that's uncomfortable in the most delicious way—and parting them, angling them so he can examine the small pucker. He sticks his face close and I can feel his hot breath against my sensitive skin. Nerve endings I didn't know I had come to life.

"All done," he mutters, abruptly getting out of the water and leaving me there, confused. I watch him, unsure of what to do, holding my vulnerable and erotically charged position, really confused about why we're not having sex. Picking up a large sheet of fabric that looks like a towel, he rubs himself down and then turns back to me. "Come here, my Tribute."

Wet towel, ick. But when he wraps me in it, it doesn't feel wet and the fabric soaks up every drop of water. He rubs another over my head and my hair is mostly dry by the time he's done.

"Go to the foot of the bed and wait, hands on your head," he orders, and I obey, though I'm getting tired of these inspections. He leaves for a moment and returns with a jar of goopy cream. Dipping his fingers into the stuff, he rubs it in, and it disappears into my skin, leaving a silky sheen. I suck in my stomach as his hand glides over my chest. Typically male, he's extra thorough around my nipples, spending triple the time around my breasts as anywhere else. When his hands swoop lower, he pushes my legs apart further and kneels. I can't hide my excited quiver as he dips his head to inspect my pussy.

Bogdan

THE NEED TO touch my Tribute is strong.

It is my duty, and I must learn her responses, her alien body, but deep down I also know that I am enjoying myself. I can feel my body urging me to bury myself inside of her, to fill her with my seed, to complete the bond. And when I am touching her, when I am distracted by her sweet scent and soft skin, the guilt stays away. It will rise again when we are done, but for now I am unburdened.

She moans as I stroke the soft petals of her body, wetness coating my fingertips. The tantalizing scent of her draws me inward, pulling me closer. My tongue flicks out.

The manuals said pleasure with mouths and tongues was possible and her moan, as my tongue slides up her center, confirms it. She tastes even better than she smells and I realize my chest is vibrating too. I am moaning, sinking my tongue into her and lapping at her essence like I am starving. Indeed, it almost feels as though this manner of touch is far more intimate than using my fingers.

I groan, my *seela* writhing in almost desperation to get at her and suckle at the soft folds of flesh protecting her channel. Her *pussy,* as the manuals called it. The word is soft, just like her.

Ignoring my thrashing cock, I feast on her, my fingers digging into her soft flesh, my only focus on exploring her with my tongue. When I move my mouth up to her second opening, licking at the crinkled hole, she gasps and tries to jerk away.

I slap the rounded curve of her bottom. "Hold still, my Tribute."

"Sorry... I just... wasn't expecting that." Her voice is breathy. Soft. Full of desire. She arches her back, offering her body up to me, her Master.

I drag my tongue over her sensitive crease again, pressing harder against the small opening, and she wriggles and gasps but doesn't move away. The whimpering is very pleasing to hear.

"Please..." She begs me sweetly. "Please, Master, fuck me."

She wants me to mount her. To fill her and seed her. To bond with her. Of course, she does, she is a Tribute. That is her purpose. But I feel my resentment stir anyway, even though I know she is only following her instincts.

Everything about my Tribute tempts me... she does not just tempt me to ignore my duty, she threatens the memory of *her*. With my Tribute's scent now imprinted on my brain, I realize that I can no longer remember *her* scent. Could I before my Tribute's arrival? I am not sure. I did not try to forget *her*, exactly, but I did not try to cling to the memories either. They were too painful.

Now it feels as though my Tribute's presence has begun to erase *hers* in the only place she still exists... my memory.

Everything inside of me rebels. Even my unruly *seela* quiet as I finally realize exactly what effect having a Tribute is having on me—it is everything I feared. My chest clenches and I pull away from her.

"Master?" She begins to lift her head. In a moment she will turn and look at me and I cannot have that. I do not want her to look at me. I do not want to see her liquid brown eyes, full of desire and temptation.

A mere thought makes the nanotech from the Bride Trainer flow over her skin, from her hips to all her most sensitive parts. I make them buzz, catching my breath as she cries out and drops her head again.

"Do not tell your Master what to do, Tribute," I say harshly, thickening the parts of the belt inside of her and she moans in response.

Relief eases my tension. I do not need to touch her to pleasure her. I will distract her with her training. She will climax and then she should need to sleep again. When she wakes, I will feed her and then train her until she needs to rest again. That is what the High Commander ordered, is it not?

And during this time, I will find a way to both do my

duty to my Tribute and to preserve my memories of *her*... of my Harai.

Pareena

FREAKING BELT...

The Bride trainer is doing things for Bogdan that Frllil had *never* made it do. Things I'd never even guessed it *could* do.

The buzzing tech isn't just covering my pussy and ass, it's pushing inside of them, stretching me and filling me far more than his fingers had. Not only that, but some of it is sliding up my stomach and moving to my breasts. It tickles the sensitive underside of the hanging globes before seeking out my nipples.

Who needs nipple clamps when you have kinky alien technology?

I cry out as the pinch reaches the point of pain, making pleasure throb through me, and the belt begins to buzz and hum inside of me. My ass feels almost uncomfortably full, my pussy doesn't have a millimeter of nerves that isn't being stimulated, and now my nipples are pulsing in time with my swollen clit.

Collapsing, it feels like all the strength is being sucked out of my muscles. My orgasm wraps around me like a giant cocoon of ecstasy, smothering me in erotic bliss.

8

Pareena

I WAKE in a tangle of blankets, my legs spread far apart so that nothing touches the swollen, over sensitized flesh between them. Even with the Bride Trainer covering my pussy, I don't want to close my legs.

No one ever told me how painful multiple orgasms could eventually become. Begging hadn't stopped Bogdan. He'd kept playing with the belt, finding new horrifically deliciously creative ways to stimulate my body until I'd been mumbling and insensible.

I turned my head, which is about the only part of my body I feel strong enough to move right now. I scowl. He's gone. Again. No big alien hottie lying next to me.

And he *still* hasn't actually done the deed.

As soon as my pussy recovers and I have the chance, I

am going to jump him. Although, with Bogdan I might need a sneak attack approach. *Surprise! I tripped and fell onto your dick!* He might be mad at first, for taking control away from him... He seems very big on control.

Wait, I'm the one in control... this is my fantasy. Right? I keep forgetting because... well, because I don't feel very in control.

My stomach roars like a dragon. I'm starving again. It feels so nice to be hungry. Food would be even nicer, but I need Bogdan for that. At least, I think. All this advanced alien technology, surely there's a fridge somewhere. Or a minibar.

Sitting up, I see the filmy gown I'd worn earlier still pooled on the floor. I put it back on and move to the door.

The lights are on low throughout the chambers. Tsenturion officers must rate extra nice quarters. Bogdan has a large living space in addition to a large sleeping and separate bathing chamber.

He's kneeling in front of a wall section that has one of those removable panels. Their version of a closet? A small box, intricately carved out of something like mahogany wood, lies open before him. I can't see what's inside, but whatever it is, Bogdan stares at it like any moment it'll jump at him like a snake. In the quiet the only sound is his harsh breathing.

My stomach chooses this moment to gurgle.

Bogdan slams down the lid and rises, spinning around. *Yeesh, he's fast.* Gotta be those warrior reflexes. I back up when I catch the expression on his face, my heart tripping. Even in the picture Frllil had shown me, he'd never looked like this... like he was ready to attack. Behind him, the panel closes with an audible click.

"What are you doing?" His voice is harsh. His helmet appears between one second and the next, obscuring his face and the glittering anger in his eyes. The scary spines that pop out from the shoulders of his Batman-like suit make me want to run. Which is a bad idea. For the first time I feel a little uneasy and unsure of my safety.

Then I remember that's silly... this is all happening in my head. It's not like he can actually hurt me. Except... everything feels so real. If he did try to really hurt me, would I feel that the same way I do the spankings and the orgasms? Would my own brain do that to me?

"I..." I swallow audibly. "I woke up and w-was hungry." He is silent and I draw myself up, feeling very strange. I don't understand what his problem is, and I don't understand why my brain has created a problem, or a secret, or whatever. I should treat this like it's real, though right? Like everything else. "I didn't mean to intrude or spy on you or whatever." I flap my hand at the closet-thing behind him. "If it's personal—"

Without a word, Bogdan spins on his heel and leaves. Not just the room—his entire quarters. He heads to the main doors without pausing. They slide open just in time from him lumber through. The last I see of his giant form is him striding down the empty hall. The doors slide shut.

Well, crap. Now what?

Bogdan

LOOKING at the few keepsakes I have left from Harai has thrown me off balance. This is why I rarely acknowledge their existence. Normally they stay tucked away in my keeping place and just knowing they are there, safe, is enough. Now my Tribute knows they are there as well.

She would not touch them, would she?

My forward momentum grinds to a halt. Spinning, I move over to one of the wall consoles and use it to pull up a visual of the interior of my cabin. She is there, not looking at the keeping place, just pacing back and forth before she moves to sit down, looking thoughtful. Perhaps waiting for me to return with food?

I should get food.

I meant to go and retrieve a meal for her, before she could wake up, but I must have been lost in my memories for longer than I realized. The carefully pressed night flower Harai gave me on our last visit, to symbolize our promises to each other, to find each other at the Mating Festival upon my return. The small *suuki* rock, which the superstitious believe keep the owner safe from harm that she gave me the first time we parted. The lock of her hair tied with a ribbon. It is even softer than my Tribute's skin, but touching it gives me no pleasure.

"Bogdan? Where is Pareena?" Tribute Dawn's question makes me jump. I was so preoccupied I did not even notice her presence.

She is staring at me, her brow furrowed and confusion in her blue eyes. The pale strands of her hair are pulled back in what she calls a 'ponytail,' leaving her face and neck exposed. Beside her, Arkdhem, who is often her companion when the High Commander is on duty, is also staring at me but his expression is blank.

"I... she is back in my room. I needed... a respite. I am unaccustomed to sharing close quarters for long periods of time."

"Oh, well that makes sense," Tribute Dawn says, smiling at me. "It's definitely a bit of an adjustment. Of course, it's an adjustment for her, too. I was hoping to meet her, but Gavrill told me not to bother you two these first few days. But since you're out here without her..." Her voice trails off and she looks at me hopefully.

The idea of sending Tribute Dawn to entertain my Tribute is appealing, especially because the High Commander will not be able to chide me when I've made his Tribute happy. It will give me time to recover my equilibrium and ensure that my Tribute is not left alone for too long. Arkdhem's presence is decidedly less welcome, but at least there will be a guard.

Despite my insults to him, I know full well that he would be willing to lay down his life for both Tributes. He is not the fighter that I am, but he is highly ranked for a reason.

"If you would like to visit my Tribute, I have no objection."

Tribute Dawn sighs. "*Pareena*, Bogdan, her name is *Pareena*."

"I know that." I frown at her. I do not understand why she thinks I have forgotten my Tribute's name already.

"So why don't you use her name?"

It is not the first time Tribute Dawn has said something incomprehensible to me. From the exasperation on her face, this means something to her.

"She is my Tribute." Why would I use her name? Her name means nothing to me. That she is my Tribute means everything.

"Right. Never mind." Tribute Dawn shakes her head. "Okay, well, I'm going to go visit *Pareena*."

"Thank you for taking the time to visit my Tribute." I try to smile at her. Not just because she is being kind, but because I don't want Arkdhem to know how much it chafes to send him to look after my Tribute, even indirectly.

As I walk on, Tribute Dawn mutters something under her breath. It sounds oddly like 'hopeless.'

~

Pareena

I COULD REALLY USE A THERAPIST RIGHT NOW.

The irony is not lost on me. But truthfully, a lot of psychologists and therapists see one themselves. I did both before and after I became sick. We know and value the importance of mental health. Despite the fact that I know this is all in my head—at least, I think I know that, I'm starting to question whether or not I *really* know since I keep forgetting—I could really use someone to talk to.

I feel an emptiness in my chest that makes me ache and... I swear it's not just coming from me. Is it possible to feel someone else's emotions?

Except that Bogdan isn't someone else, he's a figment of my coma dream. A really, really, strong figment of subconscious imagination who sometimes acts like my greatest fantasy come to life and sometimes acts completely different from what I want.

There's a teeny, tiny part of me that almost wonders if maybe I'm not in a coma and this is actually all real. That's why I need a therapist. I think I might have delusional disorder, because this bizarre delusion is starting to seem more like reality. I know I'm not schizophrenic, or at least I wasn't, but is it possible something has happened to my brain chemistry while I've been comatose?

Or maybe I feel this way because to my brain, it feels like I've been on this alien fantasy ride for weeks now. Living in it. Immersed in it. And it doesn't change. The only time it changes is when I 'fall asleep' and then 'dream.' Except obviously that must just be me going deeper into my coma. Or my subconscious resting from weaving this elaborate new life.

My thoughts are going around and around, trying to remember everything I can from my old life and the details of delusional disorder, as well as everything I know about nearing death awareness and near-death experiences. Hallucinations are common.

But do they always go on this long?

There's not really anyone who can tell me that. And until, and unless, I wake up, there's no way to know how long I've actually been experiencing this. It reminds me of the old stories of the Fae, where people would be kidnapped or accidentally stumble into a faerie mound and time warped. They could spend a thousand years there, only to return and find that mere minutes had passed—or the reverse.

The knock on the door is a welcome distraction. I jump to my feet and then realize I have no idea how to open it. Bogdan just walked over to it, so I do the same, but nothing happens.

"Hello?" I call out.

"Hi!" The cheerily feminine, slightly muffled greeting nearly makes me tear up. It's Dawn. Just hearing her makes me realize exactly how much I've craved friendly female companionship over the past weeks. Frllil hadn't exactly been the kind of being I could gossip or talk with and Bogdan definitely wasn't.

This also seems like proof that this is all my subconsciousness' doing. I wished for someone to talk to and *poof!* Here she is. Sure, she's not a therapist, but hey, I can't have everything. Although, the fact that I can't actually get to her is a point against my proof...

"I'm sorry, but I can't seem to open the door," I call back apologetically. "Is there a button or something?"

The door slides open and I jump back, startled. Dawn beams at me, a looming Tsenturion warrior standing just behind her. She's very California girl from head to toe, other than the long gown she's wearing and the collar around her throat. Actually, in some places in California, the collar wouldn't be at all unusual. Long blonde hair pulled back in a ponytail, blue eyes, and a bit of tan on her skin, which is impressive considering that she's on a spaceship.

Except that I'm imagining her, so I guess she can have a tan if I want. Trying to remember that this isn't real is starting to confuse me. Maybe I should just take Dumbledore's advice. I smile back at her. I'm just going to go with the flow and pretend it's all real so my brain can stop running around in circles about it.

It's real to me.

"Hi, I'm Pareena." I hold out my hand.

Dawn launches herself at me and I find myself laughing as she hugs me tightly. I hug her back and marvel at how good it feels to just hug someone. I can't remember the last time I did that either.

"Oh... I should have asked if you're a hugger," she says, almost directly in my ear, although she doesn't let go of me either. "Sorry... I just... I really needed this."

I laugh and both of our arms tighten before we break and step away. There are slight tears in her eyes.

"You have *no idea* how good it feels to not be the only human on board," she says, grinning broadly. "Especially when I'm outnumbered by mountains of testosterone." She gestures behind her. "This is Arkdhem. He's my... well, I guess he's my bodyguard but he's also my friend."

"Hello, Tribute Pareena." Arkdhem smiles at me and steps forward, offering his hand. "It is nice to meet you." I take it and he pumps it up and down three times in very controlled movements. From the proud expression on Dawn's face as she watches the interaction, I'm guessing she taught him how to shake hands. It is pretty cute how he makes it somehow overly formal.

"Nice to meet you too. Um... I guess, do you two want to sit down?" I gesture toward the couch thing.

"I will, but Arkdhem is going to go get us some food," Dawn says, smiling brilliantly at him. "Right?"

"Nothing with meat, please," I say automatically. It hadn't even occurred to me earlier when Bogdan had brought me food. Of course, since it's my brain creating the menu, that makes sense.

"That's right, you're a vegetarian?" Dawn asks, still beaming at me. Arkdhem doesn't say anything, just tilts his head and listens to our conversation. "Are you Hindu? Is that why?"

"I'm more spiritual than religious, but yes, my parents were vegetarians and so I was raised that way. I did try some meat when I was a rebellious teenager, but I never actually liked any of it and eating something I didn't like for the sake of rebellion didn't appeal to me, so I just went back to being a vegetarian." I smile at the memory. My parents hadn't known about my illicit meat intake, but that hadn't been the point. It was better they hadn't known. If they had and disapproved, I probably would have felt compelled to keep eating it.

Dawn claps her hands excitedly. "Oh, I'm so excited!

Maybe we can do yoga together?" The expression on my face must have communicated my complete disinterest in the practice.

"I'm more of a runner," I said. At least, I had been, before the cancer. I liked movement. Going places. Staying in one place and breathing in different poses had been about as appealing as eating a meal of meat. Meditation is good for the soul, but I tended to find my meditative state on park pathways with my feet pounding against the earth and the sounds of nature all around me.

"Oh..." Dawn looks a little crestfallen. "I used to teach yoga... if you'd be interested in learning." She glances at Arkdhem. "And maybe we can figure out a path through one of the cargo bays or something." She looks back at me. "Unless you do sprints?"

Arkdhem looks confused. "Running? From what? There is no need to run from anything here. I will protect you."

Oh geez. Dawn covers her mouth as she begins to giggle helplessly, and she shrugs at me.

"Um, running for fun and exercise," I try to explain. "Just... just to run." Arkdhem looks more confused. My stomach chooses that moment to let out an embarrassingly large growl.

"Okay, I'll try to explain later," Dawn says, patting his arm. "Go get us some food for now?"

"Yes, Dawn." He smiles down at her, bringing his fist up to his chest, before exiting back out the door.

Then Dawn's stance changes entirely, to one of uncertainty, and she takes a deep breath as she meets my gaze.

"Okay, so now that we're alone, I have a confession to make," she says, the words coming out in a rush. "And if you hate me afterwards I totally understand although I hope you won't because you seem really nice and we're both stuck here and it would really suck if the only other human in this part of the galaxy hates my guts, but I don't want to start off a friendship with a lie. It's my fault you're here."

9

Pareena

I BLINK, trying to process Dawn's confession. Her fault that I'm here?

Here where? Stuck in my head? Is this some kind of manifestation of whatever part of my body is responsible for my cancer? Or possibly a manifestation of my id, confessing that it's sent me into a coma dream of my deepest sexual fantasy?

"I don't understand."

She takes another deep breath, visibly steeling herself. Every line of her body reveals how anxious she is, and I have to stifle my urge to immediately reassure her that everything is fine when I'm not sure what she's talking about.

"I was the first Tribute. I meant to fight, to escape, but... well, it's not exactly easy," she says, hunching in on herself a little. I can practically see the guilt weighing her down. "I've been here for weeks and I still don't see a way, or I would totally help you."

"It's okay," I say soothingly, automatically shifting to the tone I'd always used with distressed clients. In the back of my mind, a part of me wonders exactly how Dawn's confession fits into this dream. Maybe some portion of me feels guilty over not accepting the reality of my impending death? "We can't always escape the situations we find ourselves in. Sometimes all we can do is make the best of where we are, and there's nothing wrong with that. You're one human, on a ship filled with warriors, alien technology, and no help. No sane person would expect you to be able to escape from that."

Because winning the fight against overwhelming odds doesn't always work. Not everyone could be David and Goliath. Sometimes, you were Braveheart or Boadicea and that is just part of life.

Dawn fidgets in her seat, wringing her hands in front of her. "But... when I realized I couldn't escape, and I couldn't keep them from abducting more women, I helped them choose *you*. You fit all the parameters, you were dying, we could save you... I was so excited because I wouldn't be alone anymore and even though the Jabol matched you with Bogdan, I thought, 'hey that has to be better than dying, right?'"

I sit up a little straighter, frowning at this insult to Bogdan. "What's wrong with Bogdan?"

Hearing my indignation, her eyes widen, and she holds up her hands in front of her in a placating manner. "Nothing!" Then she shakes her head. "No, that's not true, we're going for honesty here." She looks at me curiously. "He didn't exactly want a Tribute. In fact he's been the most outspoken against it. Actually, he's been the *only* warrior against it. Some of them don't seem interested in having a Tribute, but he's the only one who actively tried to stop the program. And... okay, I'm just going to say it—he's kind of a dick."

Maybe, but he is *my* dick, and so I can't help but feel a little pang in my chest when she says he didn't want a Tribute. That explains a lot, actually.

Except... wait, it only explains it if this is real. Why would my ideal fantasy be a hot alien who doesn't actually want me?

"Oh God, I'm sorry, I'm making things worse, aren't I?" Dawn asks, looking miserable. "Look, maybe we should talk about something else. Bogdan is a hardass but he's come around. I haven't heard him say a single thing against the program in days. I mean, not that I talk to him that much but—never mind. Still not helping. Want to talk about Earth? I miss being on a planet so bad, traveling in space seems really cool but I miss weather, and animals, and television. They've got a decent selection of spanking books here, but that's about it, and I try not to encourage Gavrill to pay too much attention to those because then he gets ideas that I don't need him to have. The hot sex makes up for a lot, but I still just miss *home*, you know?"

I blink. Most humans don't refer to anything other than intercourse as sex anymore. If they mean oral, they say so. "Hot sex? Like, actual penis in vagina sex?"

She gives me a strange look. "Well, yeah."

"Bogdan hasn't actually had sex with me," I admit, a pit opening up in the center of my stomach. I put my hand over it. He didn't actually want a Tribute... if we don't have sex, will we bond the way we're supposed to? Is this his way of keeping me at arm's length?

Dawn gapes at me. "Then what have you two been doing in here?"

"Pretty much everything else. He uses his hands, his mouth, the training belt... but I haven't even seen his dick," I confess. Normally I wouldn't be this open with a stranger, but this is different. If this is real, Dawn is the only other human around, and if it's all in my head, then she's just part of my subconscious.

"Oooo, they're so weird! They kinda look like a cobra snake, and they have tentacles instead of pubic hair, and the tentacles have little suckers on the end that feel *amazing*." Dawn looks thrilled at being able to impart this knowledge and I can't help but feel envious at the way her eyes go glassy at some memory.

Except that it's not really her memory, right? So it has to just be a manifestation of what I want sex with Bogdan to be like.

So maybe some part of my brain just wants me to have to work for it?

Who knew coma dreams could be so complicated?

Bogdan

With Tribute Dawn on her way to entertain my Tribute, I find myself walking to the training arena. It is constantly filled with warriors, working to keep their skills sharp, so I know it will be easy to find a sparring partner. Working off the excess energy that my Tribute has left me with sounds appealing. Not nearly as appealing as working off the energy with her and actually finding a release... but since I can't bring myself to do that yet, I might as well do this.

A good sparring session should help clear my mind as well. I must refocus myself on my duties, my people, my vengeance. Then I can return to my Tribute with a clear mind. Perhaps that will help me control myself with her. At least long enough to reconcile my duty with my memories of Harai.

Entering the training arena, I immediately head to the sparring mats. This is one of the biggest rooms on the ship and, other than the dining hall, often the fullest. Today is no exception. I am aware of my fellow warriors pausing to look at me. I do not need to hear their whispered words to guess that they are wondering why I am here rather than with my Tribute.

As soon as I reach the sparring mats, Jakar and Volim, who have just finished a bout, approach me, curiosity in their eyes although it is not reflected in their armor. They have superb control over their emotions.

"Commander." They both salute.

"I did not expect to see you here," Jakar says, giving me the option of explaining my presence or of shrugging his comment away. Those warriors within hearing distance all pause, waiting to see if I will answer. While Volim is not interested in a Tribute, Jakar is and I cannot help but think that perhaps he is hoping I might not keep Tribute Pareena. I have been vocal in my protests against the program, even if I agreed to do my duty once she was assigned to me.

The idea of her being reassigned to someone else, even an honorable warrior like Jakar, sends a flash of jealous heat through me. He would be a better choice than Arkdhem, but yet... I cannot bear the thought of it. She is mine. My body feels it even as my mind and heart struggle.

"Tribute Dawn wanted to meet her," I say by way of explanation. It is close enough to the truth and it appeases all the listening ears. I see several nods out of the corner of my eye. Jakar and Volim chuckle and nod their heads in understanding as well, before moving off.

Since her arrival, Tribute Dawn has disrupted the natural order of things on the ship more and more every day. There is a reason Tsenturion Warriors did not take mates until they were ready to cease their military duties. Our lives are split into parts—childhood, service, and then mating and family. Trying to combine our service with mates and family is not only unwise, it is against the manner of our people, but the High Commander has spoken, and I seem to be the only one truly against the Tributes program.

Although, my feelings on that are now mixed too.

How could they not be when my Tribute was saved from death by the program? The idea of a universe without my Tribute in it is too uncomfortable to contemplate. I grit my teeth, eyes moving around the mats until I see Polixan looking back at me. He jerks his chin up at me and I move to his mat, my armor sliding down to the short pants.

Tsenturions do not fight in armor unless they mean to kill.

~

Pareena

As Dawn tells me the details of the Tributes Program, half-reluctant and half-anxious for my approval, Arkdhem returns with our food. The tray contains a lot of the same things that Bogdan brought me before, but some new things to try as well. All of it is delicious.

"So, you convinced them to only take women who are about to die, but you still feel guilty?" I ask, prompting her to talk more about the emotions I see playing across her face.

"I can definitely tell you used to be a shrink," she says with a strained laugh. She sighs. "Yes, I still feel guilty. I mean, technically we give them a choice with the survey, but who would actually believe that they're risking alien abduction? Did you?"

"Well, no..." I admit, thinking back to it. I'd thought it was a distraction, that answering might lead to something else which would entertain me and keep me from thinking about how weak and ill I felt and my impending death. Then I'd fallen asleep into this coma dream. Or I'd actually been abducted by aliens. Was it weird that I was starting to think the latter might actually be a real possibility?

Yeah, super weird.

That's how detached from reality I've become.

Maybe I shouldn't have taken Dumbledore's words so seriously.

"I did the best I could." Dawn sighs and looks at me with miserable eyes. "Do you forgive me?"

"Of course!" I say it immediately, firmly. I'm not surprised she asked. Dawn is wallowing in guilt over my presence, especially because having another human on board ship makes her so very happy.

"See, I said you were worried for nothing," Arkdhem chimes in, smiling at Dawn and nudging her with his elbow. There is something brotherly about his manner with her, which makes me smile. He is much more relaxed than Bogdan. He turns to look at me. "She has been fretting for days now, vacillating back and forth between being very excited and very anxious about your arrival. It has been most unpleasant." The last part is said in a teasing manner, which makes me laugh as Dawn groans and rolls her eyes.

"He's not wrong," she admits, sighing and setting down her empty plate. She looks around the room. "So... I kind of thought Bogdan would be back by now, if I'm being honest. I'd say we should give you a tour of the ship, but I don't want him to come back to an empty room. Find out where he is?" I blink before realizing she's asking Arkdhem, not me, to locate Bogdan.

Tilting his head as if listening to something we can't hear, Arkdhem nods his head after a few moments. "He is sparring with Polixan in the training arena. Would you like to go meet him there?"

"Yes!" Dawn's eyes light up. She grins widely at me. "Trust me, you're going to want to see this."

"Okay." I have to admit, I'm very curious now just because of her reaction. And it would be nice to see more of the ship and the Tsenturion warriors. Maybe I can see or find something that will help me determine whether this is a coma dream or reality.

Maybe it doesn't really make too much of a difference in the end, as long as it feels real, but I still want to know.

Bogdan

As Polixan and I hit and kick at each other, I can hear the warriors around us talking. Their words flow over me, but I will contemplate them later. The Vgotha are eluding us again. We have picked up another trail, but it is leading in a direction that no one expected. Everyone is worried because the Vgotha have been acting out of character for weeks now. Even before Tribute Dawn joined us. She insists that the Vgotha leader wants to meet with the High Commander, but no one believed her.

Now, after weeks without action, the warriors are starting to wonder if there was some truth to her words. We have never gone this long without a battle and it has everyone on edge. That my Tribute has joined us, a second representation of the hope for our future, a few of them are starting to wonder if perhaps we should try to speak with them. I shake my head, but the words do not impact my emotions. I am too focused on keeping Polixan outside of my guard. I will contemplate their words later.

But then I almost fall over when I feel my Tribute's presence impinge on my consciousness, allowing Polixan to get in a harder blow to my shoulder than he should have been able to land. For a moment, I think I must be imagining things, because I shouldn't be able to actually *feel* her without the bond, which we do not have. Then I realize it must be her nanotech, alerting me, and I have just confused it with thinking I can feel *her*.

A murmur sweeps across the arena and Polixan steps backs, turning to see what everyone is looking at. Swallowing a grimace, I turn as well.

Possessiveness sweeps through me when I see my Tribute making her way across the arena, Tribute Dawn at her side and Arkdhem walking just behind them. He is watching over them as if they both belong to him. It does not bother the High Commander that Arkdhem treats Tribute Dawn so familiarly, but I feel my ire rise at seeing him do the same with *my* Tribute. He reeks of desperation and I curse myself for leaving my Tribute in his care. I should have heeded my instinct not to trust him.

What did they talk about? Did he say anything to her about me? Would he try to turn her against me?

There are a multitude of eyes now on my Tribute, admiring her, and she is looking back at them. Not just looking, *admiring*.

Pushing down a snarl, I stalk toward them. Seeing me coming, my Tribute's dark eyes open wide and her gaze travels over my body, her tongue flicking out across her lower lip. I can feel her arousal surge and I send a quick order to the training belt. It begins a low hum against her flesh, and she gasps.

As I come closer, Tribute Dawn frowns, sidling next to my Tribute. "What's wrong, Bogdan?"

"You should not be here," I growl, glowering at Arkdhem and addressing him rather than Tribute Dawn. "You did not ask my leave to remove my Tribute from my quarters."

Arkdhem just stares back at me insolently as Tribute Dawn's mouth drops open in indignation. "She's an adult, meathead!" Tribute Dawn says. "She doesn't need to ask permission to go anywhere!"

"She does, and *he* needs my leave to escort her," I respond, still glaring at Arkdhem. On Tsentur, no unmated male would escort another male's mate unless they were family, or her mate had agreed to it. I had allowed him to accompany Tribute Dawn to my room, because the High Commander had set him as her guard, but that assent did not extend to *leaving* my room with him.

"It's fine, Dawn." My Tribute steps around Tribute Dawn, her eyes on me. The focus of her gaze soothes something inside of me, something that riled when I saw her looking at the other warriors. "I should have realized that I would need to ask my Master for permission to leave the room." There is a small smile on her face, but I do not think she is being insincere.

"But—" Tribute Dawn begins to protest and my Tribute glances over her shoulder at her.

"The courtship manuals, remember?" My Tribute says to her. Tribute Dawn sighs and shakes her head. The High Commander is far too lenient with her. I am proud that my Tribute already knows her place better than Tribute Dawn ever has.

Holding out my hand, I stand stock still as my Tribute comes over to me. When she places her fingers in mine, I am relieved that my armor is mostly retracted. I do not know that I could have hidden the flash of pleasure that surges through me at her touch.

"Come," I say, pulling her against me. I give Arkdhem a dark look before turning my full attention to my Tribute. "We will go back to my room now."

"Yes, Master," she says cheerfully.

The emotion that rises in my chest, warming me throughout, is not entirely welcome.

10

P areena

WITH ONE HAND on the back of my neck, Bogdan leads me back to our room. His room? I'm not really sure. He keeps saying 'his' room. Part of me wonders if that's another way to reject my presence in his life. The unwanted Tribute that he was forced to accept... but for someone who doesn't want a Tribute, he's awfully possessive.

I have to admit, that little show of jealousy in the training arena cheered me right up.

He must feel *something* for me, or he wouldn't have cared that Arkdhem was walking around the ship with Dawn and me. Or that I'd been ogling the other warriors in the training arena. Not that he needs to worry on that front. I might enjoy the scenery, but I don't want any of them. No, for some reason I want the grumpy, brooding warrior who supposedly didn't want a Tribute at all.

"So what now?" I ask, after the silent walk back to his room. I didn't want to ask in the halls, in case I didn't like the answer, but a girl can only take so much quiet.

"You left the room without permission," he says, his tone dark as he steers me toward the bed. "You've earned a punishment."

"You didn't tell me I couldn't," I point out, although I know that I probably could have figured out that he'd like a heads up. I've barely known him for twenty-four hours, but I already know that Bogdan might be the biggest control freak I've ever met. Or imagined. Whatever. Like it matters at this point.

He frowns and I swear I can feel his disappointment. Was he looking for an excuse to spank me? Hmm. Maybe I shouldn't have pointed out the flaw in his logic. According to what Dawn was able to tell me before Arkdhem returned, Tsenturion warriors were big into spankings and then sex. Or at least, her Tsenturion warrior is.

"You are correct, the fault was mine. From now on, do not leave the room without me or my permission. And you will not speak with other warriors."

"What if they speak to me first?" I ask. Not that any of them had. They'd all stopped to look at Dawn and me when we'd entered the training arena, and we'd passed quite a few in the hallways who had all bowed their heads to us before looking away, but not one had tried to speak with us. Well, except Arkdhem, but after Bogdan's little speech in the training arena, I got the feeling that he was an exception due to his position as Dawn's bodyguard. Or escort or whatever he was.

"They should not speak to you. You are mine." He pulls me to him, pressing my body against his, and I can feel my pulse begin to race again. There is no way I should be horny again already, and yet I am. One hand pets my hair, tugging it slightly so that I turn my head up towards him, while the other strokes the small of my back. "Medik and the High Commander are exceptions."

Okay, well that makes sense.

"What about Arkdhem?"

His hand fists in my hair, and my eyes widen as he pulls my head back more, baring my throat to him. It is an extremely dominant and seriously sexy move. If I had on panties instead of this stupid training belt, they'd probably hit the floor. What? I like a little bit of caveman in my men apparently. Even if he's not actually a human.

"What about him?" Bogdan growls the question—and is that my imagination or did I see a flash of red streak through his armor?

"He seems nice," I say cautiously. I don't want to prod his jealousy needlessly, but I don't want to lie either. "And if he's with Dawn all the time, I'm probably going to see him again. Am I supposed to ignore him? That seems rather rude."

Bogdan

NICE? He is a dung-eating *slythin*, a belly crawling reptile that lived in the wetlands of our home planet. That is perhaps an exaggeration, but in this moment, hearing my Tribute compliment him, that is the first thing that flashes through my mind. He wants my Tribute. I am sure of it. He wanted Tribute Dawn too but would never disrespect the High Commander by overstepping his bounds.

The way he took my Tribute from my room after I

allowed him to accompany Tribute Dawn for a visit, it is clear I will not be afforded that same respect. I trust the other warrior to have my back in battle, but obviously I cannot trust him with my Tribute.

"Stay away from him."

She makes a huffing noise with her breath, putting her hands on her hips as she pulls away from me, as much as she can while her hair is in my grip. Something about the stance seems fairly aggressive and I cannot decide whether to smile at her spirit or punish her for being disrespectful to her Master. Since we are alone and there is no one to see her, I decide not to punish her. But I do not smile either. I don't want to reward bad behavior.

"He came with Dawn. She said he goes everywhere with her when Gavrill is unavailable. So am I not supposed to see her either?"

That would be unfair to her, I admit. But he would help himself to my Tribute if he could and that is unacceptable.

"I will speak to him." I grind out. My Tribute should not be deprived of another Tribute's company just because Arkdhem does not know how to behave himself. I force myself to loosen my grip on her hair, letting my hand drop. Rather than stepping away, as I assume she would, she leans in toward me.

"You seem mad," she murmurs, running a finger down my arm, following one of the red streaks. My body tightens immediately, shifting from frustration and anger to arousal without a single stop in between. The energy I'd hoped to burn off with sparring is back as if it never left.

"Come. We have been apart for some time. I wish to inspect you." That is not what I really wish to do, but it is the closest I can come to it. For now.

"Is it really necessary?" She sighs but complies when I

pull her toward the bed and point to the floor where I wish her to stand. She makes no protest when I unhook her gown and let it fall into a filmy pile at her feet. The beauty of her body is now exposed for my pleasure. The training belt slides away from her intimate areas, turning into a belt in truth. She should always be naked in this room.

When I run my hands up and down her sides, her eyes half close. I stroke her up and down, over and over, tugging her close so I can trace the line of her neck and jaw, even her ears.

"Mmmm," she hums when I rub the small flange between my fingers. Her expression is dreamy. I have never been so fascinated with an ear before, but suddenly I must taste it. I tilt her head close and run my tongue along the edge. She shivers when I probe into the delicate channel and catch the soft lobe between my teeth, tasting it. Her legs shift and I draw her back to the bed, sitting down and pulling her into my lap. To my delight she sinks against me, curling up as if I am a particularly comfortable chair. The position puts her most enticing parts within reach.

Soon. Not yet. I turn her head and nibble at her other ear. She sighs and wriggles on my lap, stimulating my cock delightfully and making my *seela* strain toward her.

My arousal is matched by her own. Her nipples are tight beads, her breath coming in pants. I am sure that if I dip my fingers between her legs, they will come away wet with her arousal.

I dip my head to whisper to her. "Are you primed for me, my Tribute?"

"Always, Master." Her mouth is half open. I rub my thumb against the pad of her lip, and she tilts her head, drawing it into her mouth and giving it a good hard suck. My seela almost burst from my armor.

"I wish to see you climax," I tell her, and she wriggles again on my lap, setting space between us.

"I wish to see *you* climax," she responds. Her hand reaches between my thighs and strokes the bulge there. The touch is shocking, both because it is unexpected and because no one else has touched me there in so long. The need to be buried inside of her rises up inside of me, pushing at me, but I push back. I am the master of my emotions and actions, just as I am the master of her. I will not be manipulated by either.

I catch her hand and draw it up behind her back, forcing her breasts up and out. "Do not touch me without permission."

"Why?" Her breathy voice teases me. "What will happen?" She writhes in my grip, her intent obviously not to get free but to shake her breasts under my nose. Another attempt at manipulation. I cannot touch her there or she will think she has won. A pity, as I would have enjoyed playing with the soft mounds.

"I will punish you."

She squeals as I tip her over my lap. Yes, this is much more pleasing. I can watch her cheeks grow pink as she shifts on her belly, stimulating my cock, and she will know she is not in charge. I palm her backside, feeling her bottom wriggle as she kicks and squirms, trying to get free.

"This is what happens to naughty Tributes." I crack my palm on her bare bottom over and over, enjoying her shrieks. Finding pleasure in the way she writhes against me. Her bottom must be more resilient than Tribute Dawn's, considering the amount of punishment she can take. She's not distressed by the discipline, although indignant, and when I check her for arousal, she is perfectly primed, dripping wet with sweet passion for me. "What's this? Do you enjoy your discipline?"

She moans as I dip my fingers in and lifts her hips, trying to direct my fingers toward her pleasure nub. Of course, I will not allow her such a treat when she is being disciplined.

"You know I do." Her voice is sassy, and I immediately move my fingers away from her wetness. My Tribute moans in disappointment and then shrieks as I begin to spank her again, much harder this time.

SMACK!

SMACK!

SMACK!

"Is that how you address your master?"

"No! Sorry! Master, please."

She shudders and begs when I dip my fingers into her slick channel and gather the juices. I stroke the furrows of her sex, avoiding touching the fleshy protrusion that is the hot button to her pleasure. The manuals spoke of the clitoris as being impossible for most male humans to find but I locate Pareena's easily every time. Another reason Tsenturions are superior to other males. The ones that do find the clitoris don't understand the fleshy nub is only a small part of pleasure-receptor filled tissue.

Not every female will enjoy direct touch on the small, sensitive bud. Pareena seems to prefer indirect stimulus. She jumps when I apply too much pressure, but purrs when I stroke beside it. It is best if I do not get too close right away, but spend time teasing her until she is primed and beyond begging.

I do this now, alternating with sharp smacks to her bottom. This isn't a true punishment, only a reminder of who's in charge. Judging by the way she's now pushing up to meet my palm, she's enjoying it more than she lets on. I apply a round of swats to the top and bottom quadrants of each cheek and plunge two fingers into her tight channel. She throws her head back with a throaty moan.

"Do not climax without permission," I advise her. "You will not like the consequences."

"Will you belt me, Master?" She wriggles her bottom. Cheeky Tribute. I lift her and position her on the bed, her legs hanging over the side and hips propped on a pillow. When I return with the strip of *kurdzu* hide she calls a belt, I present it to her lips.

"Kiss it. And when I'm done you will thank me." I run a hand down her taut back to calm her. She is not afraid, but excited. Her juices are running down her leg.

"Count," I order and snap the belt against her warmed backside.

"One," she cries, her legs straining for the floor. I steady her with a hand on her lower back and lay careful stripes on her bottom and thighs.

Pareena

I MIGHT REGRET THIS TOMORROW...

The pain is delicious, but deep down I know I am over-doing it. I just don't care. The tears sliding down my face feel freeing. The arousal curling in my core is turning me into a horny, spanking-crazed slut. In the best possible way, of course.

Every crack of the belt across my ass makes me scream, and yet as soon as the burning sting fades from the initial impact, I crave another. I moan when he pauses, stroking his fingers through my arousal again, circling my clit and teasing me with a touch that is too soft to bring me satisfaction.

"Please, Master," I beg.

But his hand lifts again and my head drops down in disappointment.

Then he slaps my pussy.

I cry out as the tips of his fingers snap against my clit and the surrounding area, the exquisite agony making my toes curl. He does it again and again, as if he knows exactly what the stinging slaps are doing to me. My orgasm swells, close to bursting, but not quite making it.

"Please, please, please," I beg, chanting the word over and over again. Then his fingers press down over my mound, rubbing the whole area and my entire body jerks.

"Come for me, my Tribute."

The order, his deep growling voice, set me off and I scream with release as he moves his fingers in a circular motion. Ecstasy pounds through my body, taking every ounce of pain and twisting it, turning it into spectacular pleasure.

My arms collapse, leaving my upper body resting against the bed, quivering from the intense orgasm. Bogdan's fingers make one last swirl around my throbbing clit and then move away. I swear I can feel him staring at my pussy, like he wants nothing more than to thrust inside me, but something is holding him back.

Should I say something?

Do something?

Torn with indecision, I bite down on my lower lip and wait.

It doesn't matter that I just had an orgasm—I still want

him. I almost feel like I *need* him inside of me, like there's a gaping emptiness that won't go away until he fills me.

"What do you say?" he asks finally.

"Thank you, Master."

I hold my position. Waiting. Hoping.

Finally, I turn my head to look at him over my shoulder. I was right. He is staring right at my upturned ass, but he's not moving. The expression on his face is conflicted, but full of desire. Then he notices that I'm looking back at him and his gaze lifts to meet mine.

"What is it, my Tribute?"

"Do you want me to really thank you?" Before he can stop me, I flip around, so that I'm kneeling facing him rather than looking away from him. His eyes lock onto my breasts and I put my hands on his thighs. The alien cock that Dawn described is right in front of my face, just his armor between us, and I swear I can see it move. "Let me pleasure you, Master."

"No." He steps back, turning away, and I let my hands drop, trying not to cry as the feeling of rejection wells up inside of me. Turning away, he moves to hang the belt back up on his Wall of Pain.

What am I doing wrong? Why doesn't he want me? I gather my courage. We can't keep going on like this.

"Master, I have a question." I'm pretty sure I see his shoulders tense at the question, but I persevere anyway. "Why haven't we had sex yet?"

Rather than answering me, Bogdan turns back around and walks past me, heading for the door while gesturing for me to get into the bed. "You should rest."

I scramble up to follow, ignoring his hand gesture. It's not like he gave me an order or anything. "Did I do something wrong?"

Black slides up around his body, his armor going back into place as if it can shield him from me. Hurt wells up in my chest. Dammit.

I catch up to him before he reaches the door to leave our quarters.

"Where are you going? Master?"

"You do not have permission to leave the room. I will be back soon."

The door opens and he whisks away, leaving me standing there feeling utterly rejected. I dig my nails into the palms of my hands, determined not to cry. Taking a few deep breaths, I push down the ache in my chest.

Talk about *wham, bam, thank you, alien.*

I guess I'm not getting an answer right now. Why doesn't he want to have sex with me? Dawn was surprised by it. We didn't talk about it with Arkdhem there, but maybe I should have... no. That would be a bad idea. Something about Arkdhem definitely rubs him the wrong way. I don't need to put more obstacles between us.

I'd think that maybe something is wrong with his equipment, but when I touched him earlier, he was hard and there seemed to be extra movement as well. I'm not sure what a cock surrounded by tiny tentacles is supposed to feel like, but it seemed to fit Dawn's description.

I pivot in a slow circle and go to pick up my gown. I would kill for jeans and a t-shirt right now, but regardless, I'm not just going to stand around here naked. I feel vulnerable enough already. My alien fantasy is starting to feel a lot more complicated than I ever expected. Another point to it being reality? I still can't quite swallow that though.

I wonder how much time I have before Bogdan returns. I suppose I could just walk out without him, but without Dawn I'll have no idea where I'm going. Plus, I doubt making him angry is going to help. I nibble on my thumb-nail, a nervous habit that I've never quite managed to grow out of.

This isn't at all ethical but... I want to know what's going on and he's not talking. Dawn doesn't know. And this probably isn't even real, right? It's not really snooping if I'm imagining all of this.

And if I'm not?

I shake my head. My mind is made up. Hey, even Hermione knew that you have to break the rules sometimes.

I'll start with the secret panel on the wall where he hid that box. I was going to try and respect his privacy, but he's not talking and I'm getting pissed. And hurt. Besides, if he comes back and what's the worst he can do—punish me?

11

Bogdan

I MARCH DOWN THE HALL, acknowledging passing warriors' salutes and scowling when they congratulate me on my Tribute. I do not wish to think about my Tribute when my cock and *seela* are bellowing for relief. My jaw clenches and I rub my chest. I feel a kind of pain there, but it is a strange pain, as if it is not my own.

I do not like thinking about the look on my Tribute's face when I left the room.

Part of me wishes the Vgotha would appear, simply so I could justifiably stay away from her. Just for a little bit. Also, surely a fight with the enemy would take the edge off my constant state of arousal, where sparring did not.

Why haven't we had sex yet?

I do not have an answer that would satisfy the High

Commander, so I do not think it would satisfy her either. I am unable to even explain it to myself.

I would not be betraying a mate. I have no formal allegiance to Harai, who is long gone and was far too kind to deny me happiness in the future. And yet every time I begin to get caught up in the moment, something holds me back.

It feels wrong to me, to have Tributes when we have not yet defeated our enemy, yet I seem to be the only one who thinks so.

My Tribute intrigues and challenges me at every turn and I enjoy her spirit as much as her body... but to bond with her... to breed with her...

Are we to create a new generation of Tsenturions when we cannot even guarantee their safety against the Vgotha threat? I shake my head, shoving away the panic and crushing guilt that threatens my composure. The decision has already been made, no matter that I disagree with it.

I will do my duty.

Somehow.

The scent of food and echoing loud voices signal an end to my walk. I stride into the mess hall to find more edible vegetation for my Tribute.

When I enter the cafeteria, several warriors hail me, acknowledging my presence. I nod but quickly look away from them to be sure none approach. It works; I have several moments of solitude to review the food lists and find ones I think my Tribute will enjoy.

In the end, the only Tsenturion other than High Commander Gavrill who would dare interrupt me when I obviously wish to be left alone steps up to my side. Medik is older, wiser, and not a warrior. He is an anomaly, a man who finished his service, mated, fathered children, but then came with us when our Medik was injured on duty. He was supposed to serve one mission and then return home... but there was no home to return to. During the mission, he'd preferred to go by his title, but after the Great Devastation, he'd given up his name entirely, demanding to be known only by his title, as his mate had been the last to speak his name and he did not want that taken away from him.

His loss was greater than any of ours individually, yet somehow, he has more hope than I do.

"Greetings, Bogdan. How goes the bonding of Tribute Pareena?"

"My Tribute's training is going well enough." I respond, my voice even. I specifically don't mention bonding. There has been no bonding yet. A feeling of guilt suffuses me, because there are many warriors who would love to bond with a Tribute, and yet I am fighting the bond with mine. However, the idea of bonding with her also fills me with guilt. There is no winning this scenario.

Medik just smiles.

"Is your Tribute unsatisfactory?" he asks.

"My Tribute is perfect." I snap the words out defensively before I realize it was probably his intention to goad me.

Medik cocks his head, a twinkle in his eye. Not a very soldier-ly gesture, but he has always been more expressive than the rest of us. "Perfectly suited to the Tribute program or perfect for you?"

"Is there a difference?"

Rather than answering, he just chuckles and continues on as if I had answered him. "I had hoped the altered questionnaire would yield good results. Dawn's input was invaluable. Has Pareena shared anything about her past life with you?"

If he were anyone else, his familiar use of my Tribute's name would rankle, but since it is Medik, I let it pass.

"The subject has not come up." Was that not what her file was for? What more do I need to know?

"Hmmm," Medik sips his drink, studying me. "It might be good to discuss life events before her arrival. Hers and yours."

I come close to blurting out how she found me looking over the contents of the betrothal box. Which is odd. I have never felt the need to share my personal experiences before. At times Medik has asked questions about my mental and emotional state, but I assured him my mental faculties would not interfere with my warrior duties. As long as my physical health is in peak condition, I have no need to review my memories.

"What purpose would it serve?" I scowl, as if displeased by the idea, but truthfully, I am curious. After all, he is the only male other than the High Commander who has ever been mated. In many ways, he has served as a paternal guide to all of the warriors in our fleet. We all lost our fathers and mothers to the Great Tragedy, and he stepped into the breach.

Medik is used to my severe expressions and, as usual, ignores this one. "She will surely wish to know more about the warrior she's been given to. I understand you are, ah, busy getting to know her in other ways," Medik's cup barely hides his smile, "but when you rest you might talk to her about each other."

"Perhaps I shall," I murmur. Now that he has suggested it, I cannot help but wonder if there are things the file did not reveal to me. Besides, knowing more about my Tribute can only be a good thing. The more I know, the easier I can train her to bend to my will.

"Excellent," Medik exclaims. "I wish you all success. Let me know if I can assist you."

I could protest that I have no need for his help. My Tribute will respond to my questions in a satisfying manner because she is obedient and acknowledges me as her Master, but I have another issue to tend to.

Before he can turn away, I catch his arm.

"There is a matter you can help with."

"Oh? Not a medical issue, I hope?"

"Of a sort. My Tribute does not eat the flesh of animals. I was able to provide a meal for her earlier, but I do not know if it was adequate for her needs on a continuing basis. What plant-based dishes provide the most nutrients for her system?"

Several minicycles later, I enter my quarters laden with two large platters of nutritional plant-based dishes. Medik was happy to help me select them.

I frown when I do not immediately see my Tribute and set down the platters. I feel strangely uneasy and sad. Am I feeling what she is feeling? Where is she?

"Pareena?" To call her 'my Tribute' when I am addressing her feels too strange and I remember how Dawn insisted I use my Tribute's first name, seeming to think I had an objection to it. I like my Tribute's first name. It rolls off the tongue in a pleasing manner.

A choked cry, on the other side of the bed, makes me rush forward. My Tribute is kneeling again, by the wall. When she looks up at me, tears are streaming down her face. The source of the uneasy sadness is clear. Somehow, I know what she is feeling. But I cannot focus on that revelation now, not when I can see her distress.

"What is wrong? Are you hurt?" I crouch and run my hands over her clothed body.

"I'm fine," she sniffles. "I'm fine." She catches my hand and presses it to her chest. "Oh, Bogdan, I'm so sorry."

"You are unhurt? Then why are you crying?"

She shakes her head, unable to answer. I gather her into my arms and hold my Tribute as she weeps. My insides feel as if they have been scrambled. I wish to fight but there are no threats in the room. What could have disturbed her?

My eyes fall on the open panel that usually hides the compartment where I keep my memory box. She's taken out the gifts from Harai, as well as the only items I have left from my parents and ancestors. I have not looked at the vid pics of my sisters and younger brother in decacycles, and seeing their faces now sends a pang of grief through me.

Pareena

As SAD As I was feeling before, just looking at the pictures of children and realizing they must have all been killed when Tsentur was destroyed, is nothing to how I feel, watching as pure grief etches itself across Bogdan's face.

"I'm sorry," I whisper, leaning into him, holding onto him. I'm terrified he'll pull away from me, but if anything, he seems to sag against me. The anger he felt when I saw him looking through this box the last time is nowhere to be seen, and somehow that makes me feel even worse. "I went snooping."

"It... it is understandable." His words are stilted. Tight. I cannot tell if he actually means them or not. "You wish to know more about me."

I thought I felt his grief, but now I just feel a kind of emptiness, as if all emotions have shut down.

"You're not mad?" I ask, tentatively.

"No."

I hold my breath, but it doesn't seem like he's going to say anything more without prompting. "Who are they?"

We both look at the pictures simultaneously. I can guess who they are, but I think it will probably do him some good to talk about it. Maybe that's the shrink in me, but I've never seen anyone more bottled up than Bogdan is.

"My sisters. My brother. My family."

I swear I can feel the sadness coming back to fill the emptiness, as though just saying their relation to him has somehow breached the barrier against his emotions.

We are both silent again for a long moment. Sometimes silence is all that is needed to get someone to open up.

"Do you wish for me to tell you what happened?" His voice is reluctant, but that's not entirely unexpected. Still, I almost sigh in relief that he's making the offer. I wasn't completely sure he would, which *should* have been fine but... it's easier to maintain a professional distance when I don't have a personal stake.

"Would you?" I ask softly.

To my surprise, Bogdan leans back against the wall, pulling me onto his lap. I snuggle in, pressing myself against his body and doing my best to serve as a comfort during what I know will be a difficult talk for him. Frllil told me about the Great Tragedy. But it's different hearing about an event from someone who wasn't affected by it versus someone whose life was radically changed by it.

I can feel the rumble of his voice through his chest as he begins to speak.

"It was planting time. Night blossoms signal the time for the Mating Festival. Our fleet was late returning to Tsentur, which had never happened before in living memory..." His voice trails off, as if the pain is too much to bear and instinctively, I lean into him. I can already feel the tears gathering at the backs of my eyes again. Clearing his throat, his arms tighten around me. "I was to leave my duties as a soldier and return to the planet, where I would rejoin my family and travel to the Festival."

He falls silent again. Lost in the memories perhaps.

"Were you going to find a mate?" I ask gently.

"I had already found one."

The answer surprises me and I am glad he has me wrapped tightly in his arms, because I'm not sure I could have contained my shock. That was the last thing I'd expected, especially because I was told that Tsenturions could only bond with a mate once. But, of course, he didn't get a chance to bond with her.

My heart aches and a fresh wave of tears spills from my eyes. It's so incredibly tragic and yet I feel anger rising too. Not at Bogdan, but at the Vgotha. The unnecessary loss is so devastating, so infuriating, that even I feel it. Bogdan shouldn't be here. He should be happily mated, possibly with children. No wonder he didn't want a Tribute. It wasn't personal to me at all.

"Did you love her?" I keep my voice soft, calm. My therapy voice. Although the way my fingers stroke over his chest, trying to soothe him, isn't at all professional. I can't seem to make myself stop though.

"I did." The pain and sadness in his voice make me want to hug him for the rest of his life. "We had not bonded, but I was looking forward to our life together."

I choke a little, and then I realize that I'm crying a lot harder than I thought I was. My chest heaves, but I don't seem to be able to make myself stop.

"Hush." Now Bogdan is the one comforting me. Holding

me tightly, he begins to rock me slightly. "Do not distress yourself. It was a long time ago."

"It's so sad. You all lost so much." And no matter how long ago it was, I can tell it still affects him. It still affects all of them. How could it not?

12

Bogdan

I TRY to thumb away my Tribute's tears, but there are too many of them.

"It was a long time ago," I repeat the only thing I can think of to say, to try and comfort her.

"It still hurts," she whispers.

I cradle her head to my chest and let her cry, because she speaks the truth. *It still hurts.* No matter how long it has been, it still hurts. I rest my cheek against my Tribute's head. She fits into my arms perfectly, her slight weight replacing the heavy feelings I've carried for many cycles. The burden is still there, but fractured, like a stone broken into many pieces. Smaller pieces more easily dealt with. *It still hurts.* But perhaps not as much.

I have never cried before, yet my Tribute is weeping far

too vigorously for just discovering my betrothal box. Could she be sensing my grief?

Whatever it is, I feel calmer when her sobs quiet. I pull the box closer and sift through the contents to find the ones not related to Harai.

I lift out a small jeweled dagger. "This was my grandmother's. She carried it always, until I came of age and she gave it to me." I thumb the pommel where a stone is missing. "She let me play with it when I was young, but I dropped it and broke the main setting. So, she took the jewel and added it to our family crest." I pick up the brooch she'd made from it. The black stone glitters in the bronze setting.

"This looks like onyx." My Tribute tentatively lifts her hand and I let her take it from me. She turns it over, inspecting it. Her eyes and nose are puffy and slightly discolored, but she seems to have calmed as well. She holds it up to my chest and giggles. "You should wear it. It matches your suit."

Because both are black. A small smile of amusement curves my lips.

"What about this, Master?" she asks, emboldened by my sharing. She reaches past me and touches the golden lock of hair, although she does not pick it up.

I remain silent for a long moment, staring at Harai's hair, feeling the ache... feeling the guilt of having my Tribute in my lap as I look at my intended mate's last gift. The High Commander has bonded with his Tribute, but I have not bonded with mine. Part of me still feels that the very presence of non-Tsenturion mates makes a mockery out of what had been a sacred bond on our planet. Yet, I still want my Tribute now that I have her.

"Was it hers?" she asks gently. I nod and a muscle in my jaw clenches. I am unable to speak, too overcome with conflicting emotions. My Tribute sets the brooches and dagger back in the box and twists around to cup my face. "It's okay, Master. I know you don't want a mate. I'm not trying to replace your lost love."

I blink. How did she know my thoughts?

"It was wrong of me to pry," she says, her fingers softly stroking my cheeks. I can feel the sadness in her, but also a kind of calm that creeps over me like a comforting balm. She is no innocent. She too has known grief and loss.

"Why did you?" I ask, curious. Medik did tell me to ask her more questions. I would not have thought that sharing more of myself with my Tribute would make me feel better, but it did.

"I wanted to know more about you. I want to be closer to you."

I frown, my arms tightening around her. "You are already close to me." I shift my legs underneath her for emphasis.

Surprisingly, her dark eyes twinkle with humor in response, her mood lightening. "*Closer* than that. I'm here for you, Master, Bogdan, however you want me. I understand if you want to wait."

She bites her lip and drops her eyes. My cock stirs.

Oh.

The urge to claim her wells up inside of me, stronger than ever now that she's told me that she understands... that she will wait. I don't know why, but somehow that one sentence breaks through the resistance that I have been feeling. I never fully understood my resistance either, so perhaps it is not surprising that I don't fully understand why her offer has affected it.

"I do not wish to wait," I say, abruptly standing with her in my arms. She grabs onto me, holding tightly and blinking in surprise as I carry her to the bed.

Her slight weight reminds me to be gentle. I lay her on the bed and pull off her gown, exposing her smooth skin to my touch. My cock is achingly hard, my *seela* unruly and writhing with the need to connect to her. *Yes.*

The Vgotha threat still exists, but we will eradicate it. My Tribute will just give me another reason to fight.

She can be distracting, but I have already proven, both to myself and to the other warriors, that I can attend both my Tribute and my duties.

The loss of Harai still hurts, but she is gone, and she would want me to be happy. My Tribute makes me... well, not happy exactly, but even before the Great Tragedy I was not a cheerful Tsenturion. But she makes me less unhappy. She soothes the sharp edges of pain and anger inside of me, even if she does not eradicate them entirely.

Rest peacefully, Harai.

The thought slides through my mind like a benediction, a release from a long sentence of grief and fury. Those emotions are not gone, but there are other emotions now too.

Curiosity. Affection. Admiration. Desire. My Tribute has awoken a side of me that I thought had died with Tsentur. It has been an uncomfortable and sometimes painful awakening, but now I don't want to hold back from her any longer. She is not the mate I intended to have, but she is my Tribute and she will be my mate.

I rear up over her, drinking in the sight of her lithe form sprawled on my bed. Her hair flows around her shoulders like a black river. Her gaze is lazy, eyes hooded, as she studies me as I am studying her.

Suddenly I wonder what she thinks of me. Does she long for my touch as I long for hers?

Her tongue darts out and swipes over her lips, and I have

my answer. I command my armor to retract. Her eyes widen with anticipation and then widen even more when her gaze comes to my cock. The way her lips pop open in surprise, I know that she is impressed. My *seela* strain towards her body.

~

Pareena

DAWN HAD NOT BEEN EXAGGERATING about the alien peen. If anything, she understated it.

It really does remind me of a cobra, rising up from a nest of tentacles, all of which are trying to reach me. There is one longer tentacle above all the others and my pussy clenches when I realize it's at the *exact* right spot to be able to stimulate my clit. I sit up, reaching towards them, the same way they're reaching toward me, and then I hesitate.

"Can I touch them, Master?" I ask, looking up at him.

The way he's looking at me is very human. All prideful male, pleased with my reaction to his cock.

"Gently." He threads a hand into my hair, and my mouth waters. Something about having a man's hand in my hair, his cock in my face, just always makes me want to suck it. Apparently, it doesn't matter that the cock itself is a little weird looking.

I don't go right for the gold though when I touch him, instead I stroke the longest tentacle of the moving nest while the smaller ones brush over the back of my hand as soon as it's close enough.

"They're soft." It's a really weird sensation—this whole

thing is weird—but I'm surprisingly okay with all of it. "Almost velvety."

"I am not soft," Bogdan says, sounding insulted.

"Just the skin is," I reassure him. Apparently, males have some similarities no matter what part of the universe they come from. "I can feel that you're very hard." I wrap my fingers around the shaft of his cock, just under the flaring head, and he groans, his hips thrusting forward eagerly.

Considering how many times he's gotten me off without getting himself off, it's a testament to his willpower that he doesn't do more than that. I can't help but wonder what it would take to break that steely self-control. His cock flexes in my hand. Not the same way a human's penis would. Human genitalia is more rigid and it might pulse or throb, but it wouldn't actually *bend*. The hooded head flares, its edges moving up and down and reminding me of the way a stingray looks when it swims.

Holy shit.

The possibilities boggle the mind. And then add in the tentacles...

I giggle when the little strands pull at my skin, trying to wrap around my fingers. This is seriously the whole package. And I feel a little pang of disappointment that it's really unlikely Bogdan would get the joke if I tried to make it.

I move my fingers over the shaft, pulling them out of reach of the tentacles and then sliding back down. He groans again, his hand tightening in my hair, but that is his only reaction.

I can't help it. I have a Ravenclaw's curiosity and I have to know.

Dipping my head, I swipe my tongue over the broad, slowly undulating head of his cock. His skin is more textured than a human's and I wonder how it will feel when it's sliding inside of me. Right now, though, my focus is on what I'm doing to *him*. Bogdan's body goes rigid as my tongue explores his cock.

"What are you doing?" He sounds like he is choking on the words.

I look up at him and the expression on his face... shock, desire, curiosity. It's the most open I've ever seen him. I grin slyly up at him. "Didn't the manuals cover blow jobs? Oral sex?"

"Yes..." His voice trails off slightly and I suddenly realize that he might not have completely understood what the books were talking about if the Tsenturions don't have a frame of reference for it.

This should be fun.

～

Bogdan

MY TRIBUTE'S tongue flicks out again, running along the rippling ridge of my cock. Shivers run through me, but I am otherwise frozen, watching her taste my sensitive flesh. It is strange but extremely pleasurable as her small tongue explores me.

She works her way down to my cock and envelops the tip in wet heat. The sensation is enough to nearly unman me and my knees lock in place, body arching, sending my cock deep into her mouth. Instead of drawing back, she hums, sending tiny vibrations through my synapses. The pleasure is overwhelming. Seeing her dark eyes, watching her face, as she swallows me is the most shocking and erotic experience of my life.

As she moves inward, my lesser seela suction onto her face and pull her close. I can feel her arousal more strongly than ever, feel her pleasure in serving me. She is enjoying this. Not in the same way I am, but, nonetheless. I do understand, because I enjoyed tasting her, but I had not expected her to enjoy the same. The manuals had indicated that not all human females want to perform the oral sex.

My Tribute must be a superior human female, which does not surprise me.

My prime seela strokes her face. She closes her eyes, breathing through her nose as she sheaths my cock in her throat. My fingers are still fisted in her hair, but instead of pulling her off, I allow her to work up and down on my cock until stars fill my vision. My arousal tightens like a fist. If she continues, I will not be able to claim her.

She slides her mouth off, drawing in a deep breath. My *seela* release their hold, leaving small marks across her cheeks. Marks that arouse me even more, because of what they mean. Before she can plunge down again, I tug her away.

"Not that way." The urge to claim her, to sink into her and release my seed is too strong. I will not be able to hold back if she uses her mouth for the oral sex again.

"Did you like it?" she asks, breathless, her eyes bright as if I have been pleasuring her, not the other way around.

I trace my finger over one of the circular marks on her cheek. "I liked it very much, but I want to claim you now."

"Are you sure?" she asks, and I can see a spark of fear in her eyes, feel it in the nanotech. "Because if you start and then change your mind, I think I might actually cry again. And I really don't want to cry again today."

"I will not change my mind," I assure her. "You are my

Tribute. It is time and I have waited long enough to fully claim you."

Too long, I am sure the High Commander would say. The other warriors would agree. But it is the right time for me, for us.

Pressing her back onto the bed, I move atop my Tribute, ready to truly make her *mine*.

$\sim$

Pareena

BOGDAN'S LIPS MEET MINE, taking my mouth before I can respond. His tongue slides against mine and I feel movement against my inner thighs, making me shudder in erotic anticipation. Were those the tentacles?

Yes, yes, yes, yes, yes please!

My arms move, sliding over his hard muscles, tentatively at first, because he hasn't really allowed me to touch him like this before, and then more... and more... I am greedy, exploring his body with my fingertips and he groans, rocking against me.

Oh my...

Those are *definitely* the tentacles, moving against the sensitive skin of my inner thighs, working their way to my pussy. The Bride Trainer retracts, leaving my sex open and exposed. A kind of fearful, excited anticipation fills me. What is this going to feel like?

Something moves against my pussy and then I feel it, pushing into me. The flared head is thick and strangely shaped, but I am soaking wet and it manages to push inside of me. I cry out against Bogdan's lips, my nails digging into his shoulders. It only takes him a moment to take my wrists and pin my hands down above my head, leaving me totally helpless beneath him, as he slowly impales me on his alien cock.

It *moves* inside of me, pressing against my quivering muscles in strange ways, all while his tongue strokes the inside of my mouth.

Talk about an alien invasion, I think, and then have to wonder if I'm a little hysterical.

It feels so incredibly good that I can barely stand it.

Something pulls at my labia, and I realize that the tentacles have gotten in on the act. The sensation is tingling pleasure, like bubbles traveling over my skin, and then it deepens even more, as if he's literally sucking on my pussy while he fucks me. When the super long one moves over my swollen clit, my whole body jerks in reaction.

His lips leave mine, and then Bogdan is staring down at me, watching my reaction as our groins press together. His strange cock is fully buried inside of me and his tentacles are stroking and sucking me and I can actually feel my toes curling.

"Oh... oh fuck... Please..." I beg, my need, my pleasure already rising higher and faster than I can handle. "It's like a tongue, licking... oh please... please don't stop..."

The *prime seela* that Dawn had told me about suctions onto my clit, tugging on the sensitive nub, and I scream as ecstasy surges, releasing the tension that had coiled almost too quickly and too powerfully inside of me. I writhe underneath him, my entire body quaking with the hot bliss... and then he rolls over so that I am sitting on top of him and it feels like he is even deeper inside of me.

~

Bogdan

I prop up my Tribute as her body rocks in orgasm. As much as I long to unleash the full power of my desire upon her, I am too worried that doing so will hurt her. My control is close to snapping as it is. Having her on top of me will help keep me from causing her any harm.

She cants forward, clasping her hands behind my neck now that I have returned control of her arms to her. My whole torso is rigid, muscles bunching in an attempt to control my impulse to flip her on her back and pound out my need between her accommodating thighs. She shifts up and down, back and forth, wriggling as if it will help her accommodate the thick intruder.

"You're so big," she gasps.

"You're so small," I correct her. She whimpers and I hold her close. "Just wait." Her body is opening like a flower, coating my cock in her cream and allowing it to slide inside.

"No, I need you." she strains to seat herself, but I don't let her go. For a moment she struggles in my hold, pushing at my chest and grunting with exertion. I swallow my amusement. Her dark eyes flash defiance and it makes me want to laugh.

"Kiss me," I whisper, to distract her. Immediately she leans forward, obeying her Master's command. My lips claim hers, my tongue thrusting into her mouth. She moans as she moves, rising up high enough that it stretches the *seela* suctioned to her skin, before sliding back down my cock. Her head falls back, ending the kiss.

"Oh yes..." She shudders, arching, and I curve one arm around her back to stabilize her while my other hand seeks out her breast.

"Good girl," I say, repeating the accolade I saw most often in the manuals. I am immediately rewarded when her pussy clamps down around my cock in reaction. The hot, wet pulse of her body around mine is celestial.

"More," she demands, breathing fast and struggling to move. "Harder."

For the first time in what feels like forever, my face creases into a smile. "Patience, little one."

"*Now*," she half-orders, half-begs. My Tribute is bossy and it's adorable. Instead of anger that she dare to command me, as she has clearly forgotten herself in her need for my cock, I am amused and gratified by her overwhelming desire.

"Fuck me, Bogdan, please," she begs, resting her forehead on my chin, her pussy fluttering around my cock. Rather than chastising her, I decide whenever I am inside her, she will call me by name instead of Master. I like the way she says it.

Reaching down, I trace the plump petals spread around my hard shaft, displacing lesser seela as I measure how much more of me she needs to take. My hand comes away coated with her wetness. My prime seela is nestled beside the fleshy ridge of her most sensitive spot. It undulates gently, stimulating her constantly. No wonder she is mad with need.

"As you wish," I murmur, loosening my grip so that she can rise halfway up my cock. Gravity and my *seela* tug her down, impaling her again and making both of us groan. Tremors of pleasure ripple through her.

"I've never been so full." She is panting for breath. "Harder please, Master, fuck me."

"Bogdan," I correct her.

"Bogdan," she repeats immediately, her sultry voice

turning my name into a sigh of pleasure. "Please, fuck me. I need you."

I need you.

Her words spark something inside of me, and my self-control slides away like a Vgotha ship on the run. My muscles bunch and roll as I rock into her, forcing her to ride my body like a boat bobbing on a wave. Her small body is suspended over mine, held up by my hand in her hair and my cock impaling her. Once I am sure she is fully seated again, I snap my hips and make her bounce.

A keening cry escapes her, and a flush creeps up her chest. She is climaxing. Again. What little control I had left is gone. I flip her onto her back. She is soft and wet now, her pussy adjusted to my cock. There should be no danger of harming her.

I grasp her hips and pound her, my lesser *seela* slackening and tightening to allow my movement, my prime *seela* wagging wildly against her clitoris. Her orgasm is non-stop, constant waves of wild sensation breaking in her body. I feel the feedback in the back of my mind, her pleasure and satisfaction a constant presence as my own climax grows to epic proportions, ready to crash into us both. Her mouth is slack, her eyes practically rolling back in her head, but her nails claw my back as if to urge me on.

My cock stiffens, hardening to its full length, my *seela* pulling at her flesh and initiating the exchange of bio information. Rapture erupts, carrying my seed with it into her body, leaving us shuddering together in mutual bliss.

13

P areena

A SOFT TOUCH on my folds makes me whimper.

"Easy," Bogdan soothes, rubbing cream into my sore pussy. The ache diminishes almost immediately, and I sigh in relief. When I'd told him "harder," he'd definitely ended up taking me at my word. I wonder if this is how Lois Lane feels after she gets it on with Superman.

When he's finished, he looks at me, studying my expression. Giving him a lazy smile, I reach out and trace his hard features. He smiled earlier, I'm almost sure of it. I didn't realize it at the time, I was too desperate to be fucked, but the memory floats back to me as I lie in a post-coital haze. I never thought I'd see the big, surly alien let down his guard, but here he is, fussing over me, wiping off my sweaty limbs with a soft cloth and inspecting the puffy redness of my labia.

"That's normal," I tell him. At least, I'm assuming it's normal. There's usually post-coital soreness after any vigorous sex, much less vigorous alien sex with a strangely shaped cock. "I'm fine."

"You are so tight," he muses, looking back down at my pussy contemplatively. "I will have the Bride Trainer prepare you before your next claiming."

I whimper at the thought of being filled, of going about my day constantly fucked by the Bride Trainer in preparation for my Master's cock. It sounds both torturous and unbearably arousing... actually, wait, I've done it before with Frllil and it was both of those things. But it seems like it would be even more so when Bogdan is the one giving the orders to the Bride Trainer instead of Frllil.

"I'm fine," I say hastily, half-hoping that he'll believe me, half-hoping he won't. He frowns at my dissent. "You're big, but I'm made to stretch."

He still frowns, but sits down on the bed beside me, tracing his hand over my hip as I roll onto my side to face him. I can't help but wonder how he's feeling, now that we've finally had sex. Am I the only reason for his frown or is he thinking about the Tsenturion woman he'd planned to mate?

Does he feel like he betrayed her?

It doesn't take my degree to know that he's suffering from a large amount of survivor's guilt. If I'd taken the time to think, I would have tried to talk to him about that before we became more physically involved... but thinking has not exactly been high on my priorities when it comes to Bogdan.

Wait, does this mean that I accept everything I'm experiencing is actually real and not just a really strong manifestation of my imagination?

And now my head hurts.

Bogdan distracts me by stroking his finger over my cheek, making a small circle.

"I like these," he says, sounding smug. All of my other thoughts go flying out the window.

"You like what?" I ask, confused. Breasts, ass, pussy, even thighs and lips... but my cheeks?

"My seela marks," he says. I can feel a little thrill of possession run through me, but I'm pretty sure it's not me that's feeling it. I think it's *him.* But more importantly—

"What *seela* marks?!" I sit straight up.

Amused, Bogdan brings me to the bathroom where I stare at the mirror in there. Reflective surface. Whatever. I run my fingers over the marks on my cheeks as they burn red hot with a blush.

"Oh my... everyone's going to know what I did!" Don't get me wrong, I love giving head. It's an act of service that speaks to my submissive soul, but I've never had it advertised on my face that I'd recently indulged.

Standing behind me, Bogdan puts his hands on my hips, pulling me back against him. I swear I can see the glimmer of a smile in his eyes. Males. Doesn't matter the species, they're all alike in some ways.

"I like it." Yeah, he definitely sounds smug. Turning my face to his with a finger he lays his lips against the marks. For such a big, brooding, mean-looking warrior, he's a remarkably gentle kisser. Sighing, I give in and feel myself slumping against him as the humor of the situation gets to me.

After all, who is going to judge me? I don't think the other warriors are going to. They're more likely to high-five Bogdan, or whatever the Tsenturion equivalent would be. Dawn? My impression of her is that she'll want to compare notes.

Turning to face him, I twine my arms around his neck and meet his mouth aggressively. For some time, I teach him the different ways to kiss—the fervent pull of lips and sly trespassing tongue, little nibbles on the edge of his lips and finally, the slow sucks that sends waves of heat through my body.

I end up facing the mirror, my hooded gaze taking in the sight of my brown limbs sprawled against his thickly muscled body. His large hand covers my breast, swallowing it up entirely. My black hair flows over his glittering skin in shocking contrast. Onyx and copper and gold. We look good together.

I think. I can't help but wonder if he thinks so too.

I'd wanted him to open up to me, but now I can't help but think of that memory box as being Pandora's Box. There's hope, yes, but it's also opened up a lot of other emotions. Not just emotions. Insecurities. I pull my lips away from his.

"Master..." My voice trails off, because I'm not sure how to handle this. He's not a client. It would be so much easier to ask if he was, but my emotions are involved too. Which, that's a revelation I'm also going to have to absorb, because I'm starting to believe all of this is real and not just a coma dream and the ramifications of that are something I'm not quite willing to face yet.

"Bogdan. When we are alone, you will call me Bogdan," he orders, and I pull away in surprise.

"Really?"

He stops trying to kiss me and frowns. "You do not wish to?"

"No, I'm... I'd love to call you by your first name. I'm just wondering—"

An alarm sounds in the room and I shriek, practically

trying to climb Bogdan's muscled torso. His arms tighten around me, both reassuring me and holding me in place. The lights dim in the room for a moment, and through the door I can see his console flashing a red light.

"What is that?" I squawk, a little embarrassed by my reaction, but still freaked out. In my defense, nothing like that has happened since I've come onboard the ship. I didn't even know it was a possibility.

"It's all right," he soothes, running a hand down my naked back. "It's just an emergency summons to the bridge. Be quiet for a moment."

I almost bristle and demand to know more, but from the way he cocks his head I realize that he's hearing something I can't. Someone on the bridge, I'm assuming. *Just an emergency summons to the bridge.* I almost want to kick him. What *kind* of emergency? Are we under attack? Has there been a hull breach?

Because if this is all real, like I'm starting to believe it is, and the aliens saved me from death and I'm about to lose out on a fantastic life with a sexy alien who wants to dominate and spank me, I'm going to be really ticked.

His armor rolls over him, hiding the glittering skin under the dark panels and he steps away from me. Yeah, that's not reassuring. I almost whimper at the loss of his warm body against mine. I felt *safe* in his arms, dammit. Logically, I know I'm no less safe now that he's not holding me, but that doesn't change how I feel.

"I must go," he says, his voice deep and full of an emotion so deep it feels wrong to just call it 'anger.' That is what centuries of grieving, of loss without justice, of a burning need for vengeance sounds like. There is nothing in my education, nothing in my experience, to help prepare me for dealing with someone in that position. "There are

Vgotha sighted within range of our ships, which means we are within their range as well. You must stay here."

"But—" I stop, because I can't think of a good reason to argue. He can't stay here with me, when he could be somewhere else doing something useful, and I definitely wouldn't be useful. I'd be nothing but a distraction. The truth chafes, but I'm honest enough to know it's true.

"Stay here," he repeats, striding to the door.

I hurry after him. "But what if you are gone for a while? Where is Dawn, can I go be with her?"

"Dawn will most likely be confined to quarters for her safety. You will remain here until I return or suffer the consequences."

I halt, even as a quiver runs through me at the thought of *consequences.*

Bogdan sees the shiver and stops as the door slides open. To my surprise, his expression softens, and he cups my chin. The almost gentle expression on his face is at odds with the foreboding black of his armor. "Please, my Pareena. Remain here where you are safe."

His plea twists my heart. Talk about unfair. But I summon my courage. I can do this. I can sit and wait for him until he returns to me.

"Of course, Master. Bogdan." I lean into his palm as he caresses my cheek.

Then he is gone, and the door is sliding shut, leaving me alone.

∽

Bogdan

. . .

THE HALLS ARE BUSIER than normal with warriors scurrying to their posts, heeding the warning of the flashing lights. There is an almost constant update of information in my earpiece, but I won't be able to sort out what is important until I arrive on the bridge.

I enter the bridge with officers Kalexston and Zakhar. They salute the High Commander standing at the helm and take their places at their respective consoles. I march to Gavrill's side and salute.

"Bogdan." He acknowledges me with a nod. The tension threaded through his posture is reflected in his armor. "Apologies for interrupting your leave."

"No need," I respond. I will always do my duty. "Is this the same ship we picked up on scans earlier?"

The ship's signature flickers on the screen for a moment, making everyone on the bridge tense. We have followed a ship like that before, through a nebula, eventually abandoning it to retrieve Tribute Dawn. The next time we saw the Vgotha, they were boarding our ship and we still do not know how they camouflaged their ship signature.

The urge to run back to my rooms and check that my Tribute is still there and safe rises up, surprising me with its strength.

The signature on the scan solidifies rather than disappears and there is an audible sigh of relief throughout the room. These new tricks of the Vgotha are troublesome. Not just in what they can do, but how they are affecting the warriors' morale. Having Tribute Dawn snatched off of our ship, even without loss of life on our side, did not bolster anyone's confidence.

Late at night the warriors still discuss where the Vgotha ship's seemingly new technology has come from. Did they always have it? Did they purchase it from somewhere? What can it do?

The one chance we had to take apart one of their pods was lost when we attempted to follow it back to its ship instead. Like the ships themselves, it disappeared from our screens.

Which means it's very likely that we are walking into another trap.

But the Vgotha must expect us to suspect... so what is their current plan? The ramifications of all the variables are why I am glad I am not the High Commander. There was a time when I thought I could see things more clearly but looking back I know I would have acted too quickly and too rashly.

Now, with more to lose, I am more cautious.

"We are not sure," the High Commander starts to say, before he is cut off by Kalexston's excited voice.

"High Commander! We believe the Vgotha's current trajectory is going to take them to a planet!"

Everyone on the bridge goes still.

Never before have the Vgotha gone to a planet before.

Again, questions arise. Is this their home planet? A base? Or another trap? Perhaps, as the Vgotha leader claimed to Tribute Dawn when he captured her, they are hoping for a meeting on the planet's surface?

So many unknowns and all our warriors and two Tribute's lives riding on the answer. I scowl at the screens and then look at the High Commander. His jaw clenches and I do not need to ask to know he is thinking of his Tribute, back in his room.

"It might be a trap," he says in a low voice echoing my own concerns.

"That is the most likely scenario," I agree, my voice also

low. The bridge is still alive with noise, the warriors scanning for other ships all around us, still following the original ship we sighted, and plotting course alternatives. Before my Tribute I would not have cared, I would have demanded we rush to it and destroy the ship.

Now I worry about the consequences of such a rash act.

"Dawn wants me to try to meet with them. To see what they have to say." The High Commander's voice betrays nothing of his emotions, but I know he would not speak of such a thing unless he were willing to consider it.

I want to scream my rage that he would even think of it, and yet there is now a part of me that understands. We have new hope. We have our Tributes. Do we want to risk them on continuing a war that the Vgotha seem to have tired of? They have been running for so long. Yet can that truly be enough punishment for their crime?

I do not know.

But I do know that I do not want any harm to befall my Tribute.

Yet, I cannot bring myself to speak, to condone such an outrageous suggestion. It betrays everything I believe in.

The High Commander looks away and shakes his head. When he speaks, his voice is raised so that everyone on the bridge can hear.

"We will follow them," he announces. "Track their course. Keep alert. All warriors on duty should remain battle ready. Be wary of surprises, scan all surrounding space as we pursue them."

The bridge swarms with activity.

More quietly, so only I can hear, the High Commander finishes his thought. "I will decide what to do when we know if we can even catch them."

14

P areena

I DON'T KNOW how much time passes after Bogdan leaves before I become bored. I nap for a bit, and then pop up and tidy the room. After some hesitation, I pack away the box of memorabilia back into the closet, because looking at it brings up too many uncomfortable questions, for both myself and him. The next time I get a chance to ask him directly to share his past, I'll do that. It's messy to play therapist to a sexual partner, but I can't help my training. And Bogdan is obviously still hurting.

Which makes me wonder—what sort of grieving process do the Tsenturions have?

The door chimes, interrupting my musing. A portion of it shimmers to show the visitor right outside.

"Dawn?" I jump up and go to the door, trying to remember how to get it open. The Vgotha threat can't be that bad if she's out roaming. Either that or she disobeyed her Master. I don't want her to get in trouble, but I really, really want to talk to someone who isn't a reticent alien warrior.

"Pareena?" comes Dawn's muffled voice. "Are you in there?"

"Yes! I don't know how to get the door open." I search the side for a panel.

"Override," Dawn tells the door and there's a beeping sound. "Tribute Dawn." The door rolls back smoothly, making me frown. I wonder if I could even get out of the room if I wanted to. She grins widely at me, looking triumphant. "I knew asking Gavrill for an override code would be good for something. Although, technically it's supposed to be for my safety."

"I'm so glad you're here," I launch myself at her. Normally I'm not a hugger but the sight of another Earth girl is such a relief. I'm so glad my subconscious conjured up a human companion, even if she isn't a Potterhead.

"I thought you might want company." She squeezes me back.

"Are you allowed to be here?" I have to ask, wondering why I was ordered to stay in my room while she's out wandering the halls. With an override, no less. "You won't get in trouble?"

She shrugs. "Gavrill was already on the bridge when the alert issued. He's ordered me to stay in my rooms during an alert in the past, but he won't mind me coming to visit you. As long as I stay out of any potential danger areas, it's fine."

I invite her to sit on the couch-like piece of furniture on one side of the room. It's built for Bogdan's proportions, so we look a little like kids sitting in our parent's fancy parlor, but at least there's a place to sit other than the bed. "So there's a Vgotha ship?"

"Probably." She doesn't sound as concerned as I would have expected. "For now. They tend to blip in and out of the scans. This isn't the first time one has been spotted and then disappeared, but Gavrill is doing a double shift and I wouldn't be surprised if he keeps everyone on the bridge that long."

Guess I won't be talking to Bogdan any time soon. Although maybe it's better if he doesn't come back and catch Dawn here. And it will give me some time to figure out how I feel about everything he shared with me and the fact that it finally led to sex.

A little lost in thought, I suddenly realize that Dawn is studying me closely, her eyes squinting in puzzlement.

"What is it? Do I have something in my teeth?" I place a hand over my mouth. I hadn't seen anything when I was in the bathroom, but I'd been a little distracted... Oh. I realize what she's looking at.

"Um, no, not your teeth..." Her eyes widen as she realizes what marks she's seeing. "Ohmigosh, Pareena. Are those *seela* marks?" She looks like she is trying not to laugh. I appreciate the effort, but I end up giggling anyway, blushing madly as I do, and then she's giggling and we both end up laughing.

"Is that what those tentacle sucker things are called?" I ask, trying to sound innocent. I feel almost like a teenager again, gossiping with a girlfriend about sex for the first time.

"Yes." We erupt into another spate of giggling and Dawn shakes her head at me, her eyes sparkling. "You wicked thing, you." She sits back with a knowing grin. "I hadn't even thought about that side effect... what was it like?"

"You mean you never..." I wave at my face, still blushing,

but my embarrassment is fading. While Dawn is clearly curious, she's not at all judgmental.

"Only a little bit." She shrugs. "He's never let me do more than lick or suck it for a few minutes before he pulls me off. I don't really argue, especially since it feels so good um... elsewhere." Now it's her turn to blush, but I know exactly what she means.

"The... *ah*... tentacles were very nice," I comment primly. Dawn and I exchange looks and burst into giggles like schoolgirls.

"Look at us, using euphemisms like old Victorian women," she chortles.

"Tentacles are just a lot to get used to." I mime wriggling them at her with my fingers, but of course, fingers can't do them justice.

"They're called *seela*," Dawn reminds me. "And then there's the big one, the *prime seela*—"

"Oh, yes," I nod enthusiastically. "Um, that's my favorite."

"Mine too," she says, grinning widely at me. Her eyes get a little bit of a hazy look, like she's not really looking at me anymore. "And if he takes you from behind—"

"Oh, that's genius." My mind reels with possibilities. Bogdan taking me doggy style on the bed, the little suckers tugging on my labia and freshly spanked bottom, the *prime seela* teasing my asshole...

"Mmmhmmm." Dawn nods knowingly, making me blush further. There's a long pause while we're lost in our own daydreams. She reaches over and pats my hand, breaking the moment. "I'm so glad you're here. It's nice to talk about this stuff with someone."

Which reminds me of the burning question of the day: what can I do to help Bogdan?

"Dawn..." I hesitate, not wanting to bring the mood down so quickly, but she's my best source of information. Who knows how long we have before Bogdan comes back. Plus, if she gets into trouble for coming to my room, I might not get this chance again for a while. "Can I ask you something?"

She looks amused. "Sure, ask me anything. Since we started the conversation with the beneficial uses of tentacles during sex, I feel like there's not much that can top that."

"The ice is definitely broken," I agree, smiling a little at her levity. "But this is more serious. Has Gavrill ever..." *Wait, that might be too personal.* I change tack slightly. "Do you think the Tsenturions grieve?"

"What do you mean?" Her eyebrows flash surprise, but she settles back onto the couch as if preparing for a long session, her head already tilted in thought.

"It's just... with the loss of their home planet... there was a lot of personal loss, too. I'm wondering how the warriors handled it. I'm particularly worried about Bogdan."

"Because he's so broody?"

"Yes." I wince internally at talking about his private life without him, but I need perspective. "I think he has a hefty dose of survivor's guilt and possibly other trauma layered on top of that. I'm not sure though, since they're not human, but they do seem to feel things in a similar manner to us. You know them better, though, and I've only really spent time with Bogdan and a little bit with Arkdhem now. What do you think?"

"That makes sense to me." She nods, warming to the subject as she continues. "When you think about it, these guys had their entire species blown up thousands of years ago, but then they were off chasing the enemy and functioning in war mode. I don't think they've ever stopped to grieve. Aren't there five stages or something?"

"You're talking about the five stages of grief postulated by Elisabeth Kübler-Ross," I say, automatically shifting to a more lecturing mode. I'm too well acquainted with it on a personal level to be able to talk about it without either going into professional mode or breaking down as I think about how it personally affected me. "The theory is people move through different stages of grief. Denial, anger, bartering, depression, and acceptance. People can move back and forth through the stages, or even repeat them."

"Right. I saw the Simpsons episode," she jokes, and I laugh.

"Americans tend to think of it as fact, but there's a lack of peer reviewed research to support it and there are other models. Some research has been done that shows humans have natural psychological resilience." I shrug, pretending a nonchalance I don't entirely feel. "On the other hand, I went through most of the stages while I was dying." Dawn's expression turns both sympathetic and concerned, and I continue before she can ask any questions, because I don't really want to talk about that. Especially since I'm becoming more and more convinced that I'm not dreaming. "But that's humans. There's no way of knowing if an alien culture would process loss and bereavement in the same way."

"Maybe you could talk to some of them and find out?" Dawn suggests.

"Like a group session?" I'm joking, because so far, I haven't really been able to interact with any of the Tsenturion warriors other than Bogdan, and to a much lesser degree Arkdhem, but Dawn nods. Hmm. I have to admit, I'm intrigued by the idea. I'd have to adapt my technique and think of it as information gathering versus treating patients, although I could end up doing both.

"Medik and Arkdhem would do it, for sure. Gavrill's been busy with the Vgotha hunting, but I bet there are a few other officers who'd volunteer. Let's do it." Her eyes light up with enthusiasm for the idea and she stands up, which is when I realize she means right now.

"Now?" My voice rises a little in a kind of panic. I don't want to disappoint my new, and only, friend, but I also don't want to disobey a direct order. My bottom tingles at the thought and I am suddenly very aware of the wall of pain, even though it's behind me and I can't see it. "Bogdan said to stay here."

While I'm enough of a masochist to enjoy some punishments, actually disappointing him or causing him any distress would be worse than anything he could dish out physically. If it wasn't an emergency situation, I might be more willing to be 'naughty.'

Seeing my reaction, Dawn pauses and then grins widely. "Maybe you can't leave, but did he say anything about entertaining visitors?"

My lips quirk in amusement. Dawn is definitely what the BDSM community would define as a brat. She's also very good at getting around orders that she doesn't want to follow. I bet she keeps Gavrill on his toes.

"No." I draw out the word, because he didn't. It probably hadn't occurred to him that he would need to. I already know him well enough to know that he probably won't like it. On the other hand, it's not something that will interrupt this emergency or disappoint him, even though I'm following the letter and not the spirit of his order. "He didn't say I couldn't. I'm okay with exploiting this loophole."

My bottom tingles again as I say this. Some sort of brat-ting sixth sense warning me that I'm not going to come out of this unscathed.

But who knows... he might not even find out. And I need something to *do*. Being his sex toy is fun, but if this is all real, that's not going to be a fulfilling life for me. From how possessive he seemed in the training area; this might be a case of 'better to ask forgiveness than permission.'

Plus, I don't want to disappoint Dawn.

Yes, I can be a little subby when it comes to my friendships as well. Recognizing the fact doesn't always help me avoid it.

"A woman after my own heart." Dawn is all smiles. Maybe the High Commander's more lenient with her? Or she just likes being naughty. Come to think of it, we never really talked about punishments, I just assumed. I'll have to ask her later. "I'll go gather who I can and be back soon. We should be done before the double shift ends."

"Sounds good." I glance around the room. We can't all sit on the couch. Bogdan seemed to be able to conjure up new furniture with his mind. "Maybe I can figure out how to make furniture..."

"I'll bring chairs," Dawn waves a hand and the door opens. She steps into the hall as I remember something.

"One more thing—" I race to her, stopping just inside the door.

"Yes?"

"Bring back cookies." I grin at her. "A proper group session should include snacks. And cookies make everything better."

~

Bogdan

. . .

THE PLANET LOOMS AHEAD, its curvature blocking out the sight of the Vgotha ship.

"Faster," the High Commander orders, his tone full of frustration. It is not the first time, but it is already too late.

I grit my teeth, slamming my fist against my thigh in anger. We are going to lose them again. When we passed by the planet, all signs of the Vgotha ship had disappeared. The screens were empty, there wasn't even a signature to follow anymore. It was like the Vgotha ship had never existed.

Except that we'd all seen it.

When I find out who they got this new tech from, I am going to hunt them down and kill them with my bare hands.

"Put us in orbit," the High Commander ordered, his voice tight.

There are a myriad of possibilities before us. The Vgotha ship could also be in orbit, using the planet to hide their presence, just far enough ahead of us that we cannot see them, and they do not appear on the scans. It could have disappeared, using that technology they seem to sometimes utilize and sometimes not. Or they could have gone down to the planet itself. There should be some sign though...

Or perhaps not. If they can disappear from our scans in open space, perhaps they have a way to land on a planet without leaving a trail. Since we have never encountered a Vgotha on a planet before, there is no way of knowing. This might not even be new technology.

I peruse the large display of the planet. With its sheltering atmosphere and large expanses of water, the planet looks much like Tsentur. I swallow a knot of pain and longing and turn to the scans. "They could be using their deploying cloaking technology."

"Or they disembarked planet side," the High Commander says. He studies the scans of the planet. "There are plenty of forests for their kind to hide in." The Jabol told us that the Vgotha are very fond of wilderness. They did not have large population centers as we did but preferred to be a part of nature. Even after so many cycles on a spaceship, they could be more adept in such surroundings than any of us.

"But which is the trap?" Kalexston murmurs. A wave of unease ripples through the bridge. No one is comfortable with the new Vgotha tactics, and this one is more confusing than the others.

"Speed up our orbit and scan the planet," the High Commander orders Zakhar before heading to his seat. "All warriors on duty to defense positions."

In the past, a mere sighting of the Vgotha would not mean such measures, but I understand and approve of the High Commander's increased sensitivity to the threat. The last time we intercepted the Vgotha, they infiltrated our defenses, managed to board the command ship, and captured Dawn. It was a cowardly tactic, but the Vgotha have no honor.

I will fight to the bitter end to ensure they do not threaten Pareena. The Vgotha might be good at hiding, but they can't run forever. We will catch them, avenge Tsentur, and secure a safe future for our Tributes. There is no other option.

15

Pareena

ABOUT TEN MINUTES after she left, Dawn returns with three warriors, including Arkdhem, and each of them is carrying a chair. Arkdhem is glowering at her, making me worry because the last time I saw him he was nothing but patience and smiles, but she catches my expression and waves her hand.

"Don't worry about the grumpy cinnamon roll, he's just mad because I went out without him."

"I must protect you," Arkdhem says fiercely, with an urgency that reminds me very much of Bogdan. There is an undercurrent to his words that makes it seem as though there is more to what he is saying than mere words. Possibly part of Survivor's Guilt? That would make sense. "I cannot protect you if you wander about without informing me. Do you wish to be captured by the Vgotha *again*?"

Wait, what's this about Dawn being captured? That hadn't come up when we talked before and that seems like a pretty big thing! I look at Dawn, startled, but she isn't paying any attention to me. Instead, she sighs and puts her hand on Arkdhem's shoulder. "I told you I was sorry. I just wanted to get some one on one time with Pareena, human to human."

She smiles winningly at him and Arkdhem scowls, but now that I look more closely, I can see that he's more fearful than angry at her. The expression resembles that of a put-upon older brother, doing his best to look after an unruly sibling that he's been put in charge of. Since I know he's basically her bodyguard, that makes sense.

"Anyway, this is Borodem and this is Corin," Dawn says, smiling at them. They don't smile back exactly but they do look at her fondly. "They are off duty and willing to be part of our experiment."

"Anything for the Tributes," Borodem says seriously, bowing his head slightly. Corin nods, just as serious.

"If there is a battle, we will protect you with our lives."

They aren't as broody and closed off as Bogdan, but they aren't as open as Arkdhem either. On the other hand, Arkdhem is also nodding in agreement at Corin's comment, just as serious as the other two. Maybe being serious is just a Tsenturion trait, even if Arkdhem smiled more when it was just him, Dawn, and me.

"Come on in and sit down," I say, gesturing. As they move past me, I pull Dawn to my side and whisper. "Did you tell them what the 'experiment' is?"

"No," she admits, whispering back. "I wasn't sure they'd come if I did."

Great. Well this should be interesting.

I move over to the bed so the warriors can put down their chairs facing it, giving Dawn and me a comfortable and more informal place to sit. I don't want this to be a formal thing, since I'm going to be asking questions about emotional stuff.

"What would you like us to do?" Arkdhem asks as he sits down. His annoyance at Dawn seems to have dissipated entirely and he is smiling slightly at me, waiting to hear what he's been called there for. I can understand why he and Bogdan grate on each other—they are very different. While Bogdan broods and holds grudges, Arkdhem doesn't seem to let anything keep him down for long.

Before I can speak, Dawn plops down on the bed and smiles sunnily at him. "Well, Pareena and I were hoping you could tell us about Tsentur. We're trying to be the best Tributes we can be, but sometimes our mates aren't always big on talking, you know."

She winks and Arkdhem shakes his head, sighing with a kind of resignation. Both Borodem and Corin shift uncomfortably.

"What about Tsentur do you want to know?" Corin asks, his voice deep and slow.

"Bogdan told me about the Mating Festival," I say, because that's the main thing I know about and that will hopefully lead in the direction I'd like to go in. All three warriors flinch. It's a tiny movement, but when done in unison it's very noticeable. I hurry on. "Were any of you preparing for the festival as well? Or did you have more years to serve as warriors?"

It does not surprise me that Arkdhem is the first to answer. Both Borodem and Corin look like they're already regretting agreeing to be a part of this, but Arkdhem... there's something about him. I do believe he truly cares for Dawn in a brotherly fashion, but there's something more. Like he's also motivated by something else, as if he's trying to impress both Dawn and me. I'm absolutely willing to use that to my advantage right now though.

"I had more cycles aboard the fleet to serve," he says, before leaning forward and speaking much more earnestly than Bogdan ever has. Again, I am struck with the impression of a young man, eager to impress a woman. But is that actually how the mannerisms translate between species? That is the unknown. "Now, though, all of us have served well beyond that and are ready for mates of our own."

He smiles widely at me. Corin and Borodem both nod. They aren't as eager and earnest as Arkdhem, but the longing in their expressions echoes his, even without the smile. There is a desperation there that shouldn't surprise me, but for some reason I hadn't expected it. Perhaps because Bogdan has been so standoffish from the beginning.

It's possible these three are more representative of the rest of the warriors though, since Dawn told me Bogdan was the only one outspoken against the Tribute program. I really wish I had something to write down notes on, but I hadn't been expecting to do this today. I'll just have to make an effort to remember everything that I can and make notes later.

I turn my attention to Borodem, smiling as warmly as I can and hoping he'll be receptive even if he's not as eager to share as Arkdhem is. "And what about you?"

∼

Bogdan

.   .   .

WHEN I AM DISMISSED from the bridge, I find myself hurrying back to my room, much more eager than I normally would be. In the past, it would not have been uncommon for me to continue to work long past my shift. Now, all I want is to return to my Tribute.

I step out of the lift, grateful the hall to the officer's quarters is empty. As I approach my room, I retract my helmet. I am tired. I want to return to my quarters, remove my armor and spend time with my Pareena. Seeing her will be a balm on an otherwise wasted cycle. We spent every moment scanning for the Vgotha and found nothing. It is possible they have left the quadrant. Either that or they are on the planet. The only thing we are sure of is that they are not in orbit around it.

A sobering thought.

The planet itself is highly interesting. Dense forests and no discernible civilization.

We have a sample from the escape pod that returned Dawn to us. It was organic based—similar to plant matter. Perhaps organic matter from a planet such as this. Of course, that type of ship will not be not easy to find on a lush tropical planet, such as the one we are currently orbiting. Even if this planet is not the source of their new technology, it makes a good hiding spot for them.

If they are there.

The uncertainty is maddening.

My steps quicken as I approach my room. Time with my Tribute will ease me. I sent word earlier to Medik, asking him to bring her a meal and tell her to rest. I am not so tired that I cannot make good use of my pleasure trophy before resting. She seemed to enjoy bathing me. Perhaps we will start with that...

My door slides open, but instead of the quiet of my

quarters and the gentle presence of my lovely Tribute, I am greeted by a shocking sight: a group of Tsenturion warriors inside my room, seated in a circle, with my Tribute.

I halt abruptly. My first thought is that I have somehow lost my way and come to the wrong room, but no, a second inspection informs me I have entered my quarters. My quarters, which are full of other warriors and two Tributes. The Tributes are seated on my sleeping platform. Tribute Dawn sits cross legged with her head propped on her hands while my Pareena sits on the edge, leaning forward. The rest of the warriors are facing her. None of them seem to have even noticed my arrival.

The sound of a low keening, like the dying sounds of a *kurdzu,* the four-legged beast that we hunted on planet Tsentur, fills my ears. It's coming from one of the warriors.

"And how does that make you feel?" My Tribute leans forward and places her hand on the arm of the warrior closest to her. I cannot see his face. Across from him, another warrior sobs, his suit flashing with grief and pain. It takes me a moment to recognize Borodem, a normally stoic warrior.

Next to him, Corin hunches in his chair with a sorrowful expression, his armor dark grey with misery. Sitting slightly separated from them is Medik, a platter of food resting on a table in front of him, as he observes my Tribute. Apparently when he brought my Tribute her food, he did not leave.

I grit my teeth at the invasion of my quarters, the open grief on display grating at my already tired senses, and the closeness of other warriors to my Tribute.

"What is the meaning of this?" I half growl, half shout.

Dawn shoots up like a warrior caught sleeping on shift, eyes wide and startled, full of guilt and a touch of fear. As well she should be. When the High Commander discovers she has wandered from his quarters, she will not be able to sit easily for a cycle. Corin winces and puts a hand on Borodem's shoulder. Together they rise and salute me, Borodem choking back his grief. I look away from him, the display of such open emotion making me extremely uncomfortable.

My eyes fall on my Tribute and my entire body stiffens with fury when I see that the warrior she is talking to, the warrior whose hand she is holding, is Arkdhem's. Touching *any* other warrior would be bad enough. That it is him, after I specifically forbade her to go anywhere near him, is enough for my suit to flash with red threads of possessive fury.

I step toward them. "*Get away from my Tribute.*"

To her credit, my Pareena does not flinch, although she does jolt, as if just now realizing that she's touching Arkdhem. Immediately her hand falls away from his. She straightens but remains seated, gazing at me steadily with her dark eyes. Arkdhem steps in front of her, as if shielding her from me, and I nearly launch myself at him. I would have, if not for Medik.

"Ah, Bogdan, is your shift over already? My, my, the cycles spin faster and faster the older I get." Medik rises and putters over to the food, beginning to clean it up. A defusing tactic, as it puts him directly between me and Arkdhem. Now I cannot attack him as I would like. I could still behead him in three moves.

"I will ask again," I bark. "What is the meaning of this?"

"We're having a group therapy session," My Tribute answers steadily. She has not looked away from me, not once, even though she is having to look at me over Arkdhem's shoulder. A feat that would be impossible were she not on my sleeping platform.

"What is that?" I demand to know. I ask the question of

her, but it is Medik who answers. Corin and Borodem are wisely silent, obviously realizing how close I am to violence. Surprisingly, Arkdhem is too, but his gaze is insolent, and I think if Medik had not stepped between us, we might have fought right here and now.

"A kind of experiment," Medik says. He extends a plate of brown discs in my direction. They smell good, although I do not know what they are. "Cookie?"

"No," I snap out. I do not know what a cookie is, but I do not want it.

I want my room to be empty other than my Tribute and me, I want some rest, and I want to know what the Vgotha are doing. I do not have the patience for any of this.

"We can wrap up," Tribute Dawn says quickly. "I think we went long enough for the first time."

My Pareena nods, still watching me.

"Why were you touching him?" I grit out. Arkdhem smiles widely at me and I nearly snarl. *I will cut that smile off his face if he is not careful.*

"A normal human gesture, meant to comfort," she explains smoothly. Arkdhem meets my gaze, his smile turning to a smirk, his own suit shimmering smugly.

I will paint the walls with his blood.

My Tribute walks towards me, skirting around him, her eyes fixed on mine. They are soft, like her voice as she tries to soothe me. "I missed you. This was only meant to kill time until you were free. And, as Medik said, it's an experiment."

"An experiment?" I test the word.

"Yes. I was wondering whether Tsenturions had a grieving process. These warriors were kind enough to share."

I remember that we're not alone in the room, and glare

at everyone.

"But we're done now," my Tribute soothes. "So maybe you don't need this?" She motions to my right arm and I realize my armor has produced a long, double-edged blade in anticipation for battle.

"Fine," I grunt and let it melt back into my suit before drawing my Pareena close. To my relief, she tucks herself against my side and wraps her arms around my waist. I meet Arkdhem's gaze. He's watching my Tribute closely. When he notices my challenging look, he tilts his head and raises his brows.

I will blood you, my look says.

You will try, he tells me with his hard gaze.

"Well, that was fun," Medik finishes fussing over the food. "But I better get back to the med bay." He hoists the half full platter. "My patients will enjoy these," he announces to no one.

"Our apologies for the intrusion," Corin says with a salute. "We meant only to indulge the Tributes' request."

I grunt and jerk my head toward the door in dismissal.

Corin and Borodem move past me. Their armor is still tinged with grief, but they bow their heads to my Tribute as they go, with something like affection in their expressions.

Medik thanks the Tributes and smiles at me as he leaves. I let him go even though I am angry he did not inform me of the meeting in my quarters as soon as he discovered it. There is no sense in trying to chastise him. As the elder on board, and the best physician despite training other warriors to one day take his place, Medik does as Medik pleases. Even the High Commander cannot gainsay him when he decides on something.

But I can still kill Arkdhem. It would be most satisfying. Then I would never have to see his stupid smirk again.

Pareena plasters a hand against my chest and I realize I'm growling.

"I guess I better go too," Tribute Dawn says cheerfully, sidling toward the door. "Gavrill will probably be wondering where I am."

Both Arkdhem and I look at her and then each other. He nods and I shake my head. Of course, he informed the High Commander where Dawn was. He is charged with her safety. Why she would think anything different is a mystery. Arkdhem might be a piece of *kurdzu* dung but he knows his duty.

That will not save him if he keeps behaving dishonorably with my Tribute. My gaze hardens again and his does as well, our brief moment of unity over as quickly as it began. The threat of violence hangs in the air again, and this time Medik is not there to relieve it.

But my Pareena slides her hand over my lower belly, squeezing me tighter. "I missed you," she says again, gazing up at me.

And I decide Arkdhem will live another cycle. If only to cover the bridge while I spend time with my Tribute. Something which I am very eager to do, although my plans for our activities have changed slightly due to her 'experiment.'

"Out," I order just as the doors to my quarters hiss open. The High Commander stands just outside.

~

PAREENA

The dark expression on the High Commander's face makes me cuddle up closer to Bogdan. I'm pretty sure I'm in trouble, but he's still less scary than the High Commander.

"You were supposed to remain in your quarters." The

glower he levels at all of us becomes more intense when it finally lands on her.

Undeterred, Dawn runs to him, jumping up to fling her arms around him and kissing him on the mouth. The dark colors of his suit shift and it glitters, like stars on a clear night. The effect is beautiful. Even though he is clearly unhappy with her disobedience, he holds her against him and kisses her back.

Out of the corner of my eye, I see Arkdhem go very still, and I turn my head slightly to see what's wrong. His suit doesn't give me any clues, but I can see the longing, the envy, on his face, his expression momentarily unguarded.

As if sensing that my attention has strayed, Bogdan's fingers slide into my hair and he turns my head to face him. Arkdhem's expression becomes tinged with anger, but then I can't see him anymore because Bogdan is kissing me. Deeply. Possessively. I realize that he is claiming me in front of Arkdhem with the kiss.

Wanting to do my best to soothe the savage beast—and maybe get myself out of some of the trouble I'm in—I kiss him back just as passionately. I press myself against him, sinking into the kiss, wanting him to know there is no reason to be possessive. There is no reason to doubt that I want anyone but him.

I hear the door slide and I pull away, turning my head. I catch a glimpse of Arkdhem's back before the door closes again.

There is a part of me that feels a little guilty over the blatant display between Bogdan and me. From talking with the three Tsenturion warriors, I now know how much each of them long for a Tribute of their own, for a family. I also understand Dawn's mixed feelings on the subject. If this is real, then I won't be the last woman abducted from her home. On the other hand, if the women are dying like I was, and they are given a choice...

Yet, is it really an informed choice? I'm still questioning whether or not this is even real, because the whole idea is so fantastical. Who could really believe that they're signing up to be an alien's mate?

"Did your shift go well?" Dawn asks Gavrill, her voice innocent.

I lean into Bogdan as the alien leader growls under his breath. He still looks displeased with her.

"Did you find the Vgotha?" I ask, hoping to distract both of the warriors. If Gavrill punishes Dawn the way Bogdan punishes me, I have a feeling we're both going to be sore soon. Might as well try to put that moment off for as long as possible. Plus, I'm curious.

"We are still searching," Bogdan says, his voice tight. "They have disappeared again. Possibly on planet, possibly deeper into space."

"Do not worry," Gavrill says, almost right on top of Bogdan. His arms tighten around Dawn even as his expression darkens even more. "They will not take you again."

I feel Bogdan's arms pulling me in even closer to him, as if he can't bear the thought of me being taken. I'm not too fond of the idea either.

"I still want to know more about that," I say, feeling a little put out that I'm the only one who doesn't know what happened. The amount of things Dawn has left out of our conversations is a little shocking. Then again, I suppose it's not exactly easy to know what to prioritize when you've been abducted by aliens and a new friend shows up. We both put alien peen pretty high on the list, but I would think a kidnapping by and escape from the enemy should be up there too.

Dawn just rolls her eyes. "I'm not that worried," she says, shaking her head. "I told you, Tor wasn't that bad. Just super sexist and a little bit of a jerk." She looks at me. "Obviously I escaped. Their ship even helped me."

"It helped you?" How... Why... What? That made no sense to me.

"It was a trick," Bogdan says immediately, his voice tight with anger.

"Some trick, sending me back unharmed and without getting what they wanted," Dawn mutters, rolling her eyes at him. I immediately get the sense that this is an argument they've had more than once. As much as I want to soothe my warrior, I have to admit, I'm inclined to agree with Dawn. She tilts her head at Gavrill. "So, what's this about a planet?"

The two warriors exchange glances and then Gavrill nods. Letting Dawn slide down the front of his body, he ushers her over to a screen on the wall, Bogdan and I following.

Bogdan makes a gesture at the console, and a giant hologram of a planet appears. With all the blue and green and white wispy clouds, for a moment I think its Earth... but then I blink and realize that the land masses are wrong. But it's so close that it hurts.

"They approached this planet and then disappeared behind it," Gavrill says. "We are uncertain if they continued on, using the planet to mask their flight, or if they landed."

"Oh, how beautiful!" Dawn exclaims, the longing clear in her voice. I feel that same longing, deep in my bones. "Can we visit?"

Excitement threads through me at her question and I look up at Bogdan. The expression on his face is not encouraging.

16

B ogdan

VISIT? Both Tributes on the same planet where Vgotha might be? The very thought makes me want to stab something. My chest tightens and I can feel something like a scream bubbling up inside of me.

"What? No!" The High Commander barks out the words, thankfully able to speak, unlike myself. "It is not safe."

"But if you scan the planet for Vgotha and they're not there... wouldn't it be safe for us to visit?" Tribute Dawn asks, pouting. I recognize the look she gives him. It is the one she often gets on her face right before he gives in to whatever insane idea she's come up with.

"We have more scans to run. Many more," I say quickly, before he can be swayed by her big, pleading eyes. I have to avoid my own Tribute's gaze as well.

Before, I had thought the High Commander had grown soft with how often he allows his Tribute to do as she pleases, but now I understand better. They are not Tsenturions, they have their own culture and way of doing things. Sometimes they must bow to our way but sometimes, every so often, we should bend to theirs as well. Because we want them to smile and be happy.

"Yes," agrees the Commander immediately. "And they will take a long time."

My Tribute reaches up to cup my face in her hands, so that I can no longer look away from her wide, dark, pleading eyes.

"Please?" she asks. The hopefulness in her voice, the longing, is almost more than I can bear.

As if sensing weakness, Tribute Dawn chimes in. "Please? If you don't find any Vgotha on it? Just for an hour, I miss being on a planet so much... please, Gavrill, I rarely ask for anything..."

The sincerity in her voice is too much for the High Commander to bear. I know it as soon as I hear her plea. She is also correct that she rarely asks for anything. Which is why she so often receives whatever she asks for.

Drakk.

"Please, Master," my Tribute whispers, pressing herself against me. "I'll do anything you want."

I do my best to harden myself against her pleas. "You will do whatever I want anyway."

A little smile curves her lips. "That's true, but wouldn't you like to see what I could offer that you don't know to ask for?" She licks her lips, reminding me that she has already shown me something new. The little marks my *seela* left on her cheeks are already faded. The idea intrigues me.

But...

"I will not risk your safety for pleasure," I say roughly.

"But if the Vgotha aren't there, then we'll be safe," Tribute Dawn says, still pleading. "And we won't go without you. You're great warriors, strong enough to protect two tiny females."

The High Commander sighs. Even though he sees through his Tribute's tactics, he is not immune to them. "I will think on it." Then his gaze sharpens, and he picks his Tribute up, hefting her over his shoulder as she squeals. "Excuse me, Bogdan. Tribute Pareena. My Tribute and I need to have a discussion about obeying orders, which she has already delayed for long enough."

"Understood," I say, putting my hand on the back of my Tribute's neck. "I believe I will be having a similar discussion with my own Tribute right now."

~

Pareena

THE FIRM HOLD of Bogdan's fingers on my neck is somehow both comforting and threatening. Watching Gavrill cart Dawn off over his shoulder like a sack of potatoes, and her just hanging there rather than talking back, convinces me that she's probably about to get her butt blistered too. And that, like me, she doesn't want to make her punishment any worse than it's already going to be because she doesn't even put up a token protest.

Although she does raise her head and wave to me as they exit, a rueful, resigned, and yet somehow excited expression on her face.

I know exactly how she feels.

I *know* what's coming. I *know* I'm in trouble. I *know* the Wall of Pain is in my future. But I'm not scared. At least, that's not my only emotion. I am a little scared, a little anxious, but I'm also turned on. Bogdan's finger is stroking the pulse on my throat and my nipples harden as he turns to me, looming over me, looking down at me.

It's strange how he can make me feel so safe and at the same time, so vulnerable.

"What did I tell you about Arkdhem?" It sounds less like a question and more like a whispered threat, his lips close to my ear, his body moving to press into me from behind. Goosebumps crawl over my skin and my bottom tingles in anticipation of punishment.

"I—" Before I can say a second word, the Bride Trainer comes to life between my legs, humming against my clit and pushing against my anus. I groan as the nanotech pushes into me like a plug, thick and punishing with how fast it stretches the tight ring of my sphincter. My knees tremble and I cry out at the sudden invasion, the shocking fullness... all while my pussy throbs emptily.

Using his hold on my neck to spin me around, Bogdan puts his forehead against mine. His eyes seethe with emotion that he somehow manages to keep from showing in his armor. Possessive anger. Hot jealousy.

I shouldn't have tried to comfort Arkdhem physically.

It had just felt so natural in the moment. He'd been upset, talking about his longing for a Tribute, for a family, and I had responded in a wholly human, if not entirely professional way. In that moment, I hadn't been thinking about Bogdan's orders or who Arkdhem was, I'd just reacted.

"I'm sorry, Master," I say simply, rather than trying to make an excuse. "It will not happen again."

I messed up and I know it.

Something flashes in Bogdan's eyes.

"I am pleased to hear you understand your transgression, my Tribute." His voice remains hard, grating. "That will not be enough to save you from punishment though."

To be honest, I hadn't really expected it would be.

Bogdan

THE SUBMISSIVE ACCEPTANCE I see in my Tribute's expression startles me. Tribute Dawn fights against the High Commander's dominance constantly and part of me expects my Tribute to do so as well. But she not only understands what she did wrong, she is willing to accept my discipline.

"I accept my punishment, Master," she says, her pupils dilating, her voice calm. There is a sense of serenity to her, one that I am coming to recognize.

My Tribute enjoys my dominance over her. She wants to submit. Unlike Tribute Dawn, who would aggravate me to death with her constant rebellion, my Pareena enjoys being taken in hand. No wonder the Jabol felt we would be well matched. She is perfect for me, in every way.

The calm that washes over me matches hers, my anger sliding away. I understand that it is me she desires, me she wants to submit to, not Arkdhem. I will still punish her for disobeying an order, but I am no longer choking on possessive fury.

My cock aches, my *seela* beginning to writhe in anticipation. Dropping my gaze to her pouty lips, I decide to work off the edge of my lust before punishing her. It will leave me more clear-minded and keep me from rushing through the process just to relieve myself.

"On your knees, my Pareena," I order.

I feel the responding heat of her arousal just before she obeys, her nanotech informing me that her bottom has clenched around the belt invading her there. Yes, I will make that part of her discipline as well. I remember what the manuals said about 'naughty girl sex' and my Tribute has been very naughty indeed.

Reaching down, I knock the straps of her gown away from her shoulders, baring her beautiful breasts to me. Hefting one in my hand, I pinch the nipple tightly, making her moan as she stares up at me. The lust in her eyes is echoed in my body.

My armor retracts and my cock undulates before her, my *seela* reaching for her, eager to latch onto her skin and leave their marks. I will ensure that no warrior will be able to look at what is mine without seeing the clear signs of my possession of her.

"Take me in your mouth." I cannot disguise the eagerness in my voice for this strange, human custom.

The touch of her tongue on my cock is just as heavenly as before, the warm suction igniting a storm of pleasure inside of me. Seeing her on her knees before me, one hand on her breast, the other entwined in her hair, my cock sliding between her lips while my *seela* pull at her skin, is highly arousing. Because of her belt, I know that I am not the only one so affected.

Still, this is supposed to be punishment. I pinch her nipple harder, twisting it slightly, while directing the belt to slide up her front, taking the place of my fingers. She whimpers, first at my fingers, and then at the way I have the belt tighten around her budded nipples. Now both of my hands are free to play with her hair while I use the belt to torment her body.

Thickening the portion of the belt filling her ass, I groan at the sensation of her crying out around my cock, pushing it in deeper until I hit the back of her throat. She rocks slightly, her hands coming up to press against my thighs and steady herself, but she does not protest or try to pull away. If anything, she sucks me harder, intent on pleasing me. This is how a human Tribute apologizes to her Master.

My cock stiffens, my need pounding through me. There is no reason to withhold my ecstasy and I climax with a loud cry, my fingers curving over the back of her head as I force her mouth down on my length. She submits willingly, her tongue and throat muscles working to pull every drop of my seed from my body.

I shudder and relax, panting slightly from the exertion of passion. When I open my eyes and look down at her, her skin is flushed, her eyes glazed with her own pleasure, and her cheeks are again speckled with the dark marks of my *seela*.

"Good girl," I say, caressing her head. She beams up at me, although her expression falters at my next words. "Now go bend over the bed. I must decide what I am going to punish you with."

∾

Pareena

WAITING for Bogdan to pick out an implement of torture is a torment in and of itself. As if my needy arousal wasn't punishment enough. Or the thick plug now shoved up my ass. Or the tight pinch on my nipples. I hadn't even known the belt could *do* that. The only difference between the belt and nipple clamps is that when I bend over the bed, my upper body resting on the mattress, the pressure does not increase the pinch.

I'm almost a little sad about that, because right now my needy pussy is throbbing so forcefully that any distraction from it seems welcome. How long I'll feel that way once my punishment actually gets started, I have no idea.

"I think you enjoyed the *kudzu* belt too much last time," Bogdan muses aloud, walking in front of the Wall of Pain and inspecting his options. I can see him out of the corner of my eye and my bottom immediately clenches at his words. Which makes me pant, because my muscles are already almost painfully stretched around the tech invading me.

Talk about an alien probe.

I giggle.

Bogdan whips around, his eyes narrowing at me and amusement flees.

"I'm sorry," I immediately say, babbling out the words. "I really am taking this seriously, I promise, I'm just nervous. Or something." Because sometimes my sense of humor has extremely unfortunate timing.

Looking away from me, he picks up not one but *two* implements of discipline. They look like a paddle and a cane.

Ouch.

Yup, all amusement successfully chased away, to be replaced by quickly growing anxiousness.

He puts the cane looking thing down on the bed in front of me. I can see that it's not made of wood, but I'm not exactly sure what material it's made out of. Something shiny.

"What did I tell you about Arkdhem?" Bogdan asks, his voice deep and growly. Even though I'm pretty sure I assuaged any insecurities he has about the other warrior, I can still hear the possessiveness in his tone.

"To stay away from him."

And instead, I'd forgotten to ask Dawn *not* to bring her bodyguard back with her and then I'd let him sit closest to me out of all of the warriors during the session, and *then* I'd touched him. All in Bogdan's room. After being given a direct order. While I've never been the type to let someone else dictate my relationships, Bogdan had literally only told me to stay away from *one* warrior. Not a friend, just an acquaintance. If nothing else, out of respect, I should have at least tried to adhere to his wishes.

I'd gotten so caught up in what I was doing. I was distracted by thinking that this all might actually be real. Trying to figure out how aliens would deal with grief, I had let it slip my mind.

Truthfully, I also hadn't realized how long we'd be there talking.

I'd thought I wouldn't get caught.

Maybe Dawn isn't the only one who is a bit of a brat.

But I don't have much more time to think about it, because there's a whooshing sound, followed by a loud *thwack!* and I cry out as both cheeks of my ass sting with sudden flames.

17

Pareena

WHATEVER THAT PADDLE is made out of, it *hurts*.

I start to jerk upright, an instinctive reaction to the painful blow that just landed across my entire ass, but a strong hand immediately pushes me back down, right in between my shoulder blades, and I'm pinned to the bed.

THWACK!

"Ow! I'm sorry!"

THWACK!

"I'm sorry, Master!"

THWACK!

It doesn't matter what I say, Bogdan paddles my bottom with measured, implacable strokes that have tears already sliding down my cheeks. I writhe on the bed, thankful that my movements don't affect how tightly the belt pinches my nipples. Thankful that the paddle doesn't do anything to push the belt deeper into my ass.

I'd wanted a distraction from the aching need in my pussy, but I'd been wrong. I'd take the needy pussy throbbing back now, because the way my bottom is now painfully throbbing is so much worse. Then I feel the plug in my ass come to life.

Oh fuck.

It's vibrating. So close to where I need it to. Too far to give me any satisfaction.

THWACK!

The pleasurable vibrations do nothing to make the paddle less painful upon initial impact and I cry out. Warmth spreads through my lower body, the licking burn from the spanking but also the needy flare of my arousal coming back online as the belt hums away. My nipples prickle, the pinch loosening and then tightening again, rhythmically tugging, like the nanotech is sucking on them.

THWACK!

My body tightens, my bottom clenching. Moaning, I dig my fingers into the softness of the bed. It feels like every sensitive part of me is throbbing, aching from the stimulation. The sensations are piling up until I can't tell which are pleasure and which are pain and I can barely breathe from the assault on my senses.

Bogdan

MY PAREENA'S pussy is swollen and shiny with her arousal even as she cries out in pain from her punishment. The *bokarr* swings easily in my hand, its length crossing her entire bottom, nearly wide enough to cover her cheeks completely. Her training belt is a thin strand bisecting her now dark red mounds. It parts into two strands to frame her pussy while staying well away from the sensitive inner folds and swollen clit.

The nanotech filling her ass hums against her clenching muscles, readying her for the final part of her punishment.

Putting down the paddle, I rest one hand on a swollen cheek, feeling the heat flare from her chastised skin. Despite my recent orgasm, my cock is already swelling again, reacting to her cries and her arousal. I shift my stance slightly and several of my *seela* reach out to stroke her hot flesh, sending a shiver up her spine at the light touch. I find it most pleasing as well. My *seela* crave contact with her and my cock swells even more, ready to impale her.

But her punishment is not yet complete.

She tenses when I pick up the *talin*. It is long and mostly stiff with just a little bit of bend, perfect for raising painful welts. I will be very careful with it for this first punishment though. From the manuals, I know the humans have something similar, but I do not know *how* similar.

So, I will be gentle.

"Three strokes with the *talin*," I tell my Tribute, picking it up from the bed. I'd deliberately placed it where she would be able to see it while I'd spanked her with the *bokarr*. The manuals had indicated that such a tactic would increase her apprehension and regret for misbehaving. I can feel her anxiety spike when I pick it up, so it seems to be working. "Then we will have the naughty girl sex."

~

Pareena

. . .

THE NAUGHTY GIRL SEX.

If I'd had any doubts as to what he meant, the way the plug pulses inside of me, making it feel even thicker, makes it very clear. My pussy quivers in response. 'Naughty girl sex' makes me hot. Not that I'm going to admit that to Bogdan when he clearly thinks it's part of my punishment.

But first I have to get through the cane. Because that's what the *talin* is and I know it.

Bogdan's hand drifts down from my shoulder blades to just above my ass, which is already burning fiery hot from the paddle. My cheeks feel swollen, like the skin is stretched too tightly, and I know this is going to hurt.

Snap!

A thin line of fiery agony blazes across the center of my ass and I scream into the soft padding of the mattress.

Snap!

Snap!

Two more strokes pop against my ass, just as hard and just as fast. I sob out the strikes, gasping for air as the initial bite fades and mutes, turning into a pulsing—but ultimately bearable—pain.

Then something buzzes against my clit and I moan as my poor, confused body comes alight with erotic yearning. I feel a little bit like a yo-yo, bouncing back and forth between extremes.

"Good girl," Bogdan croons and I shiver as I feel the belt sliding away from my ass, leaving me emptier and needier than ever. The buzzing on my nipples and clit intensifies. It doesn't make the pain go away, but it does distract. Ameliorates. Makes it feel almost good.

Something hot and hard and slick presses against my

anus. I whimper as it presses forward. The ways in which Tsenturion cocks differ from human cocks has never been so starkly apparent. The tip is thinner and more pointed than a human's, but it widens a lot faster, and now it's nosing its way into my tightest hole, making me feel ashamed and aroused at the same time.

Naughty girl sex.

Because *good* girls don't do anal.

Good girls don't like it when someone shoves a cock up their ass.

But *naughty girls* get it anyway.

And *really* naughty girls, like me, get off on it.

The stretch of my sphincter to accommodate Bogdan's broad head stings and burns in a completely different way from how the flesh of my bottom does. I moan, pressing my forehead against the mattress, panting for breath as he pushes deeper. I can feel all the strange bumps and ridges along the length of his cock rubbing against my sensitive nerves.

The fullness is as disconcerting as the way his cock moves inside of me. Then his *seela* writhe over the reddened, sensitized flesh of my bottom and I cry out at the touch. It hurts... it feels good... and he's still sliding deeper into my ass.

Bogdan

My Tribute's second entrance is even tighter, hotter, than her pussy. I can feel her muscles clenching around me, making my movements harder. Thankfully the oil I slicked over my cock before I began to push it inside of her helps, otherwise I think this might be a painful endeavor for both of us.

Although it is somewhat painful for her anyway. Even if I hadn't just reddened and striped her ass, it would be uncomfortable.

Yet, she is taking it, without protest, for me.

The power I have over her does not feel half as sweet as her willing submission to me. It flavors my physical pleasure and I can feel the connection between us growing. The more she takes for me, the more I give to her, the more I can *feel* her.

Feel her pain, her pleasure, the sheer joy she takes in doing something that gives me pleasure. I could never have imagined that taking a Tribute, taking a mate, could feel like *this*. Would never have thought that a punishment would lead to such closeness, such intimacy.

I thought she would make me weak, but instead she makes me feel stronger than ever.

Then my cock bottoms out in her clenching ass, the heat of her cheeks searing my groin and *seela*, and any introspective thoughts are lost in the pure pleasure of being buried so deeply inside of her alternate hole. I grip her hips, groaning and shuddering at the way her entrance grips the base of my cock, so tight that without the oils on my shaft, I do not think I would be able to move.

I hear her gasp when I begin to pull out, her muscles moving over my length, my cock undulating inside of her, stroking the sensitive walls of her channel. My *seela* slap at her already reddened skin, exploring the welts the *talin* left, and I can feel the way her pain and pleasure intermingle, almost as though the sensations are my own. The high it gives me is intense and I find my own muscles tensing as I thrust back into her and begin to ride her hard. The way her body contracts around me, squeezing me so tightly, is exquisite.

I understand why the manuals made such a big deal out of this act now. Tsenturions fuck to breed—and for pleasure, but we know that breeding is always a part of it. It would never occur to a Tsenturion female to use her mouth. Tsenturions do not have a second opening, as our digestive systems are different from a human. This second hole, right beside her first, to be used purely for her mate and master's pleasure... It fascinates me. My Pareena has already made good use of her mouth and now she has submitted this entrance to me as well.

Even though she has been naughty, I reward her for her submission now, increasing the pleasurable buzzing on her clit and moving some of the belt to cover and then slide into her pussy. To my surprise, I can feel the tech as it pushes into her, almost as though it's rubbing along the underside of my cock as well.

Groaning, I dig my fingers into her hips and pump harder, faster, increasing the vibrations of the tech filling her pussy at the same time. Both of us will be able to enjoy it and I smile at her gasping cry of shock and desire.

~

Pareena

OH FUCK, *oh fuck, oh fuck...*

It feels like my entire body is curling in, the way my toes curl during a really good kiss, because of the chaotic mix of agony and ecstasy rioting through me.

Not just me. Through Bogdan too. I can feel his rising

rapture, the way his possessiveness has become joyful rather than angry, the hot bliss he feels as he thrusts into my ass.

The movements of his cock inside of me are driving me wild and every full thrust makes me burn with the stretch. His cock is widest at the base and so my muscles are not able to fully adjust, but are forced open again and again and again... The stinging slaps of his *seela* are like little pinpricks of pain, somehow making the pleasure feel even more pleasurable.

I've had anal sex before, but I never felt this overwhelmed... this submissive. Now I understand why some people say that sex can feel like being *claimed*. That's exactly how I feel right now. Like I will never be able to completely separate myself from him again. He's too deep inside of me, his emotions and pleasure too intricately intersected with mine now.

With my pussy being filled, the vibrations humming along my nerves, it's like every inch of me is being stimulated. I am so full, so needy, and so completely caught up in an erotic haze of lust and pain that I can barely see straight. Tears are still filling my eyes, not from the spanking or from disappointing Bogdan, but because I am so overwhelmed by the sensations that my body is overloading.

"Please," I beg. "Please, Bogdan... Master... please, I need to come..."

He groans and thrusts hard, making me whimper at the jolt of painful pleasure that stabs through me. I can feel his cock stiffening even more inside of me, the way it does when he's close to his own climax.

"Come for me," he orders, and the tech around my nipples and clit contract painfully, vibrating madly, as my pussy is filled and emptied, like a cock thrusting in there as well, rather than just filling it.

I scream at the double assault, my orgasm rolling over me like a tsunami. My entire body feels like it shatters apart in erotic euphoria. When his *seela* latch onto my punished skin, I no longer even have the air to breathe, much less cry out. I can feel his seed pumping into me, a wet wash of heat inside of me, as my body finally gives out and darkness spirals.

18

Bogdan

CURLING around my Pareena's sleeping form, I trace my fingers down her soft skin. Her bottom is still darker than the rest of her skin, but the color is already more muted than it was earlier, and her sweet curves are snugged against my groin. My *seela* gently stroke the raised welts the *talin* imprinted on her skin. Those should remain longer than the color the *bokarr* left.

I was not easy on her, but it seems the pleasure affected her more deeply than the pain.

I am not sure that Naughty Girl Sex is as much a deterrent as the manuals suggested it would be. Perhaps that is my fault though. I wanted her to enjoy it. Besides, she had already been punished enough.

I am more in tune with her emotions than before. It did not escape my notice that she was more upset by disappointing me than she had been being punished by me. Not that she enjoyed the bokarr or the talin, at least, not on their own, but she felt the worst about how she made me feel.

And I am not immune to being touched by her concern.

I feel her stirring against me.

When I first realized she had fallen unconscious I had panicked, thinking I had overdone her discipline, but a quick communication with Medik had assuaged my fears. Despite being altered by the Jabol to be healthier, stronger, and longer lived, our Tributes are still prone to some human weakness. Apparently Tribute Dawn has suffered the same, on occasion, when overwhelmed.

I kiss the back of my Pareena's neck, caressing her stomach as she wakes. She makes a happy sound in the back of her throat and then winces as one of my *seela* slides along the welt across the center of her bottom. I can feel that she is still sore, but the pain is not great.

"Ouch..." she mutters before turning her head slightly to look at me over her shoulder. Her dark eyes meet mine, still sleepy.

"Have you learned your lesson, my Pareena?" I ask her, keeping my voice stern. She blushes at my words and then groans, moving her hand back to curve her fingers over her bottom, wincing at her own touch. Why she would want to cause herself further discomfort I do not know, but I do not stop her.

"Ten points to Slytherin," she says under her breath.

I frown. "What is Slytherin? What points?"

The look she bestows upon me now is almost sad. "We're going to have to get you all some more reading materials other than alien abduction romances. Although, since you don't have Urban Dictionary, that still won't explain everything."

Ah. She is trying to distract me. I narrow my eyes at her as I slide my hand over her bottom and cup it just hard enough to apply some real pressure on her welts and she gasps.

"Perhaps your punishment was not as effective as I'd hoped," I say thoughtfully, but there is no real menace in my tone. Although I do not understand everything she says, I realize that her attempts at distracting me are also a joke. I can feel her slight embarrassment at being asked to discuss her discipline. "Have you not learned your lesson?"

"No, no, I've learned it," she quickly reassures me, wriggling to turn over and face me, as if such an act will protect her tenderized bottom from my intentions. "I will talk to Dawn and tell her I can't interact like that with Arkdhem again."

My arms tighten around her, pulling her into me. My seela begin to explore the juncture of her thighs. Idly and without purpose, but she still sucks in a sharp breath as they stroke her swollen pussy lips.

"You will not touch him or any other warrior, either." I growl.

"I won't. I promise it didn't mean anything."

"It meant something to me."

She reaches up to cup my face, her dark eyes searching mine, for what I do not know. I can feel her soften in my arms, her expression becoming sympathetic.

"Hey, I'm yours, okay?" She snuggles into me, holding me so tightly that my seela barely have room to move. It feels strange but nice. I do not object. "I have no interest in Arkdhem. He's not even really interested in me. He just wants a Tribute. Any Tribute will do. But you... I know you see me."

Playing with her hair, I know she speaks the truth. I can feel it reverberating through my chest.

~

Pareena

WHO KNEW Bogdan would be such a cuddle bug?

I definitely need to introduce him to Harry Potter though. Maybe we can even get access to Urban Dictionary somehow, but if I have to explain that '10 points to Slytherin' means butt sex, then I will. Because I think if I have to be mated to someone for the rest of my unnaturally long life span, he should at least get my jokes. And for that, he needs to read Harry Potter.

Does this mean I'm accepting that I'm actually not about to die and that, instead, I'm going to have a really long life in space?

My mind shies away from thinking about that too hard. Because if it's real... I'm starting to realize that I almost don't want it to be. If this is real, I've gone from having nothing to lose to having everything to lose.

So instead of dwelling on it further, I do exactly what Bogdan just accused me of doing—I distract. I'm distracting myself though, not him.

"Are you really going to let us go down to the planet?"

"You heard the High Commander say he would try. If there are no Vgotha." He adds the second part hastily and with a little bit of relief.

Hmm. I get the feeling he doesn't actually want me on the planet, Vgotha or no Vgotha. My eyes narrow suspiciously. "Do you expect there to be?"

Rather than answer yes or no, he sidesteps the question again. This time he leans forward as he does so, to brush his lips over my shoulder—which also helpfully breaks our eye contact. Helpful for him that is.

"The scans will tell us more."

"I'd really like to go." My tone is wheedling, caught somewhere between whiny and pleading. "Get some fresh air... I was stuck in the hospital for so long..."

My chest tightens because I'm not one hundred percent sure that I'm not still there... or what it really means for me if I'm not.

I feel Bogdan still as he contemplates the implications of my words. He's a bit of a creampuff, my Bogdan, even though he doesn't look it. That hard, brooding exterior was protection for the sweet, fluffy middle that makes up his real self.

"As long as it's safe." There is a firmness to his voice, and I know there's no arguing with him. "Your safety means more than anything to me."

Okay, well I definitely can't really argue with that. I melt a little bit too. I know part of it is that he has a need to keep me safe as part of his survivor's guilt, but I can also feel that his need is personal to me. Which is supposedly part of the bonding process... or I can feel it because I've made him up and he is me. Yeah, let's get back to that alien planet thing. Because real or not, there's no way I'm missing out on a chance to be outside again.

"But if the scans don't find evidence of any Vgotha... then it's safe, right?"

"We will run more scans to be sure. Many cycles' worth. And send advance scouts to make sure the scans don't miss anything."

My lips twitch and I raise my eyebrows at him. "And then you'll take me to the alien planet?"

"Maybe you should convince me," he suggests, a wicked glint in his eyes, and he pulls me on top of him, making me laugh.

My ass is still sore from last night, my nipples feel over-sensitive, and my pussy... is absolutely ready to earn ten points for Gryffindor.

But, even though I'm a Ravenclaw, we're definitely never earning sex points for my house. Hm. Maybe I shouldn't try to access Urban Dictionary either. I don't want to give him ideas.

~

Bogdan

THE PLANET SCANS and advance scouts recover no sign of the Vgotha. I grind my teeth. While we are all uncertain of our scanners, the advance scout reports are more concrete. There was a small blip on the scans, on one small island, that we couldn't account for, but the scouts found nothing. Arkdhem led them and announced it as being completely clear, possibly the safest place on the planet to take the Tributes because they were able to explore every inch of it. No matter how I feel about him, I know he and his warriors were thorough.

Multiple sweeps were made.

The planet is clear.

Yet I feel a rising anxiety. Perhaps just because a planet is so out of my control.

"You know what this means." The High Commander rubs his forehead. "I don't like it."

We would only allow our Tributes in a safe area, well-guarded, but still... I don't like it either.

"We should scan again," I say. There is no logical reason for my uneasiness, but I find I cannot brush it away either.

"The results will be the same." The Commander blows out a breath. "Dawn has been hounding me, accusing me of breaking my promise. I will not have her think me dishonorable. Have Miths prepare a landing shuttle suitable for a crew and our Tributes."

"It is perfectly safe," Arkdhem speaks up, frowning fiercely at us. He does not like being questioned. To do so shows our doubt in him... but it is actually not doubt. Just fear.

Fear of what I cannot control.

I grind my teeth. The island is small, we have scanned it, explored it, and found nothing. But suddenly it seems like the most threatening thing in the galaxy. So much could go wrong. Colors flash across my armor before I can wrest it back to black.

Arkdhem narrows his eyes at me. I hope the flashes were too fast for him to interpret. I do not want him to ever see my fear. I stare back at him, my expression impassive. I will not let him see me uncomfortable either.

The Commander shakes his head. "Prepare the shuttle. Arkdhem, you are dismissed to rest for now. When the shuttle is ready, I want you back to guide us."

Pressing his fist to his chest, Arkdhem nods and leaves the bridge. My fists clench at my sides as I stare at the screen. The planet, which had seemed so beautiful, now looks like a threat.

I want to believe in the superiority of our warriors but

faced with the possibility of harm coming to my Tribute, I cannot deny the emotion that the Vgotha so often make me feel. The emotion I have tried to run from since the day Tsentur was destroyed.

I am afraid.

~

Pareena

WHEN DAWN KNOCKS on the door, I'm reading one of my favorite 'manuals.' Calling them that makes me snicker to myself. I hurry over to open it, only to find that I'm still locked out. Note to self: I really need to get Bogdan to give me access to it. In my defense, I got a little distracted. Not just by the punishment and sex, but also by the lure of the planet we're currently orbiting. I want to go down so badly.

"Override," Dawn says, and the door opens to her beaming face. I'm so shocked by her outfit that I barely even notice Arkdhem standing behind her, as usual.

"Where did you get that?" I ask, pointing at her jeans and t-shirt, suddenly very aware of the very pretty, flowing, and nearly see through gown that I'm wearing. I have an entire closet full of these gowns in varying colors but nothing else —and until now, I hadn't seen Dawn in anything else either.

Dawn beams at me. "I had a feeling Bogdan hadn't given you anything but gowns. Neither did Gavrill, but he let me use the replicator and eventually we figured out how to make some Earth clothing. I thought you might want a different outfit for going down to the planet."

"Are we going down to the planet?" I ask, trying to suppress my excitement in case the answer is no. Bogdan has been on the bridge for hours now and I haven't heard from him.

"Yes," Arkdhem says from behind her, smiling widely at me. "I have just returned from leading a scouting mission. We have scanned and thoroughly explored the island on foot. There are no Vgotha. The High Commander has already ordered a shuttle to be made ready."

Squealing with joy, I bounce in excitement and the next thing I know, Dawn's arms are around me and we're squealing and bouncing together. Arkdhem is still smiling as he watches us, his head tilted almost as if he's confused— or at least amused—by our reactions.

"Okay, so come on," Dawn says, pulling away from the hug and grabbing my hand. "We need to get you properly outfitted. There's no way you can explore an alien planet in that."

"There is nothing wrong with the gowns," Arkdhem murmurs.

We both give him a look as Dawn drags me past him.

"You would think that," Dawn says. Typical male.

The door swishes shut behind me and my bottom tingles, reminding me of the punishment I received not that long ago.

"Wait—" I manage to grind us to a halt. "Bogdan told me not to leave the room, remember?" He hadn't reinforced that order when he left for the bridge, but I don't want to take my chances. Especially since I'd be leaving in Arkdhem's company, even if Dawn is with us too.

"Well, you can't wear that," she says, gesturing at my outfit. Turning to Arkdhem, she gestures imperiously. "Call Bogdan, we'll get permission for Pareena to leave the room."

Oh yeah, Arkdhem calling Bogdan to get permission to take me out and around the ship. Especially, since I've technically already left the room, even though it's only by a couple of steps. That should go over great. But I don't protest. I can't help it that Arkdhem is Dawn's constant companion. And she's right, if we're going off ship, I want something different to wear.

"Yes?" Bogdan's voice, much surlier than he ever uses with me, makes me jump about ten feet in the air. Then I realize that Arkdhem is holding up his arm—using his armor to communicate with Bogdan and allow us to hear him.

"Hey, Bogdan, it's Dawn," she chirps cheerfully. "I want to take Pareena to the replicator to get some clothes for going planet side. Can she leave her room, please?" The way she says 'please' is rather pointed, almost like she's warning him that he better answer yes. My lips twitch in amusement before I wonder if I should make sure he knows that Arkdhem is coming with us too.

Then again, he must know, right? Arkdhem is the one who contacted him and he's almost always at Dawn's side when the High Commander isn't. I found out during the group session that he wants to learn as much about human females as possible, so that he can be a good mate. It's a very sweet sentiment, and I have to admit, he's far more charming than Bogdan or Gavrill are. Hm. Maybe that's why Bogdan doesn't like him very much.

There is a long pause.

"Pareena?" Bogdan asks, jolting me with his use of my name without the word 'my' in front of it. I don't think he's ever just called me by name before. "You wish for a different garment?"

"Just for being on the planet," I say, resisting the urge to move closer to Arkdhem. Bogdan can hear me just fine from where I am. "I'd rather wear boots, pants, and a top that's not flowy. It will be easier to move in and if there's any vegetation that might irritate my skin, it will be better to be covered up." Because I don't have any interest in encountering the alien version of poison ivy. Especially since, because it's alien, it might be even worse than the Earth stuff. Who knows what's down there?

There is another long pause.

"Fine," Bogdan says gruffly. "Just to the replicator and back. The shuttle should be ready soon. Stay close to Dawn." I take that last sentence as a reminder to stay away from Arkdhem.

"Woo-hoo, let's go!" Dawn cheers and grabs me by the hand. This time I don't resist at all.

I get new clothes! Planet clothes! I can't wait.

19

Pareena

"THAT. IS. AWESOME." Dawn stares enviously at my newly manufactured Ravenclaw shirt. I grin and drape it over my arm, along with the jeans that we made. I'll have to try them on when I get back to my room, but I can already tell the fabric should be stretchy enough to fit. We couldn't figure out how to get images from Earth—apparently, the Jabol only sent over the manuals and our files... go figure—but the shirt is blue and has my house motto on it. That's good enough for me. "I didn't even think about anything like that."

"What house are you?" I ask, curious now.

She hesitates. "I'm not sure. Um, definitely not Hufflepuff or I probably wouldn't have been picked up by the Jabol. My lack of close relationships was a big part of the reason they thought I was an ideal candidate."

"I think you're a great friend," I say immediately reaching out to take her hand. "Maybe you're Gryffindor? You seem pretty adventurous."

"That's true." She brightens. "And I always liked Hermione."

"What are you two talking about?" Arkdhem asks, sounding completely lost.

"Harry Potter," Dawn tells him. "It's a book series that a lot of people really love back on Earth."

"And you love this series?" he asks, looking back and forth between the two of us.

"Always," I say immediately.

Dawn laughs, getting the reference. "I liked it a lot, it was fun."

Arkdhem wrinkles his forehead thoughtfully. "So, I should read these books?" Dawn and I exchange an amused look. I'm pretty sure that if we told Arkdhem he should paint himself purple, because it would impress his Tribute, he would do it. He's very goal focused.

"Not everyone loves it, and not everyone loves it as much as I do," I admit. "If you want to make sure you connect with your Tribute, you should wait to find out what her interests are."

He nods thoughtfully, but honestly, I'm not really sure he gets it. The way he talks to Dawn and me, he's always looking for whatever will make his Tribute like him. There are definitely a few things the majority of women look for in a potential mate, but he doesn't seem to quite understand that a woman's choice is highly individual. That being said, the Jabol must be doing something right, because Dawn and Gavrill are a good match from everything I've seen, and I think the same is true for Bogdan and me.

"Excuse me, Tribute Dawn?" We all turn to see a warrior; one I don't recognize, which is no big surprise. He's looking at Dawn hopefully. "I know it is not class time, but would you have a minicycle to spare—we need some help." He gestures down the hall to a small area where there is a small group of warriors, all of them in what look like various yoga poses.

Dawn lights up. "Of course!" She glances at Arkdhem and me. "I'll be right back!"

Before I can protest—or even think about what I might say to keep her there—she's off with the warrior, leaving me there with Arkdhem. Crap. This is *not* my fault, dammit. But will Bogdan see it that way?

"Um, let's go watch," I say, trying not to show how anxious I am to get away from him, because that seems pretty rude, and it's not *his* fault that he makes Bogdan feel insecure.

"Pareena, wait," he says, and I jump when I feel his fingers close around my arm, pulling me back to face him. Instinctively, I try to jerk away, but his grip is too strong. Not that he's hurting me, he's very gentle, but I'm no match for his strength. A little trickle of fear slides through me before I push it away. No matter what, I do not believe that Arkdhem would harm me.

Even if he were the type, to do so with Dawn and a small cadre of other warriors so close by would be the height of stupidity.

"Please let go of me," I say, keeping my voice calm but firm.

To his credit, he immediately releases me, but the intense way he's looking at me still makes me feel anxious. That and the fact that I'm definitely not supposed to be spending time alone with him, but here we are. Maybe the fact that the others are nearby will be enough to counter Bogdan's possessiveness?

"Pareena, please listen. You were given to the wrong warrior. You were to be with me." He puts his hand on his chest, staring soulfully into my eyes.

"What?" I step back. Had there been some ambiguity about which warrior I was matched with? That would explain Bogdan's insecurity about Arkdhem.

"Bogdan didn't even want a Tribute," Arkdhem says quickly, scowling. "The Jabol matched you with him, but they did not understand what they were doing. He is incapable of love."

"That's not true," I snap, surprising us both with my vigor. Just because Bogdan hadn't wanted a Tribute doesn't mean that he's incapable of love. In fact, I think part of his problem is how deeply he loves, not the opposite. "Look, I know he's Mr. Grouchy, but he's a good mate. I think the Jabol knew exactly what they were doing when they matched me with him."

Because I'm not sure just anyone would be able to understand where Bogdan was coming from. Not just anyone would be as patient with him as I have been. Although some of that stems from thinking that none of this is real... but I'm starting to think that I was wrong about that. Hoping that I was, in fact. I want this to be real and I want everything being offered to me. I'm willing to fight for it.

Arkdhem's expression turns to one of pity, which makes me grind my teeth together. "He is not suitable," he insists. "You should have been assigned to me. I *want* a mate."

"That's not—you can't—" Gah! I don't even know where to begin. His retort feels so very *Arkdhem*. He wants a mate and so he thinks he should get one. That we might not actually be well matched doesn't even occur to him. Heck, he'd probably try to change himself to meet my needs, but that's not what I'd want. I need someone who knows who they are and is confident enough to stand up to me. Someone like Bogdan. But Arkdhem's desperation tugs at my heartstrings. "We'd make a terrible couple, Arkdhem. Even if I didn't have feelings for Bogdan, you and I wouldn't be good together."

"You and Bogdan aren't bonded yet, correct?" I hesitate and that gives him all the information he needs, turning his expression sympathetic. "I'm sorry."

Dang, he's good. Ready to play the sympathy card. Offer his shoulder to cry on. Was this his plan all along?

I take a deep, painful breath, ignoring the knives lining the inside of my chest. I can't sit here deliberating about the state of mine and Bogdan's relationship. Arkdhem has shown his cards and I've got to shut this down once and for all.

"That's between me and Bogdan. Regardless, I am not your Tribute. And... I love him." Which I probably should have told Bogdan first, but Arkdhem has rattled me a little. I don't know how long a bonding is supposed to take. Does it mean something that we aren't bonded yet? Arkdhem seems to think so. *Breathe in, breathe out. Don't panic. It might mean nothing.*

Arkdhem's mouth pinches. "You do not know your feelings."

Oh no he didn't. "Don't try to tell me how I feel," I snap, finally losing my temper a little. "Let's be honest here, Arkdhem, when it comes down to it, I don't think you actually want *me*. I think you want a Tribute, any Tribute, and since I'm here and you don't like Bogdan, you think I'll do. But to you, I could be any woman, who I am as an individual doesn't matter."

A shadow falls over the warrior's face and I take a step back, suddenly a little fearful. Suddenly, Arkdhem doesn't seem so harmless. There is a long pause as we stare at each other.

"Very well." Arkdhem says finally, his mouth twisted as if he's eaten something sour. "But you will regret it. In the end, *I* am a better match." He says it so fiercely that I know he truly believes it.

Spinning on his heel, he stalks off toward Dawn and the other warriors, looking so hurt that I feel a little bad. But I feel way worse because I accidentally disobeyed Bogdan. I didn't mean to, of course, but I know he won't be happy when he hears... if he hears...

Ugh. Did I invite any that? I review all my interactions with Arkdhem. If I had known Arkdhem felt this way, I would've kept my distance from the beginning, taken Bogdan's admonitions more seriously. I thought Bogdan was just being overprotective, but no, there was something there. Still, I don't think I did anything wrong, but I'm not sure whether or not Bogdan will agree with that assessment.

I should tell Bogdan what happened. But a little voice argues with me. What purpose would it serve? He already wants to pick a fight with Arkdhem. Maybe now Arkdhem will back off and Bogdan will sense that he has, and everyone will get along. A girl can hope, right?

~

Bogdan

. . .

My Tribute is hiding something.

Her worry is strong enough for me to feel, tugging at my senses, and nearly impossible to ignore. Perhaps our descent to the planet? Or the planet itself? The shuttle is already descending, it is too late for her to stay on the Command Ship, but she does not have to leave the shuttle if she so desires.

I capture her hand and squeeze. "If you are too nervous, you may stay on the shuttle."

"Oh no," she says, her mood lightening as she shakes her head at me. "You aren't getting off that easy. I want to step onto an alien planet. It's not dangerous, right?"

"We will be fine," I assure her. "This planet it heavily forested, including the island we are landing on, but we found a safe grassy area and cleared the vicinity of any predators. We set up a large perimeter for you and Tribute Dawn to explore."

"That's good." Her brow wrinkles. "You didn't disturb the area too much, I hope."

"No. The section we chose isn't populated with the larger, more dangerous fauna of this planet. And to clear the section, we set up signals that transmit a high-pitched frequency. Annoying but not fatal. All the larger beasts left already."

"Gotcha," she murmurs, but seems distracted. She tries to look around me at the rest of the shuttle crew, strapped to the sides of the narrow shuttle. I stiffen. Who is she trying to see?

Across from us, Tribute Dawn is secured next to the High Commander. Her face is split by a large smile and she wriggles in her harness, practically bouncing. I cannot make out exactly what she is saying, but she is chattering to him excitedly. Compared to her, my

Pareena is subdued, and her unhappy emotions gnaw at me.

"You need not worry," I try again. "It will be an easy trip. I will keep you safe."

"I'm not worried." But now she's chewing on her lip and glancing over her shoulder before turning back to the front and nervously fidgeting in her seat. I turn to see who she's looking at and I am fairly certain she looked at Arkdhem.

Is she trying to communicate with him?

I blank my expression and look down at my Tribute. I had given her permission to go with him and Dawn to the replicator this morning. I had misgivings about it, but the need for clothes suitable for exploring the planet seemed more important than my dislike of Arkdhem. Perhaps I was wrong to think so, although the clothing she is wearing does seem more comfortable for her. She particularly seems to like the top for some reason. I can feel a small spurt of plea-sure from her every time she looks down at it.

"Is there something you wish to tell me?" I ask.

"No, everything's fine," she says quickly.

We are not fully bonded, but I am enough in tune with her emotions now to know that she is being untruthful. Scowling, suddenly just as anxious as she is, I feel a kind of rage slipping over me. My Tribute is lying to me and it has something to do with Arkdhem. I am sure of it.

My suit flashes streaks of yellow and red. Jealousy. Anger. On display for anyone looking at me. Fortunately, no one seems to be. They have not witnessed my loss of control.

"You will tell me." I say to her, before turning in my harness to study Arkdhem. We Tsenturions are all in full armor and his is neutral gray. His face is turned away, so I can only see the side of his helmet. If he has said something to my Pareena to turn her against me... I will challenge him, and not even the High Commander will be able to gainsay me.

"Commence landing sequence," Kalexston says. There's a slight bump as we enter the atmosphere.

"Does it have to do with Arkdhem?" I growl under my breath so only she can hear.

"Later," she whispers back. "I'll tell you later. Promise."

Somewhat mollified, I lean back and brace for landing.

20

P areena

"THE SKY IS BLUE." Dawn sounds disappointed and I have to laugh.

"We could see that much from space," I tease her, but I know what she means, she wanted something very alien.

Instead, we got a planet that is slightly off somehow.

The sky is blue, but it's not quite the right shade of blue. It's close, but just off enough that I'm conscious of it and it's messing with my head a little. Same thing with the foliage. I've never been that interested in plants, so a botanist might immediately notice a lot of non-Earth fauna, but for me, I just notice that the green is a little wrong. Too deep in some places, too oddly hued in others. A lot of the plants look kind of shiny.

Enough to make me feel uneasy, despite how good it feels to be standing on actual ground, with a breeze blowing through my hair, and the sun shining down on me. I tip my head back to feel the warmth on my face.

Of course, it might not be the colors that are making me feel strange. I wonder if I'm picking up on Bogdan's emotions. He knows something's wrong.

Frankly, I'm wondering why I thought I could hide from him. He's more and more in tune with me. Thankfully Gavrill sensed the tension as well and, as soon as we disembarked from the shuttle, sent Arkdhem on a mission with several other warriors, while he and Bogdan lead teams around the immediate perimeter of the field we landed in.

Following orders, Dawn and I are standing in the middle of the field, right next to the shuttle, where they deemed us 'safest'. The woods are dark enough that I can't see into them, but I know there are warriors in there too. I'm almost a little amused at how serious they are, when I know they've already scanned the planet to death and sent scouts to explore the island. I wonder if their paranoia is symptomatic of the decimation of their homeworld or if it's just part of being a warrior.

At the other end of the field is the beach and I want to go running over there so badly. What I wouldn't give to go swimming...

"The perimeter is secure," the High Commander announces, striding back toward us with several warriors behind him. Bogdan is returning from the other side and I smile at him, although I still feel a bit anxious. He knows something's up, but I still haven't figured out the best way to tell him about Arkdhem's approaching me. Or if I even should.

Thankfully, there's no sign of Arkdhem and the warriors he's leading at the moment. They're still patrolling, taking samples of the planet to study back on ship. I feel a bit better that this little trip isn't just a jaunt to placate Dawn and me. Although, if it was, I wouldn't protest.

It feels so good to be outside. Smelling Earth-like smells. Actual ground under my feet. And every time the wind blows through my hair, I smile. The first time, I teared up. I missed this.

Bogdan says something low to Gavrill before approaching me. The expression on his face is stern, almost foreboding, and my anxiety spikes. Dammit.

"Come," he commands, holding out a hand. Guess it's our Come-to-Master talk.

"This place is nice," I mention half-heartedly as he pulls me to the edge of the field, nearly into the forest. There are big prehistoric-looking ferns and a canopy of trees with low hanging blue orbs—some sort of fruit, offering both shade a little bit of privacy. "Thanks for letting us come."

"Sit here, my Pareena," he orders, pointing to a rock that's just about the right size for a bench. I sigh and do as he says, feeling like a student called into the principal's office. Back in the middle of the field I can see Dawn and Gavrill talking, and she's pointing to the beach. Maybe she can convince him to let us go swimming. Standing in the field in the sun is nice, but the beach would be even better.

Reaching down, Bogdan raises my chin with a finger, grabbing my attention. So much for distracting myself. "You are keeping secrets from me, Pareena. And you lied to me. You are anxious and worried, and it has something to do with Arkdhem. I do not like it."

I flinch and then frown as what he says permeates.

"Wait, how do you know I'm anxious and worried? And how do you know that I lied?" That all seems very specific. True, but specific. How could he possibly be sure of that?

"I can feel you." He presses a hand to his chest. "Here. Everywhere. Can you not feel me?"

A strong sense of worry and affection surges through me. Not just mine, his. And if I'm accepting all of this as reality, and not just a coma dream, that means I'm not feeling his emotions because I made them up, it means...

"Is this the bond?" I ask, a little wondering, a lot hopeful. Because this is not the first time that I've thought I could feel what he's feeling, even though we don't have the mate mark yet. That's supposed to come later anyway though. The insecurity that Arkdhem had stirred in me earlier fades, especially as I can feel Bogdan's affection—directed at me —grow.

"I think so." He tucks a strand of hair behind my ear, his lips curving up into a smile as he gently teases me. "I have never been bonded until now."

My eyes fill with tears of happiness. Yeesh, so emotional. But maybe since I'm also feeling his emotions, maybe that explains it.

"Do I have the mark?" I look down at myself, but my t-shirt covers up pretty much everything.

"I do not think so, not yet," Bogdan says, to my disappointment. He smiles, obviously feeling it. "Do not worry, my Pareena, it will come." Wiping away my tears, he lifts me, positioning himself to sit on the rock and arranging me in his lap. He's so big I fit easily. We cuddle like that for a moment of peace and I can feel our combined happiness coursing through me. This close, focusing on them, it is easy to tell which are my emotions and which are his, even though they are so similar. "We will discuss the bonding later. Now you must tell me what is troubling you."

I turn so I am facing him and put my forehead against

his. I know he can feel the consternation rising inside of me. "You have to promise not to hurt anyone."

"I would never hurt you," he frowns, and I stop his lips with a finger.

"Not just me. Anyone." I give him as stern a look as I can. His body stiffens. "I mean it."

"Tell me," he growls. I sigh, realizing I'm probably not going to get him to promise anything. But chances are, whatever he's thinking is way worse than what actually happened, so maybe by telling him the bare facts it'll actually calm him down.

"Right after I finished making my clothes, a warrior came to ask Dawn for some help with some kind of yoga session he and some of the other warriors were having, which unintentionally left me sort of alone with Arkdhem for a few minutes."

To my relief, I feel Bogdan relax slightly. "I will not blame you for that, my Pareena," he reassures me, and I feel his fingers reaching up to my hair, twining a long lock around them. "I gave you permission to leave my room with him. You were in a public corridor while Dawn attended to the other warriors, you were not truly alone. Is that all?"

I tense and I feel him tense again. "Um, well, almost all. He took the opportunity of near-privacy to express his concern over our mating and put himself forward as an alternative. I made it clear that I am very happy with you and I would not be happy with him, and he backed off."

Unfortunately, this time Bogdan doesn't immediately relax the way I was hoping.

"I see," he says quietly, before I can reassure him that it's really not a big deal. "And why did you not share this with me immediately? Why did you try to hide it?"

"I didn't want you guys to fight." I give him a pleading look, but he doesn't reassure me.

Pulling me to him, he gives me a hard kiss before lifting me off his lap so he can rise up and take my hand. I trot along at his side as we move back into the clearing, toward Gavrill and Dawn.

"What are you going to do?" I ask, worriedly.

"What needs to be done," he answers vaguely, but as we enter the brightly lit meadow, his helmet covers his face, along with his full armor.

Yeah. That's... not reassuring.

~

Bogdan

ARKDHEM TRIED to steal my Pareena from me. I can tell there is more to what happened between them than what she is saying. Not that she is lying, exactly, but she is—what is the human saying?—putting the best spin on it. None of her words can hide his dishonor though.

He abused my trust of him, which was little enough to begin with. I should have known better. He should have known better. It is not unheard of for Tsenturions to compete for the affections of a shared interest, but we are no longer on Tsentur and Pareena was given to me. She is bonding with me. Even on Tsentur, his actions would be seen as underhanded, as he waited until she was in his care, and I was not present, to announce his intentions.

This insult cannot go unanswered.

Arkdhem is leading his patrol back onto the opposite side of the field and I growl as soon as I see him. My Pareena pulls on my hand, her footsteps slowing, but she is no match for my strength, much less my anger.

"Please don't make a scene," she begs. "It wasn't a big deal."

Perhaps not to her, but she does not understand our culture, our rules of courtship. Those rules are changing now that we have Tributes, but not so much that it is acceptable for Arkdhem try and sneakily steal her away from me, to attempt to undermine our bonding without publicly announcing his intentions. Even with my general lack of trust for the warrior, I would never have dreamed he'd stoop so low.

He catches my eye and straightens, staring me down. The warriors following him stumble to a halt, obviously confused about why he's come to such an abrupt stop.

"Bogdan, please," my Pareena whispers, tugging on me, but it is too late. I gently shake her off, pushing her behind me so I can storm forward, my armor sliding over my skin. I feel her hesitation and then her resolve as she begins to follow me.

"Bogdan?" The High Commander's voice cuts across the field, but I do not slow. Out of the corner of my eye, I see him and Tribute Dawn heading toward me. But I will not be stopped, and I pick up my pace.

"I challenge you," I shout, pointing at Arkdhem. All other movement in the field seems to still, the other warriors staring in shock. There has not been a challenge among our warriors since the Great Devastation. I can already see the disapproval on some of their faces, as our focus should be on fighting the Vgotha, not each other... but Arkdhem has gone too far. "You approached my Tribute and attempted to sway her interest to you, while pretending to be an honorable escort."

"What?" Tribute Dawn gasps behind me.

Arkdhem says nothing, glaring at me. His armor was already up but now a helmet forms around his head. The other warriors of his patrol are now looking at him in shock and a little consternation. Wondering at his actions. He seems surprised as well.

Did he think my Pareena would not tell me? Did he truly expect her to choose him, even in such a small manner as keeping a secret from me? Then again, had I not pressed, she might have done just that, but not because she has any desire for him. I can feel that she has nothing but platonic affection and a touch of exasperation for him. But he still tried for more.

Coming to a halt, just out of any weapons' reach, I snarl at him. "You have no honor."

The jab makes him jerk but he just glares harder. I can almost see his mind working, deciding whether or not to meet my challenge. I have been a warrior for longer and I hold my position as the High Commander's second for a reason. In a fair fight, it is highly unlikely that Arkdhem will triumph and we both know it.

Yet to forfeit a challenge before it has even begun is an admission of wrongdoing, and he clearly does not wish for that either.

"Is this true?" The High Commander comes up behind me, directing his question at Arkdhem.

Now Arkdhem does look a little ashamed, his gaze swerving away from the High Commander's for a moment before he defiantly lifts his chin and nods. "Bogdan did not even want a Tribute. He wanted to end the Tribute program and keep any of us from receiving Tributes. Tribute Pareena deserved to know she had an option, a warrior who does desire her and would treat her with the reverence and care she merits."

There is a murmur of understanding from our fellow warriors, more than one of them eyeing me because there is truth to his words. Despite the way in which he approached her, they understand why... and they agree.

"She is mine," I declare. What I am about to say next hurts my pride a bit, but it is necessary. "I was wrong about the Tributes." I do not enjoy admitting that I had erred, but it is the truth. I would rather my Pareena know that I have changed my mind than keep my pride.

"How convenient," Arkdhem sneers back. "Now that you have one, of course. Pareena should have been mine." The possessiveness in his voice, the way he casually uses her name, sets off rage I have never felt before.

With a war cry, I hurtle forward, my armor creating a long sword that swings easily in my hand, no longer caring about the rules of combat or challenges. I want his blood.

"No!" My Pareena cries from behind me. "Stop!" I hear the low rumble of the High Commander's voice, feel her frustration and upset when he catches her and pulls her back. "Make them stop!"

21

P areena

DAMN, damn, damn! I'm too late.

Bristling with spines and spikes that make him look bigger than ever, Bogdan is flying through the air at Arkdhem, his weapon aimed for Arkdhem's neck and my breath catches in my throat in fear. I don't want either of them hurt.

Arkdhem crouches at the last moment, avoiding the swing of Bogdan's sword, and he lashes out with his own weapons—knives that scrape along Bogdan's armor with an ear-splitting shriek.

"Calm down," Gavrill murmurs in my ear, holding me securely in place with one arm around my shoulders. Dawn comes up beside me and takes my hand, squeezing it tightly as we watch Bogdan stagger back. My heart feels like it has jumped into my throat. This is exactly what I didn't want to have happen! "They would have to severely damage their armor to do any actual harm to the other."

That is not as reassuring as he obviously thinks it is. I wish I had my own armor that I could don, so I could rush in to stop this madness. Although, watching them, I realize that armor might not be enough. They rush each other, meeting with a bang that makes me wince. Bogdan is bigger but Arkdhem is quicker, and I'm smaller than both of them. I'd be no match for either of their bulk. One blow would throw me across the clearing.

On the other hand, with a Tribute between them, they'd stop fighting, wouldn't they? If only Gavrill would let me go...

Arkdhem lands another blow as he rushes past Bogdan, spinning on a dime to stab his blades at Bogdan's chest and making me shriek with horror. Bogdan staggers back an inch before shaking the impact off and turning, his blade parrying Arkdhem's next thrust with a hair-raising clang and following it with a rough slash across Arkdhem's chest. Both warriors separate unsteadily.

I realize all the Tsenturion warriors are gathering to watch now. They crowd the clearing, keeping a wide circle around Bogdan and Arkdhem. Most of them have all their armor on too, in case one of the fighters accidentally slams into them, but no one makes a move to stop the insanity.

"This is crazy," I mutter as the two grapple. I have to admit, I'm starting to feel a little less frantic now that I can see the others are not worried, and especially since I can tell neither warrior's armor is giving way to the damage. "They're just going to pummel each other until one falls down?"

"Until one of them tires or lands what would be a killing

blow if not for their armor," Gavrill says nonchalantly. "So far, neither has done so."

"So this isn't to the death?" I ask, because it looks to me like they're trying to kill each other.

Arkdhem narrowly manages to deflect Bogdan's sword from slashing across his neck.

"No, we cannot afford to lose a single warrior," Gavrill reassures me. That's... kind of reassuring? I guess?

I duck my head, unable to watch anymore. A wrenching noise makes me cry out as I imagine how much damage the spines and weapons could inflict. I didn't realize I was so squeamish.

It's because I really care about Bogdan. Arkdhem too, to a lesser extent. Coma dream or no, my emotions have become entirely wrapped up in the Tsenturions.

Is this a dream though? Two burly warriors beating on each other until one succumbs... this is not one of my fantasies. Another screech makes me jump and I let go of Dawn's hand to turn and face Gavrill, grabbing onto his arm.

"Do something," I implore him, begging.

"They must fight it out. I cannot intrude without insulting their honor."

"Honor, shmonor. This is nuts! I don't want them to fight over me!"

Gavrill doesn't answer me. He turns back to the fray and I stomp my foot in frustration. Dirt flies from the gouged earth. The sky is still blue and pretty but with a soundtrack of battle cries and roars. This outing is the opposite of relaxing.

"Forfeit," Bogdan shouts.

"Never," Arkdhem shoots back and falls into a battle

crouch again. I'm pretty sure he means it. I don't even want him, dammit!

Screw this.

The High Commander's hold had relaxed to allow me to turn and face him and I take advantage of it. If no one else is going to stop this exercise in stupidity, then I will. Twisting, I slip out of his grip and rush forward.

"Pareena!" He roars my name as Dawn shrieks it. I ignore both of them, running as fast as I can to reach the fighting warriors.

"Pareena?" Bogdan turns, searching for me. But Arkdhem, seeing an opening, morphs a weapon like a club and leaps towards him.

"Look out!" I scream, utterly terrified, trying to run even faster. A millisecond before Arkdhem lands the blow, Bogdan whirls and blocks it with both weapons. With a cry, he surges up, shoving Arkdhem off balance. The smaller warrior slams to the ground, arms upraised to protect himself from Bogdan's blow.

The blow never comes. Bogdan has already turned his back and is stepping toward me, catching me in his arms.

"What happened?" he asks, morphing instantly from brutal warrior to concerned mate. "What are you doing?"

"Trying to stop this," I say, tears rushing to my eyes. "I don't want you to fight."

Sighing, Bogdan presses his forehead against mine. "You do not understand our ways. He should not have acted as he did."

"I agree with that, but I still don't want you two to fight," I insist, reaching up to hold onto his shoulders, peering at him from under my eyelashes with pleading eyes. "I don't like it. Are you hurt?"

"No. I'm fine." He lets me inspect his chest, which I know

Arkdhem's knives scored, but there's no sign of it. Other than a few smudges on his armor—from dirt, there's not a tear or indication that the nanotech has been compromised —he's whole and fresh as if he never challenged Arkdhem.

"You scared me," I half growl.

With an amused smile, Bogdan cups my face, giving a pleased rumble when I press my cheek into his big hand. He doesn't seem angry that I interrupted his fight. He switched gears immediately to make sure I was fine.

"So that's it? You concede?" Arkdhem shouts in our direction. The warriors try to shush him, but Gavrill waves them back when he wrenches out of their hold.

"I concede nothing," Bogdan says, shifting us so he's facing his former opponent, still holding me in his arms. His body is rigid even though his voice is nonchalant. His hands hold me in such a way he could easily move me aside. His helmet reappears but covers only half his face. "You acted without honor when you approached my Tribute."

"She should have a choice," Arkdhem shoots back. "I would be a better Master!"

Oh, no, he didn't.

"Enough." I snap out the word, raising my hand before Bogdan can respond. "Stop this. I'm the Tribute in question and Arkdhem is right. I *should* have a choice. No more fighting, you can just ask *me* what I want, and *I'll* choose."

The entire field falls silent.

Gavrill gives a cough that sounds suspiciously like a laugh, but when I glance at him, his face is as serious as ever and his armor shows nothing but a neutral grey. "Very well. Pareena, as the Tribute in question, you have the right to decide the warrior you would like as your Tsenturion Master. We'll uphold your decision, whoever you choose."

I raise a brow at Arkdhem until he nods, although the

movement is jerky. He already knows I'm not going to choose him, but since he's the one demanding I have a choice and I now have the High Commander's backing, it's not like he can do anything other than agree. I feel a little sorry for him, but he's the one who put himself in this position. I turn back to Bogdan and meet his gaze. He looks a little worried, as if he's not sure he'll be the winner in this contest.

Good. He deserves it after scaring me with that fight.

"All right then, I'll choose." I pause and draw out the moment. Everyone is silent, but I sense Bogdan's heartbeat. His face is blank but his suit ripples, betraying his trepidation. "When we met, I didn't like you very much," I tell him. "You were cold, abrupt and entirely too closed-off. But you also always took care of me. And even though you have the reputation of being the surliest Tsenturion, I know that you are capable of more feelings. You feel things deeper than most. That's why you blocked yourself off from the pain. And even though there are other warriors," I glance back at Arkdhem for just a moment, "who might have wanted a Tribute when Bogdan did not, I will never be satisfied with anyone else. Bogdan is mine. I'm in love with him. I choose him."

A ripple of approval goes through the watching warriors as Bogdan's love, his joy, surges through me. The black of his armor twinkles and my lips open in surprise as I realize it's no longer pure black but instead is decorated with what almost looks like stars in the night sky. Everything that makes up who he is—his grief, his pain, his surliness—is still there, but so is our love, our bond. It is beautiful.

Gavrill nods. At his side, Dawn claps her hands.

"Oh, yay." She grins, bouncing a little.

I tip my head forehead and press it against Bogdan's. "I choose you," I whisper. "Always."

In answer, Bogdan tilts his head and meets my lips. I can hear Arkdhem cursing, but I barely notice.

"So that was fun, can we go to the beach now?" Dawn asks.

∿

Bogdan

"ABSOLUTELY NOT." The High Commander and I respond to Tribute Dawn's question at the same time, although I must pull my lips away from my Pareena's to do so. Tribute Dawn makes an aggravated sound in the back of her throat.

"Oh, come on! If there were Vgotha hiding out anywhere in the ocean they'd definitely have taken advantage of the fight to come out and ambush us. None of you were paying attention to anything other than Arkdhem and Bogdan!" She points back toward the water. "An entire platoon of Vgotha could have snuck up on you and none of you would have noticed."

The High Commander and I exchange glances and then he looks back at Arkdhem. I look at my Pareena instead and almost groan when she meets my gaze with hopeful brown eyes. Tribute Dawn is not the only Tribute who wants to go to the beach.

"Arkdhem, you will spread the scouts out through the woods nearest the beach," the High Commander orders, as confident as ever, although I can hear a touch of resignation in his tone. Tribute Dawn makes a joyful sound and throws her arms around him. A small smile touches his lips, echoed in my own expression as my Pareena's excitement rises inside of me.

"Yes, High Commander," Arkdhem says through gritted teeth. He makes an abrupt gesture, signaling to the other warriors to follow his lead. With that one order, the High Commander has reaffirmed Arkdhem's place in our hierarchy, despite my challenge. I cannot be upset though, for my Pareena has chosen me. Perhaps I should even thank Arkdhem, for now everyone knows it. His pride has taken a severe blow and the High Commander must think that is punishment enough.

As the warrior whom Pareena chose to be hers, it would be ungracious of me to insist on more.

"Very well," the High Commander says, taking Tribute Dawn's hand in his. "Let us go to this beach."

It is hard not to be infected by our Tribute's obvious joy, but both the High Commander and I remain on alert as we cross the field. Tribute Dawn was not incorrect in her assessment of the distraction the challenge between Arkdhem and myself provided, but that does not convince me that the water is safe. There is so much of it and the Vgotha are not the only threat. Who knows what lurks in the depths of the waves? There was too much water to fully scan but we know there are some very large creatures residing there, with no way of knowing how close they can come to shore or if they are a threat.

But we do not even make it to the water. The moment the High Commander steps onto the sand, there is a ripple in the air before us, making him shout and push Tribute Dawn behind him, shielding her with his body. I am already doing the same with my Pareena as the rippling intensifies, an image growing and sharpening in the air. Ridges rise on my armor and my helmet encases my head, my battle blade grows in my right hand, ready to defend my Tribute, my mate.

"What's happening?" Pareena tries to come around on my other side and I push her back. I feel her hands on the back of my waist and realize she is peeking around me. It is good enough. I remain focused on the figure as Gavrill issues an alert to the patrolling warriors: Warning, intruder, beach.

The figure solidifies, remaining slightly translucent in a way. A hologram. The ugly visage grins at us and behind us, Tribute Dawn gasps in recognition.

"Greetings, High Commander." Antlers grow from his head. Otherwise, his anatomy is similar to a Tsenturion's, just covered in short grey-green fur. We have seen his face before, when he contacted the High Commander after kidnapping Tribute Dawn, demanding a meeting in exchange for her. It was an obvious trap and one we did not fall for.

"Tor." The High Commander's voice is a deep growl, full of rage.

"You can put down your weapons," Tor waves a hand at us, sounding amused. "This is only a projection. I thought perhaps you might listen better if you did not feel threatened."

"Vgotha scum." The High Commander is seething. "You dare face me after you used underhanded maneuvers to board our ship? Kidnap my Tribute? Hurt her?"

The Vgotha makes a face. "I did not mean to harm her. I did not realize how delicate human females are. Listen—"

The High Commander points his sword at the Vgotha leader. "No! I will not listen to any of your lies. We will not rest until the universe is safe from you."

"I do not wish to fight." The Vgotha actually seems frustrated. A weakness? I will have to think on it later. Right now, my focus is half on the hologram of Tor and half on scanning our surroundings. I relax minutely when Arkdhem and the other warriors come running out of the forest, heading straight for us.

"You speak as if I care what you wish."

The other warriors slow as they reach us, spreading out to surround the hologram. We need to get the Tributes back to the shuttle. But if the Vgotha can broadcast this message into our midst, what else can they do?

"We are not your enemy," Tor says. "The—"

"You weren't until you destroyed our home, our families, everything in our civilization." I snarl at him, my head jerking around, my rage swelling. "You failed though, you failed to kill us too, and we will eradicate you."

"That is what I am trying to tell you—"

"Enough!" The High Commander strides forward. Tribute Dawn tries to follow him, but Arkdhem fulfills his duties, hooking his arm around her waist and dragging her back as she curses him. At least he is good for something.

The High Commander slashes his weapon through the hologram, a vertical strike that splits the image in half and ends with a crackling screech of metal as the blade finds the source of the image. The last thing I see, before Tor's face blinks out, is murder in his eyes.

"Get the Tributes back to the ship," the High Commander roars, pointing his blade at the ocean. "Warriors, form ranks around them!"

Three Vgotha ships are rising from the water, coming just far enough forward that they are out of the range of our shuttle's weapons, and twin fears clash in my chest—mine and my Pareena's. Their doors open and Vgotha warriors jump from the openings, splashing into the shallows. With our bodies between them and the shuttle, trying to use any of our distance weapons would risk harming warriors—or worse, Tributes.

"Go!" I shove my Pareena at Kalexston, who is standing beside Arkdhem, both of their faces grim. Dawn is struggling against Arkdhem's hold, cursing at him, and he twists her around, flipping her over his shoulder.

"Bogdan, no!" My Tribute protests even as Kalexston picks her up and begins to run back the shuttle, mere steps behind Arkdhem. My heart aches at the mournful sound of her voice, but I will not fail her as I failed Harai... she will be safe, even if it is at the cost of my own life.

22

Pareena

I'M GOING to kill Bogdan.

If he survives this, that is. I'm terrified that he won't. That neither of us will.

The warrior carrying me comes to an abrupt halt, his shoulder jerking against my stomach.

"Into the trees!" I hear Arkdhem shout. Immediately, the warrior under me changes course, heading for the forest. Lifting my head up so that I can see more than the ground, I immediately spot the Vgotha ship flying above us and I push down the scream that bubbles up in my throat. Is it going to beam us up? What will I do if it does?

A feeling of helplessness rises up inside of me, the same way I felt when the doctors told me the chemo wasn't working anymore.

Because I finally really truly believe, one hundred percent with no doubts, that this is all real. I feel it down to my bones. Bogdan is real. Our love is real. This second life, this second chance at *everything*... it's real. And if I'm about to lose it just when I've fully accepted that I really have it, I'm seriously going to kill someone.

The forest swallows up the sounds of battle, the canopy hiding us from the Vgotha ship, but the warrior carrying me barely slows. I can hear Arkdhem ahead of us, crashing through the undergrowth and I groan as the 'ride' becomes even bumpier.

The breath *oofs* out of me as the warrior grinds to a halt again, his body tense beneath mine.

"Surrender, warriors. There is no need for battle. You are heavily outnumbered."

I immediately recognize the voice even though I've only heard it once before, since that one time was just a few minutes ago. My breath catches in my throat and I begin to struggle against the warrior holding me again. Dammit, I am not being taken prisoner while over some stranger's shoulder!

To my surprise, the warrior doesn't fight me. He sets me down, carefully, gently. Then I realize it's to protect me. He and Arkdhem have put Dawn and me down between them, both of them in position to shield us from the Vgotha who move out from between the trees. Four of them in total, including Tor, their leader.

"We will never surrender to you," Arkdhem says fiercely, the hate clear in his voice.

"Don't be foolish," Tor sneers back. "We won't hurt you unless we have—" Just like before, he doesn't manage to finish his sentence before the Tsenturion warrior who was carrying me springs forward with a battle cry.

Launching himself at the Vgotha standing directly in front of him, he grabs the other warrior and flings him at a second Vgotha.

"Run!" he shouts at Dawn and me, pointing at the opening between the Vgotha that he's just made.

Instinctively, we grab each other's hands as we follow his order. Panic is clawing its way up my throat and I am so, so glad I'm not wearing one of the Tsenturion gowns. A branch whips against my leg as I run, my fingers squeezing Dawn's so hard that it hurts.

I don't even know where we're running to.

But it doesn't matter.

Something catches me around my middle and the breath *oofs* out of me as it begins dragging me backwards. I claw at the restraining rope, before realizing it's actually some sort of vine. *What the—?* Beside me, Dawn screams as she fights the vine now dragging her along the ground.

The forest is alive.

I shriek, struggling, my fingers clawing uselessly at the thick vine and I can feel Bogdan's panic as he feels mine, right before the ground seems to rise up and swallow me whole.

∽

Bogdan

SOMETHING IS WRONG. I can *feel* it, even through my concentration on the battlefield. Terror rising up inside of me, yet somehow apart from me... because it is not my emotion. It is my Pareena's. She is frightened and I... *I am not with her.*

I turn toward the field, my eyes seeking her, hoping she

is finally safe... but the shuttle is still there and there is no sign of Arkdhem, Kalexston, or either Tribute. A Vgotha ship passes overhead, as though scanning the tree line, and narrowly avoiding a shot from our shuttle. A chill runs through me. Where are they? What has frightened her?

Something hits me from behind, taking advantage of my distraction, pulling my attention back to the battle. The Vgotha warriors are unexpectedly brutal fighters and my distraction could have easily ended in my death. The Jabol had told us they were cowards who would not engage us face to face, and until now that has proven true. Even when they kidnapped Tribute Dawn, right from our Command Ship, they did so sneakily. That is why they destroyed our whole planet in one blow, because they could not possibly win in a fair fight.

They have apparently honed their fighting skills since then, for they are formidable.

They are not as well armored as we, but their claws are even more vicious than our nanotech weapons and they fight like demons possessed. Where Arkdhem was unable to pierce my armor, the Vgotha weapons do not suffer the same flaw. My armor is some protection, but it is not complete. I snarl at the fiery pain that lashes across my back, turning and slashing blindly as the other warrior falls back.

Where is my Pareena?

The thought pounds through my head even as I face off against the Vgotha. I do not even wish to fight him. I do not care about killing these Vgotha nearly as much as I do about ensuring my Pareena's safety. But if I must kill them all to get back to her, then I will do so.

The Vgotha beast across from me snarls and launches himself at me. I slash at him and he actually manages to spin in midair, avoiding the blow. Quickly, I turn and lash out with my foot, kicking him just as he lands and sending him sprawling backward. His feet lift into the air and then swing, pulling his body back upright so that he lands facing me, eyes bright with furious intent.

Facing off with him, trying to ensure that no one else sneaks up on me... the Vgotha have shredded our lines and now it is an all-out brawl. The line across my back still stings. I can feel that my armor has closed around the breach his claws made but the injury remains. We lunge at each other again. I duck under his strike, managing to slash him across his side, but he catches me on his backswing, raking my thigh. Turning, I ignore the wounds as I face him again, gritting my teeth against the pain.

Before we can engage again, there is a loud blast of sound through the air, making all of the warriors—Tsenturion and Vgotha alike—jerk toward it in instinctive reaction. But when we turn back to fight, the Vgotha are running. At least two of them are carrying another Vgotha over their shoulder, although it is impossible to tell if they are dead or injured. My breath heaves out in a long sigh, confusion and dread rising inside of me.

Something is wrong.

"Come back here, cowards!" Someone yells, their voice full of anger.

But they are not cowards. I cannot think that anymore, not after fighting them. The Jabol described them as beasts, a label that rings true, but they are more than that. They have proven it today. I can tell that I am not the only injured Tsenturion warrior on the field, and I am certainly not among the worst of the wounded.

That sound we heard was a signal, a call to retreat because... because they've gotten what they came for? Horror at the realization fills me.

"*Pareena!*" Her name is a roar and I pelt toward the shuttle, my eyes scanning the field for my Tribute. Out of the corner of my eye, I can see the High Commander doing the same, yelling Dawn's name. I reach for her internally but... I cannot feel her. *"PAREENA!"*

23

P areena

"PAREENA? PAREENA!" The high-pitched way the nurse is saying my name sounds almost frantic.

I suck in a lungful of air—and moan. It hurts to breathe. The morphine must be wearing off again. I reach for the little button that they gave me to help control my drip.

"No—" I mumble to the nurse, trying to wave her away with my other hand. I'm too tired to deal with more tests. "Don' wanna—"

"Pareena, please, please wake up." Huh. The nurse sounds terrified. Weird.

"I'm awake," I tell her with a groan, forcing myself to focus. What has gone wrong that makes a nurse sound that scared?

My eyes pop open. I'm strapped down to a large table. An operating room? But this doesn't look like a hospital.

Grey-green walls, hewn out of rock. A damp, earthy smell. What the hell?

I strain to raise my head. Across the room, Dawn is chained to a wall.

Dawn. Not a nurse. *Tribute. Tsenturion. Vgotha.*

Oh no.

"Pareena! You're awake." Dawn slumps in her chains. I feel a small trickle of relief that both of us are still clothed. That's hopefully a good sign, right? "Thank fuck, I was starting to get worried."

"Wha—" my mouth feels numb, full of cotton. "What happened?"

"The Vgotha got us," Dawn says grimly.

"But where are we?" I ask, becoming more and more alert as every second passes. Unfortunately, that also means the pain in my side is increasing. I grit my teeth against it, trying to focus on what's important. "Are we still on the planet? I thought it was safe here."

"I'm guessing we're really far underground. I doubt the Tsenturions had scans to go this deep. Or we're under bedrock maybe? Or even under the water. I have no idea."

"I feel like I'm high," I mutter, shaking my head, trying to shake off the wooziness that's lingering.

"The air is different down here—probably not the right mix of gases for a human," Dawn says, although her voice isn't certain. She's definitely more awake than I am though, so she's probably had more time to think about it.

"Excellent guess, little human." The deep, rumbling voice rolls through the room. I crane my neck as the giant from the clearing strides into the room, muscles rippling. He reminds me of an elk, graceful and powerful, but bipedal and with a humanoid face. There's a kind of wild beauty to him, but he's also terrifying. Especially when I'm chained up on a table and have no idea what he wants with us.

"Tor," Dawn practically growls his name, glaring at him. "Wasn't one kidnapping enough?" She strains, tugging at her bonds. I wish I could do the same, but just trying is enough to make me stop and pant with pain. *Ow.*

"Stop struggling," Tor orders, although he sounds more exasperated than anything else, like he can't believe she's even making the attempt. "There is no escape. Not this time." Turning his back on Dawn, he walks over to me, frowning.

"You are wounded," he says, and he almost sounds sorry about it. Now that he's looking, I can stretch out enough to see that there's blood soaking through my t-shirt, just underneath my right breast.

"Oh my God..." Panic squeezes at my chest. I'm hurt and at the mercy of the enemy. Even if he does seem like a strangely solicitous enemy.

"Do not worry, little female," Tor rumbles. I stare up at him, not sure how to interpret the caring concern that I swear I see in his eyes. "Something cut you deeply when you were being pulled here. It was unintentional. I will heal you." He reaches into his shirt and pulls out a strange looking device. I don't exactly have time to look at it closely before he's pulling up my shirt and pressing it against my skin. I don't even have time to protest, just cry out in surprise at the sudden cold then hot sensation.

"Leave her alone!" Dawn shouts. Pain lances through the spot where it touches me, and I gasp in agonized shock as the blackness roils again and I pass out.

~

Bogdan

THEY ARE GONE.

I sink to my knees when I see Arkdhem stumbling out of the woods, bleeding sluggishly from the shoulder he's clutching. The expression on his face is one of horrified despair and I know... I know. The warrior might be underhanded and dishonorable when it comes to trying to steal my Pareena from me, but he would never harm either Tribute. He would fight to the death for them, if need be.

For him to look like that...

I reach for my Pareena again, but I cannot feel her emotions. Our bond is too new, or perhaps the distance too great. I feel sure that she is alive, but I also fear that is only my great hope and not the reality.

Still, the Vgotha did not harm Tribute Dawn when they had her in their clutches before. Tor had taken her to demand a meeting with the High Commander. I can only hope this time will be the same. Shame rises in me as I remember counseling the High Commander to forget Tribute Dawn when she was taken, to let the Vgotha keep her, and request a replacement from the Jabol.

Now I understand.

My Pareena is not replaceable. It does not matter that we have not fully bonded yet. I do not want any Tribute but her.

"Arkdhem..." The High Commander's voice is hoarse. "Please, tell me the Tributes are hidden in the forest."

The warrior's shoulders hunch in. "I cannot, High Commander. The Vgotha found us before we could find a safe place to secure the Tributes... they outnumbered us... we made an opening and told the Tributes to run but they did not get far. There were vines that came up out of the ground, aiding the Vgotha... we tried to fight..." His voice breaks and he suddenly sounds very young. "Kalexston did not... he... he fought honorably until the end, but the Tributes were captured."

Kalexston is dead.

Guilt swamps me. He is dead because the Tributes had been the Vgotha's goal. If I had not given my Pareena into his keeping... I had been trying to protect her, but I had made the wrong choice. I should have been there, beside her, holding her. Then Kalexston might be alive and my Pareena might be safe.

The High Commander practically vibrates with tension. "Gather our dead and wounded," he orders finally. "We will run scans. Spread the fleet out around the planet—our scouts, everything. If a single ship lifts into the air that's not ours, I want to know. Do not leave them any space where they might launch unobserved."

It will stretch our warriors and our ships to their limits, but it makes sense. They are somewhere still here on the planet. We would not have been able to miss a ship taking them into space. They must have run into the forest, to wherever they were hiding before... it's highly possible they aren't on this island anymore, but they *must* be somewhere on the planet still.

A hand claps onto my shoulder and I realize I am standing there, staring upward into the sky, as if I will somehow be able to discern my Pareena's location from the angle of the sun. I turn my head to see the High Commander's—Gavrill's—eyes looking at me with grim sympathy.

"Hope is not yet lost, my friend," he says softly, his armor glimmering with repressed rage and distress, but his voice is calm. "We will regroup and then we *will* find our Tributes and take them back." I nod at the promise in his words, although I cannot unclench my jaw to answer. I am afraid that if I do, I will lose control of myself.

I move as if in a dream, following the High Commander back to the beach. Two warriors go with Arkdhem to the forest to collect Kalexston's body. Surprisingly, thankfully, there is only one other body to recover. Borodem will never get his Tribute. A deep sadness settles over me.

We have lost a few warriors over the tsencyles we've spent hunting the Vgotha, they are not the first... but they are the first since the Jabol finally delivered on their promise of Tributes. The first since we were given *hope*.

Grief is followed by anger, but there is also relief that our losses were not greater. They could have been. The Jabol descriptions of the Vgotha's hand-to-hand fighting capabilities were highly inaccurate. If we were not constantly training, despite the fact that this was the first time we'd met the Vgotha on an actual battleground, we would have been easily overrun. We will have to train harder than ever in case we ever face them off ship again. The knowledge is both humbling and disturbing.

First new technology on their ships that allow them to elude us and now this? The Vgotha threat is greater than ever.

And my Pareena is in their hands... The last time I felt this helpless was after the Great Tragedy. The only difference is now I also feel the most dangerous of emotions —hope.

24

P areena

WHEN I COME TO, the ache in my side is gone, replaced by an intense tingling. I gasp and automatically wince, expecting shooting pain from the movement but... nothing. I sigh in relief.

"Pareena?" Dawn calls out to me. I lift my head to look at her. It's all I can lift because even though Tor did something to heal the wound, I'm still tied down. At least I don't have to crane my neck as far. The table under my shoulders has elevated a little so I'm half sitting up, which also allows me to breathe a little better.

"Present," I return weakly, giving her a lopsided smile.

"Oh, thank goodness." Dawn sags back against the wall, her hair falling in her face. "He said you would be, but... I just didn't know whether or not to believe him. I don't think he would mean to hurt you, honestly, but I could always be wrong."

"I'm okay," I reassure her, although I'm not entirely sure that I am. Physically, I do seem to be fine now, but emotionally... mentally... My brain feels like utter chaos. "Except... this is all real, isn't it? It's not a dream?"

I'd pretty much come to accept that it wasn't, but now I'm almost hoping it is. Because I don't want this part to be real. I want to be able to click my heels together and magically be returned to Bogdan. But if this is real, then that's not going to happen. Accepting that I was abducted by aliens once? That was hard enough. Accepting that it's happened again and I'm never going to see the alien that I fell in love with again? That makes me want to start screaming and never stop.

Dawn's face softens as she looks at me. "No. It's not a dream."

"You know, when I first woke up with Frllil, I thought I was in a coma. That this all was the product of my imagination. I mean, that's a lot easier to believe than something like, I was abducted from Earth via an e-reader. My cancer is cured, and I have an alien master. And now, I've been abducted a second time, and I'm caught in an inter-species feud where both sides want to annihilate the other."

"That's some imagination. You know what they say, truth is stranger than fiction," Dawn tries to joke. Neither of us laughs and her expression turns sad. "This is all real, I'm afraid. I'm real. You're here. This," she waves a hand at the room, stretching as far as the chain allows, "is happening."

"Damn."

"Yeah."

"This happened to you before, right?" I need to keep moving forward. If I stop, I'll panic. I can't do that yet. When

I'm back with Bogdan, I'll let myself freak out. "You never told me how you escaped. I think we should definitely go over that now."

"Last time I escaped because the ship helped me," Dawn says, shrugging one shoulder a little ruefully.

"What the what?" That entire sentence makes no sense.

"I know it sounds crazy, but that's what happened. I was crying in my cell and all I wanted was to get out... and then a door opened and I swear, the ship led me through itself to an escape pod and then the escape pod took me back to Gavrill." She sighs. "The Tsenturions wanted to experiment on it but I convinced them to let it go and try to follow it back to the Vgotha ships... it escaped, but I'm kinda glad it did."

"You're talking about it like it was alive." I'm fascinated by the idea.

"I think it might have been. Before Gavrill put it back into space to follow it, the Tsenturions discovered that it was made of living organic material. Like a really smart mushroom or something. I think it decided to help me."

"I guess that's why we're in a cave instead of on a ship," I reply, a little glumly, tugging at the bonds on my wrists. My head falls back as the stark reality of our situation is really driven home. Captured by Vgotha, who are obviously working to keep us from escaping the same way Dawn did the first time, and I no longer even have the faint hope of waking up in the hospital.

Part of me can't believe I convinced myself that this was all a dream. I've *never* had dreams that felt so real. I think deep down, I always knew it was happening, I just didn't want to admit it. Because being abducted by aliens to be a sex slave isn't something that's supposed to happen in real life. Considering the trauma of cancer and knowing I was dying, followed by the trauma of being abducted by aliens, believing every-thing was a dream was my brain's way of protecting myself.

Huh. I wonder if other Tributes will be more likely to handle being abducted the way Dawn did or the way I did. She wasn't already dealing with trauma at the time she was taken, unlike me. She told me she had lost her family members before abduction, but their deaths weren't recent. Maybe being in the midst of a first trauma when abducted led to dissociation.

"What are you thinking about?" Dawn interrupts.

"Oh... nothing important. Therapist thoughts." I make a face. I need to focus. Because this is real and if I ever want to see Bogdan again, we need to escape. I can't even feel his emotions right now but I'm sure he's furious and terrified... emotions that start to rise in myself when I realize I don't even know if he's alive. Swallowing back the fear, I shake my head. I have to operate under the assumption that he's alive and well or I'll completely break down. This is my second chance at life, dammit. I'm not going to let myself break down unless I know that something has happened to him. "What do you think the Vgotha want with us?"

"Before the attack, Tor said something about wanting to meet with the High Commander," she says slowly. "That's what he said he wanted last time too. I don't know why though. And I don't know why he thinks attacking them will help—"

"The Tsenturions attacked us," a deep voice interrupts. Tor strides back into the room, almost prowling, like some great beast out of a fairy tale. He swings his great antlered head my direction and I freeze like a rabbit sighting a preda-tor, suddenly unsure of myself. "Tribute Pareena. I trust you are feeling better?"

"Oh yeah, I'm doing great," I try for sarcasm, but my voice comes out breathy and scared. I shrink back on the table as he looms over me.

"Leave her alone, asshole!" Dawn yells at him and out of the corner of my eye I can see her struggling again. Straightening, Tor makes a gesture, not unlike a Tsenturion ordering a door to open on their ship. Part of the wall seems to grow outward, a grey-green mask moving almost like nanotech to cover her mouth. Her eyes are huge and frantic as her cries grow muffled, but she's still breathing.

"What did you do to her?" My voice has gotten a little shriller. So much for sounding brave.

"Nothing that will harm her. Her shrieks have begun to hurt my ears." He grimaces slightly, shooting a look over his shoulder that would make most people quail in fear. Dawn glares back at him.

"Let her go," I demand, my own fear sliding away in defense of my friend. It doesn't hurt that so far, while he looks threatening, Tor hasn't actually done anything to hurt us. Heck, he healed my side. Then again, I wouldn't have been hurt if he hadn't had us kidnapped...

"Not unless she will keep silent and allow me to speak. I have waited a long time for this audience and time is of the essence."

"Destroying the entire Tsenturion planet wasn't a good way to get their attention." I scowl at him. "Maybe you should've just left a message at the beep."

With a grunt, he waves his hand at my table. Streams of grey-green table matter flow up my shoulder, starting to cover my mouth.

"Wait," I sputter. "I'll be quiet. Just... tell me what you want with us. Maybe I can help."

He pauses. Another flick of his wrist and the gag flows away and becomes part of the table again.

Alien tech is so cool. Super creepy, but cool.

"I have been trying to communicate with the High Commander for some time. A message could not be sent over normal channels. There was no way to ensure it would not be intercepted and corrupted."

"Well, kidnapping us is not going to create any good will between you," I point out, keeping my tone reasonable. I find myself falling into my therapy voice, pointing out the flaws in his logic. "They're probably pretty upset with you right now. On top of the whole genocide thing."

For a long moment, Tor stares at me and I shrink back, thinking that maybe I've gone too far... Then he turns away and with a wave of his hand, a portion of the wall smooths out. Images appear as if on a screen—the clearing where we were. There are Tsenturions in full armor patrolling the empty space. One runs out of the woods to the center where Arkdhem stands, clenching his fists over and over again—it looks like he's giving a report. They're searching for us.

I don't see Bogdan or Gavrill and my heart aches. My heart sends a plea out to the universe that they're both unharmed.

"They'll find us, you know," I tell Tor quietly. "They won't stop looking until they do."

He snorts. "They will not find you. They did not even know we were here on this planet or they would not have brought you here. But now I have the upper hand and the High Commander will listen to my demands." Tor's dark gaze turns to the screen. "Once he is desperate enough, he will do anything. Even talk with a Vgotha."

∾

Bogdan

I TEAR A SAPLING UP by its roots and toss it aside. Beside me, the High Commander does the same. Behind us, Tsenturion warriors comb the undergrowth. I refused to leave the planet and almost as soon as he'd gone up to the Command Ship and ensured his orders to create a blockade around the planet were being followed, the High Commander returned.

Neither of us can sit by idly, waiting for news, when we could be looking for our Tributes. Even if I find nothing, I must try. All I am sure of is that my Pareena still lives. I cannot feel her emotions, but I feel sure of that.

The High Commander hefts another sapling and sends it crashing into the brush. "It's no use. We should burn this place to the ground."

"Once we are sure Dawn and Pareena are not here." We don't even know if they are still on this island, but I know neither of us will risk the fact that they might be. The only thing we can be sure of is that they are still on the planet.

The High Commander covers his face with a hand for a moment. When he drops it, his face is frozen like a mask, anguish writ in every line of his body.

"I cannot do it, Bogdan," he says quietly, so that no one will overhear. In that moment, he is not my High Commander, he is my friend, and he is in pain. "I cannot sacrifice her for our people, and I cannot sacrifice our people for her. I do not know what to do."

Clapping my hand on his shoulder, I bow my head forward until our foreheads touch in a show of shared grief.

"We do not know what Tor wishes," I say quietly. "But your Dawn was unharmed the last time he took her. No matter how the Vgotha feel about us, there is no reason to think they'd hurt the Tributes."

"We have hunted them for so long and now..." Gavrill sighs, closing his eyes. "I don't know what to do. What concessions I might be willing to make." He looks at me, pain in his eyes. "Perhaps you were right, and the Tributes are a weakness we should not have indulged in until the Vgotha threat was eradicated."

"No," I say immediately, pulling back and shaking my head. "I was wrong, and you were right. Your Dawn, my Pareena... they are worth more than their ability to bear our children. They are the hope for our future, and they brighten our lives. I cannot imagine how hard is it to have your Dawn taken from you a second time, but you cannot give up." I grip his shoulders. "Your Tribute needs you, High Commander." Although he has been speaking to me as Gavrill, I deliberately use his title to push him back into his role.

It has the effect I hoped for and he straightens up, determination firming his jaw.

"The planet is blockaded," I say. "They are here. All we have to do is find them."

There is a subtle shift in the color of his armor—it is still the bluish gray of despair and mourning, but there is something new there too. Something more determined.

I would not have expected myself to be one for rousing speeches, but my Pareena has changed that about me. She has given me something I did not have before—a reason to live rather than a reason to die. Sending her off with another was foolish. I should have gone with her. If—*when*—I get her back, nothing will ever take her from my side again.

Grief for Kalexston, for Borodem rises again. They have already been taken back to the Command Ship where their bodies will be prepared for full funeral honors. Kalexston's death especially weighs on my conscience, but I will ensure he did not die in vain.

We will tear this planet apart looking, if we must. There is nothing in the universe that will keep me from my Pareena. And then the Vgotha will pay for their crimes.

Pareena

"WHAT IS IT YOU WANT?" I ask, a little worried by the almost manic gleam in his eyes.

"We Vogtha have been persecuted and hunted unjustly for too long. The age of hiding and cringing in shadows needs to end, we need peace." The way he says it is almost a threat and I can only imagine how he thinks peace will be obtained. To be fair, the Tsenturions seem to feel the same way about Vgotha, but...

"The Tsenturions hunt the Vgotha because you destroyed their planet and everyone on it. You're the aggressors. You struck first. You blew up Tsentur. Of course, they were going to come after you."

"That is what your warriors think, the lie they were told." His face twists in anger, making him appear truly frightening. I am glad that anger is not directed at me. "That is what I want to tell them. The truth behind our supposed attack on Tsentur."

I'm a therapist, I know better than anyone that there are multiple sides to any story. The Tsenturions seem sure... but so does Tor.

"What is the truth?" Because there are a lot of things that

don't add up. I admit, I got a little frustrated when Gavrill wouldn't let Tor get a word in edgewise. He was a hologram, not even there in person, and Gavrill wouldn't let him finish a sentence. I'd wanted to know what he wanted, just from natural human curiosity.

"The Vgotha did not destroy Tsentur."

"Okay..." I draw out the word, tilting my head at him. "Do you have any proof of that?"

A grim smile curves his lips. "Not so long ago, we finally acquired some."

He waves his hand and the screen showing the Tsenturions searching for us changes. No more forest, I can now see a landing deck, much like the one where the presentation ceremony was conducted. Instead of Tsenturions, blob like creatures ride little platforms around. The creatures look like Frillil, when he wasn't trying to look humanoid.

"The Jabol," I say. "What does this have to do—"

"Watch," Tor commands, his voice deep and resonant in this underground cavern.

So I watch. The video speeds up, the Jabol racing around the platform, interacting with their computers. I don't know exactly what I'm seeing but the air feels heavy. Something bad is about to happen on screen, I can sense it.

Groups of Jabol cluster around a console in front of a large screen of their own, all of them practically vibrating with excitement. The screen in front of them shows a view of space... and then a giant planet floats into view.

"Planet Tsentur," Tor explains in a bleak voice just as the Jabol being to sway back and forth. Something on the bottom edge of the screen is beginning to glow, brighter and brighter, turning a threatening red.

And I can't breathe. Somehow, I know what's about to happen. I've seen Star Wars but... this isn't a movie. It's real.

A large beam of energy shoots out from the Jabol's ship, straight at the planet. It ripples, flaring and pulsing, and that horrifying bright red light surrounds the planet.

A minute later—probably more, because the video is sped up—Tsentur explodes. They did it. The Jabol Death Star-ed Tsentur.

25

P areena

SEEING Tsentur explode has both Dawn and I nearly limp with horror. Knowing it happened was bad enough... watching it... I can only imagine the terror of the Tsenturion people when that terrible red glow surrounded their planet. They would have known something was wrong, that something was happening. I can only hope they didn't suffer when the final blow came.

"How?" I gasp out the word, tears surging in my eyes. "How come Gavrill and the others don't know this?"

"The Jabol were trusted merchants who commonly traded with the Tsenturions. A ship of theirs would have been welcomed into Tsenturion space," Tor says darkly, still staring at the screen. "When the High Commander's ship returned home, they were there to greet him and tell him about the horrible Vgotha who had destroyed Tsentur."

For a long moment the room is quiet, but I feel like I've just survived an earthquake. My whole world view is shaken, but at the same time, I can't make sense of it. Why would the Jabol do that?

"You could've doctored that footage," I say, but I'm not certain. Across the room, Dawn's eyes are wide, and tears roll down her cheeks as well. Both of us are affected, confused... I don't know who to believe. "Why would the Jabol even want to blow up the Tsenturions' planet? Like you said, they traded with them."

"The Jabol needed protectors. They faced a new threat, risen from the ranks of the species they kept as slaves."

"What threat?"

"The Vgotha." Tor's voice echoes in the chamber, filling the shocked silence. "Have the Tsenturions ever wondered where the Vgotha came from?"

"Um..." I look at Dawn, because she's known them for longer than I have. She shakes her head slightly, eyes wide over the gag, her expression just as troubled as mine.

"They treated us as beasts of labor, enslaved for centuries." Tor snarls, shaking his antlered head. "They do not see other species as being equal, do not consider us important. The Jabol are not fighters. They focused their technology on exploiting and experimenting on other species, but they did so subtly, knowing that war would thwart their efforts. They grew complacent, thinking the Vgotha were too stupid, too ignorant to even want to be free of their tyranny. But they were wrong. We revolted. Stole ships and escaped their tyranny, and then returned again and again to free more of our people. They needed strong protectors who would regard us as the enemy, without having to explain what they had done to us."

"So, they blew up Tsentur and framed you," I whisper. It could be a lie. A trick. A trap.

But I believe him.

Tor bows his head.

"Do you have proof? That you were enslaved?" I brace for more videos.

In answer, Tor lowers his head, turning so I can see the bare skin on the back of his neck, a worn patch where no fur grows. There, in faded ink, is a tattooed symbol of a circle with three wavy lines traveling horizontally across it. I still, my breath catching. I immediately recognize that symbol, I saw it all over Frllil's facility. I never asked what it meant, I just assumed it was a Jabol thing. Well, technically I guess it is.

"This marks me as property of the Jabol," Tor rumbles. "I've bore it since birth. The slavers took me from my mother and gave it to me before I was sent to the children pens and raised for a single fate: to work and die in the mines. The Jabols need supplies for all their tech."

"They didn't use robots?" I blurt. I can't get my mind around this.

"Why would they waste their great intellect on building and maintaining machines for such a low purpose when they had easily replaceable labor?" He sneers and I know he's not speaking his opinion but repeating something he must have heard once. "Every one of my race was captured and pressed into work. Indeed, I was sent to the most dangerous places, for as a child I was small and could fit into the narrow spaces where the Jabols found the best ore."

I stare into Tor's white eyes, feeling like I've been crushed under a boulder. My stomach roils and threatens to bubble over.

If this is true, then everything the Tsenturions believe

about the Jabol and Vgotha is wrong. The race they've been hunting for years, in a misguided sense of punishment, is innocent. The real aggressors, the Jabol, control the narrative and rule the Tsenturions in their own way.

This is awful. I can't imagine someone like Frllil being so cruel... but then again, he's willing to capture human women, risk their lives by bringing them through a wormhole, to be the brides of aliens. And before Dawn got involved in the program, they didn't even ask for the negligible consent that I gave. So maybe I'm not the best judge of what Jabol ethics might lead Frllil to do... I don't like to think that he had anything to do with the destruction of Tsentur, because I *liked* him, but that doesn't mean I'm right.

Maybe the Jabol are a little like humans and there are some who are capable of committing terrible acts and some who are really good people. Or maybe they're *exactly* like humans and even the really 'nice' ones are capable of terrible things, especially when it comes to others that they think are different or less than them.

But none of that is what is most important.

"We have to tell them," I finally say. I still feel sick, but there's not time. "We have to tell the Tsenturions what really happened." The horrible image of Tsentur's broken pieces is still on screen.

"What do you think I've been trying to do?" Tor snarls. "The High Commander is unwilling to listen and now more of my Vgotha warriors have *died* because he is too much of a Jabol pawn to meet with me. I cannot send the message without risking the Jabol knowing about it. So now I have you and eventually he will have to agree to a meeting."

"Maybe but... that won't make him a better listener." I look up at Tor, meeting his gaze. "Let us go. *We* can take him the video and tell him everything you just told us. *We* can speak for you."

Tor's brow furrows, but I can tell he's thinking about it. He shakes his head. "I would rather speak for myself."

"You can't force someone to listen to you," I say in exasperation. "If you drag him, unwilling, to a meeting, he's not going to be in a listening frame of mind. Kidnapping us was an act of war, that makes you the bad guy in this scenario, even if you're trying to do the right thing in the long run. The Tsenturions lost everyone they loved long ago they're going to be too freaked out to listen to you if you're holding us over their heads the whole time."

At least Gavrill and Bogdan will be, since they're the most emotionally involved, but since they're also the top two ranking warriors in the fleet it doesn't really matter if someone else might be thinking more clearly. "But if you let us go back, it's a clear peace offering and it's exactly what they *won't* expect."

Dawn makes a muffled noise behind her gag, like she's trying to talk. Narrowing his eyes, Tor studies her.

"No screaming," he says, and she nods in agreement. With another wave of his hand, the gag recedes.

"I escaped last time, because your ship helped me," she says quickly, like she's afraid she won't be able to get the words out before he gags her again. "Gavrill and the warriors were already confused by that, confused by the fact that you didn't harm me at all, they *wondered why*. If *you* let us go, deliberately, that just makes everything you're saying more believable."

Tor begins to pace, obviously thinking about our words but unsure of changing his plan.

"Send Dawn back," I say suddenly. "I'll stay here."

"No," Dawn gasps, but I keep talking to Tor.

"I trust you. Someone has to start trusting around here. It may as well be me." And my negotiating skills might keep me alive even if this is a trick. I definitely get the impression that Tor likes me better than Dawn. "Maybe if I show some trust, you will too."

"You're a brave one," Tor rumbles, pausing beside me. He cocks his head as he looks down at me, studying my expression.

"Thank you?" It comes out as more of a question than anything else, because I'm not sure if that's really a good description for me right now. I don't feel particularly brave. Just out of options.

"I wouldn't mind a Tribute of my own." He caresses my cheek with a callused finger. Dawn chokes on a gasp.

Argh. Males. I very gently move my face away from his touch.

"I'm not interested in that sort of relationship," I say firmly. "I'm already in one and it's complicated enough."

A strange sound fills my ears, like rocks rolling into each other, and I realize he's chuckling.

"So brave. And honest. Very well. I will not claim a Tribute... yet."

"So, you agree? You'll let Dawn go?" I persist.

"No," Tor clicks a finger and both our bonds release. "I've decided. Both of you will go back."

"What's the catch?" Dawn rubs her wrists, scuttling past Tor to help me off the table.

"If I only send one of you back, it will still seem as though I am the 'bad guy,' yes?" He speaks the slang a little oddly, although he definitely gets the general idea. "So, I will be definitely not-the-bad-guy and I will send you both back. But if the Tsenturions do not listen to you, if they attack us again, we will not hold back this time. We have new ships, new weapons, and we will destroy them. I will not accept any further unnecessary losses of my people. After today, many are already unsure that we should forgive the Tsenturions for their ignorance."

"Fine." I'm not going to argue with him, I'm just going to have to hope that Gavrill will listen better to Dawn and me than he has to Tor himself. "Can you give us a copy of the video? We promise we will only show it to the high command, in a secure location." The Jabol definitely won't like the Tsenturions knowing they're really the enemy. We need to keep this a secret as long as possible. I can't keep it from Bogdan though. Thankfully, as Gavrill's second-in-command, he's part of the high command.

Dawn and I lean against each other, not so much because we can't hold ourselves up, as to just reassure ourselves that we're really okay. That we have support if we need it.

Tor motions and the wall ejects a tiny cylinder. When he hands it to me, my fingers curl around it, gripping it tightly. So much depends on this one little cylinder.

"Follow me." Tor leads us into a long corridor, the rough hewn walls glitter in the light he pulls from a pouch on his waist. The light is dimmer than I would like but it's just enough to see by. Dawn and I stumble along behind him, keeping our eyes to the ground so that we don't trip over anything.

I can't tell how long we walk or how many turns we take. I do know I couldn't easily find my way back through the caves, definitely not without getting lost. Every so often we hear voices, deep rumbling ones, and I know it must be more Vgotha. I guess Tor didn't have to check in with the others about his plan.

I have to admit, now that I'm here, I'm curious about the

Vgotha and how their society is structured. Do they live the same way as they did before they were enslaved by the Jabol? How has their society changed since they escaped? More questions pop into my head—do they have mates? Children? A home?

I keep from asking any of my questions though, unsure of their welcome. I also am not sure I want to know all of the answers. It's too sad. Too infuriating. And I can only handle so much right now.

The corridor begins to get brighter, my leg muscles starting to burn with exertion, and I realize we're going uphill. As the opening appears in the distance, Tor comes to a halt, turning to look at Dawn and me. A little worm of fear wriggles through me; he's not going to change his mind about letting us go, is he?

"Many cycles passed before the Vgotha understood why we were being hunted," he says, his voice sad. "Many more before we discovered what really happened, and even more until we could prove it. During that time, we fought to defend ourselves. But we are tired of living in hiding. My hope Is that you will be able to convince the Tsenturions to hear us out."

"We want to help," I say, speaking for both Dawn and I. She nods her head, surprisingly quiet. "Thank you for trusting us."

"If they do not believe the vid, if they do not believe you, tell the High Commander—we are no longer the easy prey they found us to be initially," Tor says, his eyes flashing even in the dark. I go very still, my breathing stuttering a little. The male is an apex predator and right now he is deadly serious. "Tell him, the Riknari gave us the vid. They gave us our new ships and tech. And if we do not prevail on our own, they *will* be back to help us."

"Who are the Riknari?" I ask, confused and a little scared. Something about the way Tor said their name made me think he was making a *really* dramatic statement.

"Just tell the High Commander." Tor nods and points to the long corridor. "Now go. Turn right when you get out of the cave."

Glancing at each other, Dawn and I instinctively reach out to grab each other's hands and we run the last long length of the corridor together, bursting out into the forest from a cave. Panting, I look over my shoulder to see that the blackness of the cave swallowed up any sign of Tor, if he is even still there watching us.

I look at Dawn. "So? What do you think?"

She chews on her lower lip. "I don't know. I mean... he *did* just let us go..."

"They did that with you before though, kind of," I point out.

"The *ship* did." She rubs one hand over her face. "But... I felt like he was telling the truth. Or at least, what he believes is the truth. Maybe he's right. Maybe this was all a frame job and the Jabol are the real bad guys."

Which is a really hard thing to swallow. Because that means *our* guys are also the bad guys in a way. Duped. Ignorant. But still fighting on the side of evil.

I reach for my usual standby of dealing with things I don't want to think about—distraction. Turning in a slow circle, all I can see are trees.

"So, I guess we go right?" Sadly, there's not a path or anything. That would be way too easy, I guess.

"Um... it does look a little less dense. And I guess if we're going to trust Tor, we might as well trust that he's not just sending us out here on the planet to die," she says. Good point. So, we start walking.

I am extra thankful that we got 'planet' clothes. I can't even imagine how much harder this would have been in a filmy Tsenturion gown. I'm not sure that Dawn is right about this direction being less dense, but it's definitely not more densely forested than any of the other directions.

I'm not sure it matters anyway.

"I think Tor definitely liked you better than me," Dawn says after a few long minutes of silence.

"Um..."

"He's kind of hot, right? In a weird, Dark Elf kind of way."

Huh. Now that she mentions it, he does kind of look like a Dark Elf. A little furrier than I pictured them, but close enough.

"Do you think he has a weird penis too?" she muses.

"It would be kind of disappointing if he didn't," I respond with a laugh.

I guess if we have to hike across a weird alien planet, looking for our alien mates, we might as well talk about weird alien peen.

Unfortunately, it's a hot weird alien planet and I'm sweaty and thirsty within twenty minutes... which is, thankfully, when we hear someone yelling our names.

26

B ogdan

"Pareena!"

I can't believe my eyes.

The High Commander had set the ships to scanning the planet at regular intervals, but we hadn't actually expected it to pick up anything. Not after the first scan when we realized the Vgotha had managed to not only hide themselves, but to obscure the nanotech signals from the bride training belts.

At best, we thought we'd catch a ship as it lifted into the air.

Instead, suddenly, the bride trainers flashed their location on our scans. They were not on the island, which means all our searching there had been useless. Even knowing it could be a trap, Gavrill and I had immediately led a team to where their signatures had been picked up.

The forest was too dense for a shuttle, but we landed as close as we could and he and I began running straight for their location, shouting their names.

If the Vgotha were there, we wanted them to know we were coming, in hopes of springing the trap. The other warriors hung back, waiting to see what happened.

"Bogdan!" My Pareena runs through the trees, joy on her face, streaking toward me. The relief that I feel upon seeing her is so overpowering that when she jumps forward and against me, wrapping her legs and arms around me, I fall to my knees. I can feel her again, feel her joy, her love, warming me from the inside out. The sparkles on my armor swirl and flash like tiny nebulas moving over me.

Close by, Gavrill and Tribute Dawn are having a similar reunion, his hands running over her as if he cannot believe that he's touching her again. I know how he feels.

"How did you get away from the Vgotha?" I ask, holding my Pareena so tightly that it is a wonder she can breathe. Pride surges through me. I already knew my Tribute was a wonder, but even I would not have expected such a wonder from her. Unless perhaps the ship somehow helped them again? I am rather skeptical of such an idea. I cannot imagine the Vgotha are so incompetent that they would fail to block an avenue that had already been utilized.

"Not now," Gavrill says, his voice snapping out as he becomes the High Commander again. "We're too vulnerable here on planet. We'll head straight back to the ship. Medik is waiting and you can tell us your story there." He turns to our other warriors. "Go back that way, find where the Vgotha are hiding and destroy them."

Strangely, I feel my Pareena tense, feel her uncertainty and... I am not certain what else, but I do not think it is good.

"Wait!" Tribute Dawn yells out and all of the warriors freeze. "Um, you should *all* come back with us, okay? You shouldn't go after the Vgotha until Pareena and I tell our story."

The High Commander gives her a long look, his face stony, but he nods before lifting her into his arms, refusing to let her walk. He looks at the warriors, who are waiting for his order. "Guard our retreat."

Since I am already holding my Pareena, I begin to move toward the ship as quickly as I can. The skin along the back of my neck prickles, as though there are watchers in the woods, but that is impossible. The scans did not see any Vgotha and there is no sign of them now. Perhaps they were pursuing the Tributes and fell back when they saw us? I tighten my grip on her, eyes scanning the trees for further threat.

"You're safe now," I kiss along her hairline, moving quickly through the forest. As soon as I get her back on the ship. "The Vgotha will never touch you again, I vow it."

For some reason, I swear I can feel her consternation increase. I tighten my grip on her, picking up my pace as the small clearing where we landed appears. I don't understand the emotions I am picking up from her and that causes me even more concern.

The shuttle door opens as we rush toward it, the warriors around us alert for another Vgotha attack. Medik is waiting inside with two warriors he's been training as his assistants. Transport platforms hover beside them. Gavrill and I both ignore the platforms, electing to carry our Tributes and set them on our laps for Medik to scan. Pareena leans against me, the side of her face nuzzling into my shoulder.

"No internal trauma," Medik announces. "And no

external wounds as far as I can see." He frowns, pausing as he runs the scanner over my Pareena's stomach.

"What is it?" I snap out the question, too wound up to be polite.

"It looks as though..."

"I *was* hurt," she says, and my chest tightens. "The Vgotha healed me."

Emotions clash inside of me. She was hurt—fury and hate. She was healed—reluctant gratitude. I might not want to be grateful to the Vgotha for anything, I might not want to think one single good thing about them, but I cannot be angry that they spared my Pareena any pain. Even if they were the ones to cause it.

"We should get some armor," Tribute Dawn says. "Why don't our belts work as armor like your nanotech does?"

"Because they were made for Tributes, not warriors," the High Commander says.

"And so we don't need armor?"

The High Commander nods. "Exactly."

"Okay, but I keep ending up in situations where armor would be handy. I'm just saying."

I growl, not liking the reminder. Perhaps we *should* speak with the Jabol about adjusting the Bridal Trainers to also have protective functions. I do not like to think that it would ever be necessary, but I will choose my Pareena's safety over my own pride without hesitation.

"Okay so..." Tribute Dawn looks up at the High Commander. She seems paler than usual, although that is not entirely surprising. Both Tributes have been through an ordeal. "When we get back to the ship, we need to speak with you and Bogdan. Alone." She glances at Medik. "Medik too, would probably be a good idea."

I would rather take my Pareena back to my room to

check her over thoroughly myself, but she's already nodding. I can feel how serious she is through our bond. As happy as she is to be reunited with me, there is something weighing heavily on her mind.

"Yes," she says quietly. "I think just the three of you to start."

~

Pareena

IT ENDS up being four of them gathered in Gavrill and Dawn's room, because Arkdhem was waiting for us as soon as the shuttle docked. He apologized over and over to Dawn for allowing her to be taken, even though she told him it wasn't necessary. I was just relieved that the warrior who had been guarding me wasn't there doing the same. She ended up telling Arkdhem to come too. Possibly to reassure him that us being taken wasn't actually a bad thing.

I don't protest because Arkdhem *is* part of the high command, but I'm glad that it's just them. This is going to be hard enough and I think it's best the leaders decide how to present the information to the rest of the warriors. Dawn and I are really only observers to Tsenturion culture, I can't begin to predict how they will react.

Gavrill sits down in his chair, Dawn on his lap, and Bogdan does the same with me. Despite the seriousness of the situation, I can't help but be a little amused. Then again, it's not like I want to let him go either. I lean against him and I'm not sure whether it's to draw on his strength or because I'm preparing to comfort him.

"What is it you need to tell us?" Gavrill asks, his expression serious.

"A message from the Vgotha," Dawn says in a rush, speaking even faster when Gavrill's expression changes. I can feel Bogdan stiffen beneath me—and not in the fun way. Neither of them wants to listen, but unlike with Tor they aren't immediately interrupting her either. "They've been trying to meet with you because they didn't dare send a message that might get intercepted. They aren't the bad guys, they didn't destroy Tsentur, the Jabol did."

There is dead silence in the room. I can feel Bogdan's emotions—they go straight to denial and fury.

"Lies," Arkdhem snarls, getting to his feet and glaring at us. Beside him, Medik sits as if frozen, his expression completely blank. "The Vgotha are dishonorable cowards, they are scum, and the Jabol are our allies. Why would you believe such a thing?"

"Because they showed us this," I say quietly, pulling the small cylinder Tor gave me out of my pocket and holding it up. It's only as I do so that I realize, I have no way of knowing how to access the information on it. Fortunately, Medik suddenly begins to move again, and he reaches across the table, plucking it from my fingers. After a long moment of examining it, he twists, and a hologram leaps out of the end of it... I recognize the scene immediately, a smaller version of what Tor showed us.

"What is this?" Gavrill asks as the Jabol start to race around in the image.

"Just watch," Dawn murmurs, interlacing her small hand with his.

I sit rigid, studying the Tsenturion's faces. I can't guess what they're thinking, although I can feel Bogdan's growing confusion and anger, his utter grief and devastation when the planet finally explodes. Medik bows his head so that I can no longer see his face.

"That's what they wanted to show us," Dawn says as the three warriors stare stone faced at the hologram showing the rubble of their homeworld. "That and proof that the Vgotha were a slave race, imprisoned by the Jabol and treated cruelly. And when the Vgotha broke free, the Jabol were afraid of their vengeance. So, they destroyed Tsentur and framed the Vgotha."

Arkdhem snorts derisively, obviously not believing any of this.

"You think this is truth?" Gavrill asks, his tone neutral.

"I do," Dawn murmurs. "I know it's crazy, but...I don't think Tor is lying." She looks at me.

"I don't either," I say. "I can understand why you'd be reluctant to believe it—"

"I can't believe I'm hearing this. This proves nothing," Arkdhem interrupts, furious. He slams his fist down on the table in front of him. "We lost *two* warriors today to the Vgotha and you come in here with this... this fake vid, these Vgotha lies—"

"Lost?!" Dawn's horrified question cuts him off. "Who did we lose?"

"Kalexston, who gave his life trying to keep Tribute Pareena from being taken," Arkdhem glares at me as my heart sinks into my stomach. That must have been the warrior who had been guarding me. Dead? He was dead? "And Borodem who fought them and fell on the beach."

"Oh no..." I breathe out the words, tears springing to my eyes. I feel awful about Kalexston, but even worse about Borodem... he'd had so much hope for the future, for *his* future and now...

"That's not the Vgotha's fault," Dawn insists, although

there are tears now running down her face. "*They* didn't attack first. *They* didn't lie to you. *They* have just been trying to meet with you and *you* didn't listen!" Realizing what she's saying, how it sounds like she's actually blaming her mate, she claps her hands over her mouth and stares at Gavrill in horror and apology.

"It all comes back to the Jabol," I say quickly. "If they destroyed Tsentur and lied to you from the beginning—"

"*If*," Arkdhem mutters, his faith still clearly rooted in the Jabol.

"Then it's completely understandable why you'd react the way you did today. But they lost warriors today too and Tor still wants to end the fighting... he let us go because he wanted to get this message to you so badly."

"The Vgotha are known for their tricks," Gavrill says, his voice still neutral.

"Known by who?" I ask gently, since Dawn still has her hands over her mouth, and someone has to ask. "The Jabol?"

Silence falls again. A muscle in Gavrill's jaw clenches. Bogdan's emotions roil so violently I can't tell what he's thinking, what he believes.

Slowly, Medik gets to feet. "I... If you will excuse me..."

"Yes, of course," Gavrill says immediately, his voice softening. "We will speak later."

Nodding, seemingly dazed, Medik practically stumbles from the room and I bite down on my lower lip. Maybe Bogdan will allow me to seek him out later. He's obviously in a bit of shock and even though it's not really my fault, I can't help but feel a little responsible.

"We cannot trust a vid from the Vgotha," Gavrill says finally, his voice gentle because he can tell he's disappointing Dawn. "They have every reason to lie."

"So do the Jabol if the Vgotha are telling the truth!" she retorts.

"It is very convenient that they suddenly have this vid now," Arkdhem says with a sneer. He is the most outwardly opposed to believing the Vgotha, but Bogdan has been so quiet, I can't tell if he agrees with Arkdhem or not.

"They said they got it—and their new tech and ships—from someone called the Riknari," I say, remembering that we were supposed to tell them that. I didn't actually expect much of a reaction, but both Arkdhem and Gavrill stare at me, completely thunderstruck, and I can feel the deep shock that ripples through Bogdan. Tor had been right—it does mean something to them. Something big. "Um... so, uh, what does that mean exactly?"

27

B ogdan

OUR TRIBUTES HAVE DELIVERED shock upon shock in a short period of time. Finding them running through the forest had been a joyful one. The vid they'd shown us was a confusing one, because watching it I could feel nothing but pain, but I also do not know if it can be believed.

The Riknari... That is the biggest shock of all.

"They're a... legend," I say slowly. I look at the High Commander and then at Arkdhem. The latter shakes his head, not believing that the Vgotha have the Riknari on their side any more than he believes in what the vid showed us. Me? I do not know what to believe. But the Riknari... it would explain so much. Why the Vgotha tactics changed. How their ships managed to hide from our scanners. Why their ship returned Tribute Dawn after she was captured.

"They're a... a fairy tale," Arkdhem snaps and I frown at

him, not understanding what he means, but both Tributes immediately nod. "They do not actually exist."

"Then how do you explain the new Vgotha ships?" I am not convinced the Vgotha's story, that the vid, is real, but... I cannot deny that it might be possible. That very possibility, knowing that we might have been working for those who slaughtered our people all these decacycles, makes me want to rage and weep at the same time.

"But what *are* they?" Tribute Dawn asks.

"They are the Great Defenders," the High Commander says. "It is said that they fight throughout the universe on the side of those who have been wronged. They cannot be bribed, cannot be deterred... they are an extremely advanced race of beings with highly advanced technology. Not much is known about them, but sometimes when a great injustice has been done or an oppressed people are fighting against tyranny, they appear to help. Sometimes with goods or weapons, sometimes medicines, and very occasionally they will aid in battle."

"Why wouldn't they have contacted you directly after the Great Devastation?" Pareena asks, sounding fascinated.

"Besides the fact that they do not exist?" Arkdhem mutters.

"We did not go seeking their help," Gavrill says. His armor flickers, too quickly for me to catch the emotion. I am sure he is as conflicted as I. Arkdhem is the only one who appears sure that this is a Vgotha trick. "It is a large universe. They cannot be everywhere. We lost our people... horribly... but we immediately had allies, tech, everything we needed to seek our justice."

Except that if the Jabol were truly the ones to destroy Tsentur, then it was not justice. And our warriors and ships, enhanced with Jabol nanotech, had been hunting innocents.

The exact type of situation in which the Riknari might appear to help.

My chest clenches at the thought.

"You'll need to do more research," Tribute Dawn says quietly. "We need to at least look into what the Vgotha are claiming. And you can't hunt the Vgotha until you know the truth... and we have to stop the Tribute program until we know."

"What?" Arkdhem barks, anger flashing over his suit.

"Please, Gavrill," Tribute Dawn begs. "Any more Vgotha deaths *will* be on our heads. Even if you're not sure, you can't claim ignorance anymore if it does turn out to be true."

"Tor lost warriors as well, but he still is trying to do the right thing," my Pareena says softly. I can feel her sadness, her belief in Tor. I do not *want* to believe, but I am not unaffected by her emotions. "He said that he is not willing to lose anymore. He said that if you attack again, he will no longer hold back."

"And he has Riknari weapons," the High Commander murmurs thoughtfully. His shoulders sag with a sigh. Before battling the Vgotha warriors on the beach, we may not have been concerned, but they proved the reputation of their cowardliness wrong. They did not harm the Tributes. They *chose* to send the Tributes back. Either it is a very good trap... or it is the truth. Finally, the High Commander shakes his head. "I must think more on this."

"You are going to treat this... this deceit as *truth*?" Arkdhem slams his fist on the table again in his frustration. I cannot fault him for his reaction. Without my Pareena's sincerity, her belief, tempering my responses, I might very well have agreed with him.

"The Tributes are correct, we must investigate," the High Commander says. Relief blows through me—a little of mine and much more from my Tribute. "In the meantime, we cannot let the Jabol know we... are questioning their version of events or that we have been in contact with the Vgotha."

"So what if we find the Vgotha? Will we just let them go?"

"I see no other alternative."

Dawn and I visibly relax.

"This is madness. You're endangering the whole fleet— your Tributes! The whole tribute *program*." Arkdhem's armor flashes his anger, his despair.

I tighten my arms around my Pareena.

It is true—if the Jabol are the perpetrators of the Great Devastation, if they were willing to destroy our entire planet and manipulate us into being their weapon, then we must do everything in our power to destroy *them*. We will need to focus all of the energy we've been using to hunt Vgotha and turn it on them instead. But we are intertwined with them... our alliance, our technology, and our Tributes.

Without the Tributes we have no hope for the future. The two we've received are not enough. But we cannot ignore what the Jabol have done either, if the vid is true. The ramifications of these revelations go far deeper than just a change of alliance.

"If this information is correct, we have been dishonored," the High Commander snaps back at Arkdhem. "If it is true, then the real killers of our people have gone unpunished and they have used *us* as their hunting animals. I will not have us further dishonored."

"Or it's a trick and the Vgotha are waiting to crush us!" Arkdhem growls the words, his suit flickering so quickly through colors that I can tell he has lost control over his emotions. "Are we just to stand idly by if they attack us?"

"No." The High Commander gives him a hard look. "But

we will not attack first again either. Not until we have had time to look into the vid and their claims. If they attack first then we will annihilate them... but for now, we will pull back from the planet and figure out our next step. Until we have decided how to investigate, none of this will be discussed outside of this room, with anyone. That is an order."

The colors on Arkdhem's armor swirl and then mute to a neutral gray. He nods his head, but his expression is stony. "Yes, High Commander."

"Yes, High Commander," I echo. "If that is all for now, I would like to retire with my Tribute."

"Permission granted," the High Commander says. "I will give the order that we are to move back from the planet for now. Arkdhem, you will take command on the bridge and oversee our... regrouping. The scout ships will need refueling by now."

Regrouping sounds better than a retreat, but we all know what it really is. Still, keeping the planet under blockade for long term, especially now that we have our Tributes back, is inadvisable. The warriors will grow weary and the smaller ships will run low on fuel. We will pull back and then... see what the Vgotha do as we decide what *we* will do.

It is not a bad plan. The lack of action chafes, but I would rather see to my Pareena than anything else right now.

"Yes, High Commander," Arkdhem and I say in unison.

As I carry my Pareena to our quarters I cannot keep my mind on my duty. The Vgotha. The Riknari. The Jabol. Those are the beings I should be thinking about. Instead, all of my focus is on my Tribute. The feel of her back in my arms. The softness of her hair against my neck. The press of her curves against my body.

The door slides shut behind us and I carry her over to the bed, setting her down on the edge. "Strip," I order her, but the command is almost gentle. "I want to inspect you."

To my surprise, my Pareena shakes her head. "I don't want to do that," she says, reaching up to tug at my armor. "Make love to me, Bogdan."

"What?" I understand the terminology from the manuals, but I am unsure of how to proceed. "But—"

"Right now." Her hands start to roam over my chest, up to my neck, and her head tilts back as if asking for a kiss. "Please, I need to feel you."

Something pulses inside of me. I can feel her desire, her need. I have heard of the mating fever as it takes soldiers after a death-defying fight. I did not realize it would be the same for Tributes. Kneeling in front of her, we are on an equal level, and I pull her into me. Her legs part for my body, but it is my stomach that presses against her core, not my cock.

"You have been through so much, my Pareena," I whisper in the small shell of her ear, nuzzling it. "I want to inspect you and then you should rest."

"I don't want to rest," she says stubbornly. "I thought my second chance at life was over. I thought I'd never see you again. I want to feel you, inside of me."

I clasp the back of her neck and press my forehead against hers. It stills her for a moment, her anxious need softening as I touch her. Everything in me hums in pleasure at the softness of her skin, the lustrous umber of her eyes. I could live forever like this, pressed close to my Pareena as she rests in the circle of my arms. "Did you mean what you said? When you proclaimed your choice before all the Tsen-turions?"

"When I chose you?" Surprise flashes over her face and her forehead creases. An off-key twang jars the smooth melody unraveling inside me. "I told everyone I loved you. Did you think I was lying?"

I can feel her temper rise, but I am honest.

"I hoped I would be your choice, that you felt the same for me as I do for you, but when the High Commander gave you leave to choose, I was not sure what you would do."

"Well you should have had more faith in me. Some-times, Bogdan, you can be a complete ass," she huffs. Although I know I should punish her for speaking to me in such a disrespectful manner, I cannot help but laugh. I enjoy her fieriness and I can tell she means it almost affec-tionately. "But no, I wasn't lying. I don't ever want to lose you. I'll be honest, when I first woke up and saw Frllil, I thought I was dreaming. In fact, I thought I was having a coma dream for a really long time, but I wanted it to be real. I thought that my mind made all of this up because it was so close to my sexual fantasies. *You're* my every fantasy, Bogdan."

She burrows closer, and I understand her desire for me to penetrate her. We both wish to be joined as closely as possible.

"This is real. And you are mine." I shift so she straddles my great body, her hair flowing around her face. "You belong to me forever." I snap my hips upward, making her bounce. Her pupils dilate, her large, dark eyes growing larger and darker. "My mate. And I won't allow you to forget it. I will show you how very real I am."

In a rapid fighting move, I flip her over, so I am seated, and she is over my lap face down. She makes a muffled sound as I peel her 'jeans' away from her bottom, almost tearing the fabric when I can't remove it fast enough. It is not nearly as convenient as a Tsenturion gown and I make a note that she should only be allowed to wear these 'jeans' on special occasions.

"Since you do not feel you need rest, I will make love to you as you wish... but first you must be taught proper respect. You should not call your Master an ass."

I am not at all surprised by the lack of regret I feel from her.

"Well then don't doubt my feelings for you," she mutters.

SMACK!

The satisfaction I feel from having my Tribute across my thighs, her soft bottom quivering from a hard slap, is immense. It soothes the anxiety that built up inside of me when I was searching for her, making me feel more connected to her than ever.

"I will not doubt your feelings again, and you will learn not to insult me," I say calmly. Immediately, I feel a hint of mischief trickle through her and I shake my head, although I do not bother to hide my smile since she cannot see my expression.

"I'm sorry for calling you an ass, Master," she says, but I can both hear and feel her insincerity. This spanking is not truly about addressing her behavior, though, and we both know it. Still, some of the formalities must be observed.

"You will be once I am done disciplining yours," I tell her and raise my hand again.

28

Pareena

I SQUEAL as Bogdan's hand comes down again and again on my ass. I could tell he wasn't truly upset with me, and considering I'd just been abducted and recovered from the Vgotha I'd kind of thought he'd go a little easier on me, but that is not the case.

Smack! Smack!

"Ow, Master, please!" I try to twist away from his hand. The spanking hovers between punishment and pleasure and I'd really prefer the latter. Instead of indulging me though, Bogdan just takes a firmer grip on my body, tipping me forward even more on his lap so that my fingers press against the floor to help keep me from feeling completely off balance.

Every stinging swat makes my pussy clench and I cry out as my desire surges. I can already feel tears gathering in the backs of my eyes. Not because the spanking hurts so much but because I'm so relieved to be back over my Master's lap, to feel his discipline... and hopefully I'll be feeling his cock very soon, too.

My legs kick out, but they're tangled in the jeans and my movement is restricted. I moan as Bogdan's hand pauses for a moment, caressing the warmed cheeks of my ass before seeking out my pussy. I can feel the nanotech from the bride trainer creeping over the front of my mound and sliding over my clit. I moan when the vibrations hit, just enough to tease me, not enough to get me off. His fingers push into my pussy, but only for a moment, just long enough to coat the digits in my wetness before he's pressing them against my ass.

The tight ring of my anus stretches, and I whimper, wriggling on his lap as he slowly sinks his fingers into the narrow space.

"I wasn't that naughty!" I protest, although my objection is admittedly half-hearted at best.

Bogdan chuckles and I can feel his amusement. "No, but you did call me an ass... I think you meant it as a hint for what you wanted."

"I definitely did not," I retort, although my toes curl as he pumps his fingers harder, stretching the small hole. The slight burn has me panting with desire. I want him inside of me so badly, but for some reason I can't turn off the sass.

"Oh, well then." He slides his fingers out of my ass, leaving me aching and hot all over, the teasing vibrations on my clit feeling so much worse now. Dammit!

~

Bogdan

. . .

I CAN FEEL my Pareena's rising frustration and I chuckle. I will not torment her for very long, though. I am too relieved to have her safely back in my arms. Even though she does not see the need for rest, I am determined she will get some. If I have to fuck her into submission to ensure that she rests afterward, then so be it.

SMACK!

I begin to spank her bottom again and she wails. Not because of the pain, as I am not spanking her nearly as hard as I could be, but because she is flush with passion and aching to be filled.

SMACK!

SMACK!

My cock rocks against her side as she writhes on my lap, my *seela* straining against the inside of my armor.

Shifting the aim of my hand, I land the next swat directly on the pouting lips of her pussy and my Pareena cries out in pain and pleasure. Ordering the nanotech away from her swollen clit and back to the belt around her hips, I aim the next swat carefully and the tips of my fingers snap against that tender bud. I can feel the aching need, the ecstatic agony, the blow produces, and I do it again.

And again.

She sobs, bucking her hips upwards, on the verge of orgasm...

Rather than giving her the final swat that she needs, I lift her up off my lap.

"Wait! No!" she cries out, scrabbling uselessly and trying to keep her position so that I will keep spanking her sweet pussy. "I was almost there!"

"I know," I chuckle, tossing her onto my sleeping platform on her back. "There are more punishments than just spankings, my Pareena."

"Stupid manuals," she mutters, making me shake my head. I am amused that she believes I would be helpless to punish her without the manuals. But perhaps I should read more of them, as they do have such interesting ideas.

I pull her *jeans* from her body so that I may spread her legs and lift the hem of her shirt up above her breasts. The rounded curves with their brown peaks are too tempting to resist and I lower mouth to the luscious bounty.

Pareena

BEING EDGED AS A PUNISHMENT SUCKS.

On the other hand, I'm pretty sure Bogdan isn't going to keep punishing me much longer. His hot mouth closes around my nipple and I moan, arching my back and wrapping my legs and arms around him. Well, trying to. He holds himself apart from me, keeping our bodies from touching the way I want them to, *need* them to, and it's driving me wild.

The sensitized skin of my bottom rubs against the sheets beneath me, my clit throbbing between my legs after being spanked, and the hot suckling of my nipple creates a maelstrom within me, pulling me into its grip. When Bogdan plucks my hands from his shoulders, pinning arms down beside my head, I feel my entire body spasm in reaction to being rendered so completely helpless beneath him. His big body is between my legs, keeping me from being able to press my thighs together and rub, and I can feel the tickling sensation of the very tips of his *seela* questing over the tender skin of my inner thighs.

"Please, Bogdan," I beg, writhing as he switches his attentions to my other nipple, leaving the first one tightly budded, wet and throbbing in the cool air. "I need you inside of me, I need you to fuck me... claim me..."

He groans around my breast and I feel his weight come down on me more, the flexible head of his cock parting my pussy and teasing the lips with its waving motions. Then his mouth moves away from my nipple and covers my lips, keeping me from being able to say anything. I open my mouth, taking him inside me the only way I can right now, sucking on his tongue and trying to rub my pussy against the tip of his cock.

I can feel his own desire, barely held back by his self-control, his determination to torment me, and I let my own emotions go completely. If I can feel him, then he can feel me, and I wallow in the passion that was threatening to overwhelm me, letting it swamp me completely.

It works.

He groans and then his cock is pushing inside of me, stretching me open so wonderfully as he thrusts forward. My pussy shudders around the bumps and curves of his shaft, my clit practically pulsing with joy when his *prime seela* slides around it. I cannot use my arms, but my legs wrap around his hips, pulling him into me until he is completely buried in my aching pussy.

I moan against his lips as he recedes, and then cry out again when I feel the nanotech from my belt trickling down the crease of my bottom and sliding into my ass, quickly thickening and stretching the tiny hole. The sudden double penetration is shockingly erotic. I am so completely full of him, our passion twisting around each other... It's like we've completely opened ourselves to each other, to our love. I no longer have any doubts that he's real and he no longer is trying to hold back from me.

That's when it happens.

The hot pleasure is interrupted by a sudden stabbing pain on my arm.

"Ow!" I tear my lips away from Bogdan, my head jerking around to see the problem. My arm throbs but the skin is unbroken. A jewel-like shape of thin golden lines appears, pulsing lightly. "What the—"

"My Pareena," Bogdan murmurs, his tone almost savagely possessive. Startled, I look up at him and see him staring at his own arm where a similar image glows. I thought I was in tune with his emotions before, but now I can feel *everything* rushing through me—wonder, ecstasy, heart-bursting happiness.

And love. So much love. His eyes are shining as he meets my gaze, a smile unlike any other spreading across his lips.

"These are our bond marks," he says reverently.

"I can feel you," I whisper. "It feels..." My voice trails off as I try to find the right words.

"Like coming home. You are my home, Pareena."

For a being who has lost his home and spent centuries without, that means *everything*. Tears spark in my eyes, choking me and I can't speak, so instead I arch my back and lift my head, pushing up to meet his lips in another passionate kiss. The mark on my arm tingles and suddenly he's thrusting into me in a frenzy.

His seela latch onto my pussy and I scream against his lips, my orgasm exploding in a fit of ecstasy that consumes me heart, body, and soul.

~

Bogdan

MY PAREENA.

Completely mine now. By choice and by the mark. I cannot decide which gives me more satisfaction. Curled up with her in my arms, our bodies sated from pleasure, I feel... at rest. Peaceful in a way that I had never expected to feel again. I mourn the loss of Harai and the life that might have been, but I think she would be happy to see me where I am now.

I am happy to be where I am now. I wish it had not come at such a cost... but I cannot change what happened to my people. All I can do is try and work to better their future.

"Bogdan?" My Pareena's fingers stroke down the center of my chest, as though she is petting me. "Are you serious about considering evidence of the Vgotha's innocence?"

I wonder if the bond allows her to follow my thoughts as well as my emotions or if the Vgotha are just at the forefront of her mind as well. "I do not know if I can fully forgive them. They have fought with us many times. And the losses of Kalexston and Borodem are fresh in all our minds."

"Mine too," she says quietly, shifting slightly in my arms so that she can look into my eyes. I see the sadness there, feel it in my heart. "But... Tor lost warriors as well. And poor choices were made by both sides that led to those losses." A small smile curves her face, although there is not much humor in it. "Neither Tsenturions nor Vgotha seem to be very good at talking."

"Then it is a very good thing that we have you and Dawn now." I brush her hair back from her face. "You are both very good at talking."

"I have a *degree* in talking," my Pareena says, and this

time her eyes sparkle with real amusement. "I just... you're going to consider what the Vgotha have said, right?"

"For you, my Pareena, I will consider anything. For you have proven anything is possible." It will not be easy, and I do not know how the rest of the warriors will feel, but for her I will try.

She leans in for a kiss, but before our lips meet, a chime from the bridge com interrupts. I still, fully alert.

"Bogdan, you're needed on the bridge." Medik's voice harsher than usual. Something is wrong.

"What is it?" I rise to my feet, shifting seamlessly into warrior mode, protectiveness surging through me.

"Vgotha ships are departing the planet."

29

P areena

THE VGOTHA ARE LEAVING the planet? Although, it makes sense. If they stay there, even hidden from the Tsenturion scans, they are vulnerable because the Tsenturions and therefore the Jabol—know exactly where they are.

"*Drakk*," Bogdan races to the door and I scramble to follow, snatching up a gown that's laying on the couch as I go. It'll be faster to put on than the jeans and t-shirt. As the doors open, Bogdan realizes I'm right behind him and he turns to face me, pointing his finger back toward the bed. "Stay here, you need to rest."

"No." My voice wobbles but I take the opportunity to tug my dress on over my head before putting my hands on my hips. "If they're attacking, I want to know. I *need* to know. I feel responsible." If he locks me in, I'll figure out a way to override the door and deal with the punishment later. "Please, Bogdan, I need this."

He hesitates for only a moment. "Very well," he says finally. "But you stay at my side and follow orders at all times. You must be silent while we are on the bridge."

"I understand," I nod vigorously. Hand in hand, we race to the bridge, passing warriors on the way who are all scrambling to reach their stations. I only hope we're not too late.

As soon as the turbo lift opens onto the bridge, Bogdan practically leaps out. The Vgotha ships on are the screens and Arkdhem is barking orders to aim weapons at them. Medik stands off to the side, his expression blank, and I can't help but wonder if Arkdhem even knows that Medik called Bogdan. My heart jumps into my throat... is Arkdhem about to start a new battle?!

I hover at the back of the room, next to the lift, not wanting to distract any of them—and definitely not wanting to get in Bogdan's way.

"Hold fire," Bogdan orders, overtop of Arkdhem. The Vgotha fleet is rising from the planet on the screen and I realize it's not a scan—we can actually see them. Arkdhem turns to glare at Bogdan, his armor streaking red with anger.

"I am not attacking," he snaps, bristling. "I am preparing us in case *they* attack."

"They are flying away from us," Bogdan says harshly, and I can feel his mistrust of Arkdhem's motives. He looks around at the other warriors on the Bridge. "We will not fire on the Vgotha unless they fire on us first."

"But Commander..." I recognize Corin, who looks distraught at Bogdan's orders. I bite my lip. He and Borodem were good friends, I can only imagine how he's feeling right now. Bogdan was right. This is not going to be easy. Even though the Jabol are ultimately the ones at fault, it is the Vgotha who have directly caused their losses. That the Tsenturions have caused the Vgotha loss as well may or may not matter to a grief-stricken warrior.

"What?" All the officers besides Bogdan look shocked.

"You heard me," Bogdan folds his arms over his chest, glowering harder than ever. *Glower Maxima!* It's almost as good as a Harry Potter spell. The officers all put their heads down and avoid his gaze. Even Corin bows his head and turns away, although I can see the muscle in his jaw clenching with anger.

The lift slides open beside me again and the High Commander strides on deck, Dawn following him a few steps behind, the same way I had done with Bogdan. She's pale and looks relieved to see me, sidling over to stand beside me. We grip hands, the same way we did in the forest, looking to each other for support while surrounded by warriors whom we know will disagree with what we think should happen.

"Report," Gavrill demands in a sharp voice.

"High Commander, the Vgotha ships are retreating from the planet," Arkdhem replies, standing at attention. "When they were visible on screen, I prepared us for battle, in case they engaged. Bogdan arrived on the bridge shortly before you and countermanded an order I hadn't yet given." He glares at Bogdan, but it's not as impressive as Bogdan's glower. I don't think anyone can glower as well as my mate.

I know that's a weird thing to be proud of, but it kind of reminds me of Alan Rickman's best Snape glare and, well... it's hot.

"Please, High Commander... Why aren't we attacking?" Corin asks, although his question is closer to a demand. He flings his arm at the screen, pointing. "They're *right there.*"

Gavrill hesitates for a long moment and the warriors stare at him, obviously picking up on the fact that something has changed. Several of them glance at Bogdan and then Arkdhem, confusion and worry creasing their brows. I know that Gavrill didn't want to tell everyone the message Tor sent Dawn and I back with, but I'm a little worried that if he doesn't say *something*, this may end up as a mutiny situation.

"It is possible…" He says the words slowly, almost quietly, and then clears his throat to speak a little louder. "It is possible the Vgotha were not responsible for the destruction of Tsentur. You all know our Tributes returned to us unexpectedly. The Vgotha let them go, sending a message for me with them."

"It's a trick!" Corin snaps out immediately and I don't miss the fact that Arkdhem immediately nods in agreement.

"It may be," Gavrill says seriously. "But until we know, we are *not* going to engage with the Vgotha. The High Command is still reviewing the message the Tributes brought us and we will decide on our next course of action soon."

"We can't just… let them go!" Corin fumes. "They killed Borodem today. Kalexston." A murmur of agreement, soft but noticeable, travels around the bridge. Dawn and I both tense. I'd known that this wouldn't be easy news for the Tsenturions to digest, but seeing it play out in front of me really drives that home.

"And we killed some of theirs. If what the Vgotha say is true, all of those deaths lie at the hands of those who made it appear that the Vgotha were the ones who destroyed Tsentur." Gavrill is very careful to talk around exactly *who* the Vgotha have accused of doing so, and I can't blame him.

The officers on the bridge are already on edge. Accusing

the Jabol... it could push them over it, whether or not they believe it's even possible. I bite my lip to keep from speaking. It is part of my personality to want to keep the peace, but I don't know if I could say anything that would help right now. As if sensing my thoughts—and he very well might be—Bogdan glances at me and gives me a subtle shake of his head.

"I will not have it!" Corin shouts, slamming his fist down. "We cannot disregard the deaths of our warriors—"

"Stand down, officer," Gavrill says sharply. The very air in the room is thick with tension and I feel like I can barely breathe. On screen, the Vgotha fleet suddenly disappears, streaking away from both the planet and the Tsenturions, and Dawn and I both let out relieved sighs. Unfortunately, that draws all eyes to us, and we immediately stiffen again.

Not all of those gazes are friendly anymore.

"You're making a mistake," Corin says acidly, turning his hostile gaze back to Gavrill. "You've become soft. The Tributes have made you emotional. Weak. They have been easily tricked with Vgotha lies, but you should be better than that."

"Officer," Medik puts his hand on Corin's shoulder in an attempt to console him, coming up to him from behind, but Corin whirls, shoving the older man away in anger. Taken unaware, Medik goes flying and falls against a console. Dawn and I cry out. Several officers rush to help the fallen older warrior. I can see the expression of regret that immediately crosses Corin's face when he realizes what he's done.

"Warrior Corin!" Gavrill's voice roars out. "You will stand down and present yourself to the brig for disciplinary matters."

Still rigid with anger, Corin flexes his fists and then nods his head. He walks briskly to the lift, and both Dawn and I shrink back as he approaches, afraid of the fury-fueled grief roiling over his armor. He doesn't even look at us as he passes. Our movement takes us closer to Medik and Dawn pulls me along with her, obviously concerned.

"Are you all right?" She asks, as Arkdhem helps the older warrior to his feet.

"I'm fine," Medik reassures her, although he doesn't have his usual air of quiet confidence about him. "He tried to pull his force at the last moment. He just caught me off balance."

Gavrill begins speaking again, addressing all of the warriors on the bridge, and we fall quiet. "We are reviewing evidence and will provide a debrief soon. For now, you will not speak of any of this outside of this room."

I wonder how many times he'll have to say that before this is all over.

There are some hard decisions to be made soon. I'm glad I don't have to make them.

Nodding at Arkdhem, Gavrill turns to collect Dawn, silently passing command of the bridge back to his third.

"Warriors, stand down," Arkdhem says. There is bitterness in his tone. Whether it's because he realizes Medik didn't trust him and called Gavrill and Bogdan to the bridge, or because he wanted to attack the Vgotha and was thwarted, I do not know.

~

Bogdan

I PUT my hand on the back of my Pareena's neck. She is staring at Arkdhem again, but now I can feel all of her emotions and I do not worry over why. She is suspicious of him and somewhat concerned, none of which sparks even the slightest hint of jealousy or possessiveness.

Of course, the mate mark on her arm does not hurt.

Guiding her away from the bridge and into the lift, I stroke her mate mark with my free hand, just as Tribute Dawn looks over at us and the doors close.

"Oh my... you have your mate mark!" Tribute Dawn squeals in delight. I feel my Pareena's surge of answering happiness. Then Tribute Dawn's eyes move to me and they widen. "And your suit has changed!"

Indeed, it has. I am surprised she has not noticed before now, but it is not a very showy change. My armor's default color is still the endless black of space, but with the glitter of a swirling nebula now in its depths.

"It sparkles," Pareena announces proudly.

What? "No—"

"It totally does!" Tribute Dawn gushes.

"I am a warrior." I glower at both of them, which for some reason makes my Pareena feel both happy and proud. I had thought the same on the bridge, but I do not understand the reaction. I glower harder. "I do not sparkle."

"If you say so." Tribute Dawn turns away but she's grinning. So is the High Commander.

"It's a little sparkly," Pareena murmurs. I give her a look. *Behave.* She shivers happily as she feels the erotic threat emanating from me.

"Congratulations," the High Commander says, his fingers seeking out his Tribute's mate mark to stroke. The two of them exchange a look and Tribute Dawn smiles, her hand moving overtop her stomach.

"We have some news of our own." Tribute Dawn blurts out. "Gavrill wanted to keep it a secret but I have to tell somebody and you two should definitely know." The High

Commander beams rather than chiding her for disobeying his wishes and a suspicion rises inside me. My Pareena is much quicker to leap to a conclusion.

"What? No!" Pareena gasps.

"Yes!" Dawn squeals. "I'm pregnant!"

Gavrill clears his throat. "We do need to keep this between us and Medik for a time." A wrinkle grows between his brows, probably because he cannot help but think of the other things that we must keep between us for now, but when he looks at his Tribute his expression softens.

"Is everything all right?" Pareena asks. "Everything's... normal?"

"So far tests are all good. I'm healthy," Tribute Dawn assures her. "Medik realized it when he scanned us after we returned and told us privately."

It was probably a good thing she did not know before the Vgotha captured her. I cannot imagine how much worse the High Commander's reaction would have been if he'd known his Tribute was breeding when she was taken. My Pareena leans in to hug her friend tightly in congratulations. I look at Tribute Dawn's stomach, but so far, I cannot see any difference.

She carries the hope of our race in her womb... and the proof of the Tribute's compatibility only makes the situation with the Jabol more fraught, but still, I feel joy at the news.

"So, what now?" Dawn asks, snuggling into her mate. "Are you going to tell the warriors about the Jabol?"

"I will have to eventually," he says, exchanging a worried look with me. As Corin and Arkdhem have shown us, not all of them will take it well. "First, I must tell them that the Vgotha may not be the enemy we thought. I will tell them about the Riknari. The fleet retreating rather than attacking will help. That they attacked in order to take you captive and killed two of our warriors..." He sighs. "It will take some time. But in the meantime, we can search for answers. We cannot allow the Jabol to know our plans, so we will have to pretend to continue hunting Vgotha, but really, we will be hunting for proof. I want to try to contact the Riknari myself, if it is possible, to see what they say."

The doors to the lift open, effectively ending the conversation. We cannot talk about any of this in the halls of the ship. Not yet.

"Are you okay with this?" Pareena whispers to me as I lead her back to our room. "It's a lot to take in."

She is right. And in times past, I would have raged louder than Arkdhem.

So much has changed. But the biggest changes are inside of me.

I do not want to lay down my weapons before I have avenged my family and my people, but my first duty is to my Tribute.

"Whatever the future holds, I will rise to greet it. As long as I have you, my Pareena," I whisper back. I feel her love wrap around me.

Despite the many unknowns in our lives right now, I feel a happiness that I had never hoped for. We have more challenges to face, but nothing feels insurmountable with my Pareena by my side.

EPILOGUE

~

Marta

In the fading light of evening, I am dragged back to consciousness with a pained groan. My forehead pulses with agony, stabbing splinters radiating through my whole body.

What happened?

A cough clutches my chest and I whine and sputter trying to breathe, the renewed pain threatening to pull me under again. At least the ringing in my ears has stopped.

Ringing from the explosion. A fucking bomb??? Fucking cartel.

Miraculously, other than a sharp knock when everything fell, my head is clear of the wreckage. My right arm flops when I try to move it to wipe dust from my face, but after a long moment I manage to get it working. My left arm throbs painfully but won't move and after an initial attempt, I don't try again. The right is enough. Grit scratches my cheek but I scrub my eyes clear enough to open them. It's just light enough that I can assess the damage... and I almost wish I couldn't.

My legs and torso are hidden, trapped under rubble of the building that practically came down around me. I can't feel them, but going by the weight they're under, I'm thankful that they're numb. That or I'm going to start feeling them any minute and it's going to be awful. This is definitely the worst situation I've ever found myself in.

I try to take a deep breath and fire flashes along my side. *Internal organ damage? Highly possible.* My right hand explores my head. *Mild contusions, probable concussion.* My left arm can't move at all. *Broken... possible shoulder dislocation.*

Situation: desperate.

Think, Marta.

My cell phone is in my pocket. It's basically a satellite phone. With the places I go, it's best to always be connected to some form of communication. I force my arm to go fishing until darkness invades the edges of my vision. When I draw my hand up, it's bright red. More liquid leaks out onto the dusty rubble beside me. A small pool, dark and growing.

That's a lot of blood. Too much blood.

I'm so fucked.

A strange sort of resigned sadness trickles over me and I sigh, leaning my head back and resting for a moment. The sky beyond the squat buildings of the Barrio is so pretty. Pale pink tinged with gold.

There are shouts in the distance, honking cars. But the cartel owns this part of town. If they blow one of their own buildings, no one will come to investigate.

"Be safe," My mother had pled with me before she died. *"That job is going to get you killed."*

She feared for me as she'd feared for my father, another fallen soldier in the fight for truth.

Sorry Mama... you were right. Again.

No one is coming to help.

No one even knew I was here, chasing a whisper of a lead about an American billionaire making bank—and not just through his pharmaceutical companies but from other drugs as well. Last time I checked in with my managing editor, I was in Mexico City. She doesn't expect me to check in for another day. There's no way I'm going to live that long.

My breath claws through my middle. I could try again to dig out my cell phone, but I have even less energy than I did before. Judging from the amount of blood leaking onto the ground, I don't have much longer.

I definitely hadn't wanted everything to end this way... on the brink of exposing corruption without managing to file my final story. I'd wanted my life to matter. If I'd at least managed to find the proof I was looking for and send the story to my editor before I died, I would have thought this sucked but... at least it would have been worthwhile. Instead, I'm going to die a failure.

And in so much fucking pain.

I force myself to relax on my uncomfortable, rubble-strewn bed, and let my breathing slow. The sun is almost gone now, gilding the horizon with fire. *My last sunset.* So beautiful. I close my eyes. I feel like it's just for a moment, but when I open them again it's full dark and something shimmers in the corner of my vision. My brain feels muzzy. Did I lose consciousness again? The minutes slipping away with my life blood...

I crane my head to distract myself, trying to see what is glowing, and a bright rectangle greets me, shining in the rubble.

My e-reader.

Huh.

I reach out and my hand falls on the smooth surface. I scrape my knuckles against the rocks but when I draw the device to me, it's unharmed. The screen has not a single crack. Unbelievable. And it's on... I guess somehow the explosion hit the power button and it didn't automatically turn off. So I must not have been unconscious for as long as it feels like.

I wipe my bloody fingers on the inside of my collar to clean them as best I can before clearing the screen of dust. I never knew who sent the mysterious device. I assumed it was a co-worker's idea of a joke, loading up a next generation reader with tons of naughty erotic stories, but when I asked around, no one confessed.

I am so glad it is here now. The home screen glows to greet me like an old friend. It has no data and can't connect to Wi-Fi—no calling for help—but its familiar presence soothes me.

At least I can die doing my favorite thing—reading. The pain I'm in is debilitating, but hopefully this will help distract me from... everything.

Before following a man that I am pretty sure runs the local section of the cartel, I'd just finished reading a hot alien abduction story. It opens right to the end of the last book in the Trilogy, but instead of the last page of the book, the e-reader screen flashes with a question I'd never seen before.

Are you Marta Flores Romero?

My lips move with the question. Huh. Weird. I should not be connected to Wi-Fi but... hey, if someone is asking, I'll answer. Maybe they can send help? The hope that rises in me is almost shocking.

Yes, I press the blinking answer.

Do you want to die today?

Holy hell.

No, I press the button. I really, really don't want to die. Duh. My lips move, forming words that I don't have the energy to actually speak. *Help me.*

Tears begin to slide down my face, blurring the screen's instructions.

<Swipe right for abduction>

I try to move my finger, but I can't. The pain is gone, the numbness spread from my lower half to my shoulders, creeping up my neck.

Marta Flores Romero, the device beeps. *<Swipe right for abduction>* The button flashes. I can't move.

Subject's vitals are failing. Initiating emergency sequence.

A pulse of light rolls over me and the pile of rubble, expanding like a sunrise.

And everything goes dark.

~

Arkdhem

Silently seething, I can only watch as the shuttle carrying the High Commander, Bogdan, both Tributes, and a small team of warriors descends back to the planet. The warriors the High Commander had instructed to find the place where the Vgotha had been hiding had been unsuccessful. The Tributes have convinced him to take them back down again to see if they can find the cave they'd been held in.

We *could* be pursuing the Vgotha fleet, but instead I am stuck on the bridge, useless, while the High Commander and Bogdan risk their Tributes yet again. We are fairly certain the Vgotha have fled the planet entirely, but there is no way to be sure. Not only that, but we don't know all the dangers that the planet offers. And the Vgotha could have left traps.

All points which I made when the High Commander informed me of his plans, and which were dismissed.

Just as I was dismissed.

Twice now, I've had the responsibility of protecting the High Commander's Tribute, and twice now I have failed. Which was why I've been left behind this time. The High Commander said it was because someone must stay in overall command of the ship, since he planned to be on-planet for as many cycles as it took to find the Vgotha's planet side base of operations, but I know it is because the High Commander has lost faith in me.

In fact, it now seems as though the High Commander has more faith in the Vgotha than he does in me, his third in command. The entire reason he wants to find their base of operations is to see if they left anything that will help prove they are innocent of destroying Tsentur. Something I find very difficult to believe.

If they are innocent, why hadn't they tried to meet with the High Commander before?

If the Jabol are guilty, why are they trying to perpetuate the Tsenturion race by providing us with Tributes?

I find it very convenient that the Vgotha are suddenly claiming innocence and providing dubious 'proof' against the Jabol. It could be completely fake. It is suspicious that right when the Jabol have finally found compatible mates for the Tsenturions the Vgotha found evidence that they were set up. If the Vgotha's goal is the complete destruction of the Tsenturions, then of course they would want to inter-fere with our matings. If they succeed in doing so, then they can just keep running, secure in the knowledge that we will eventually die out, because we cannot breed.

The High Commander acknowledged all the points I made, all the questions I asked, and then decided to go planet side without me anyway. He was far more swayed by Tribute Dawn's belief that we have all been duped. I don't blame her. We have become close and I understand she holds some resentment toward the Jabol for abducting her from her former home and life, even though she is happy now. She hadn't liked the Tribute program to begin with. But, in this, she is wrong and she is leading the High Commander astray.

The warriors look at her and Pareena and see our futures... all of which was provided by the Jabol. Everything the Vgotha claim would shatter that... it would destroy us a second time, in a blow possibly even more devastating than the first because it would be the eradication of hope.

I cannot accept that.

And I am not the only one.

Corin had not been present on the bridge when the High Commander had ordered the warriors not to speak of the Vgotha's claim. He ran into more than one warrior and told them what he knew, on his way to be disciplined after attacking Medik. Word spread quickly, and the warriors are torn on whether or not to believe the Vgotha. Most of them feel as Corin and I do—the Vgotha cannot not be trusted.

Many of them are unhappy to be in orbit above the planet, rather than pursuing the Vgotha fleet. I heard the mutterings when the High Commander opted not to follow the Vgotha fleet and investigate the planet instead. I obey my orders, though, and have not told anyone that the Vgotha have accused the Jabol of being the real attackers.

The entire fleet would have likely torn itself apart at the news, which also would have served Vgotha purposes.

By their accusations, they have set us up perfectly to destroy ourselves. Thankfully, Dawn and Pareena decided to share the message the Vgotha gave them with the high command only. The Vgotha had likely been counting on them blurting out the lies in front of multiple warriors.

Halfway through my shift, during which nothing happens because the Vgotha have fled and we are still just circling this *drakk* planet, the bridge com chimes with an incoming transmission from the shuttle. I nod at Jakar, who opens the channel. The High Commander's face appears on the main bridge screen.

"Commander Arkdhem, we have located the Vgotha's den, with the help of our Tributes. The location is secure and there are vestiges of their technology that were left behind. Their base was very large, and it will take us time to search through it."

"Yes, High Commander," I respond dutifully. "Will the Tributes be returning to the Command ship?"

The High Commander's armor flickers and he shakes his head, his expression changing slightly, to one I recognize. Dawn has talked him into something. It is an expression I've worn often enough as well. Although, I do not fight against indulging her the way the High Commander sometimes does. If—*when*—I receive a Tribute of my own, I will happily indulge her every whim as long as it does not affect her safety.

In my opinion, the High Commander indulges too many of the wrong whims of his Tribute, but it is not my place to ever express such an opinion.

"Dawn and Tribute Pareena will be staying planet-side with us," the High Commander says, sounding slightly pained. "They are the only ones who have personal experience with the Vgotha technology. They also wish to observe the Earth custom of a 'honeymoon' and spend some time off ship with their mates."

From my conversations with Dawn, I know what a honeymoon is, and I nod my understanding. This is likely as close as she thought she could get to the Earth custom. I would not allow it of my own Tribute, at least, I would have found her a much safer location. One that hadn't recently served as a Vgotha stronghold and didn't have the risk of being riddled with Vgotha traps. I've already made my opinion clear to the High Commander and repeating myself in front of other warriors will only be to my detriment.

"Deep in the caves our tech can only communicate short-range and it does not seem to reach beyond the cave system, so you will be the acting High Commander while I am on planet," he finishes with a nod.

"Thank you, High Commander," I reply, keeping my expression solemn. It is an empty gesture of faith, as he has already privately given me orders.

Keep the fleet orbiting around the planet. Watch out for incoming Vgotha or Jabol ships. Do not engage unless you are attacked first. I will return once we have thoroughly investigated their base here.

I am just here to keep the chain of command, not actually use it.

At the end of my shift I return to my room and throw myself on the bed mat. The empty bed mat that I long to share with a Tribute. I thought perhaps Pareena... but she was too enthralled with Bogdan, even though he did not deserve her. Had not even wanted her. Hadn't wanted anyone else to have one either. But now he has her... and the

Vgotha's claims threaten the ability of the rest of us to even hope for a Tribute. My fists clench in anger.

But there is nothing I can do.

My door chimes. Someone is there.

Forcing myself to my feet, I answer it, and am surprised to see Medik standing there, his expression agonizingly conflicted. I cannot recall the last time I saw him so agitated.

"What is wrong?" I ask immediately, my armor spreading over my skin in reaction. I know we are not under attack, because the bridge would have informed me, but something is clearly wrong.

Medik looks over his shoulder, stepping into my room and I step back, surprised by the furtiveness of his actions. But when he speaks, I understand.

"Frllil has contacted me. Another Tribute is ready for pickup." And he does not know what to do. How to respond. So, he has come to me, the figurehead acting High Commander while the real High Commander and his second-in-command are planet side, cavorting with *their* Tributes. I know that description is not entirely fair, but I also know that there will be plenty of time when they are *not* working and investigating. Dawn was very clear on the purpose of a honeymoon.

Drakk.

"What should we do? We can't leave her there with them... if they... if..." Medik's voice trails off and I realize that he also thinks the Vgotha's lies might be valid.

I have no fear of the Jabol. I do not believe they are anything more than our allies, but I grab onto his excuse for breaking the High Commander's orders.

"Of course, we cannot," I say immediately. It is true enough, after all. Surely if the High Commander were here, he would agree. If the Jabol are everything the Vgotha claim, we cannot leave an innocent human female in their grasp. That I do not believe the Vgotha lies makes no difference. My actions will be the same. "I will send a War Ship to collect her. The rest of the fleet and the Command Ship will remain here, in orbit, as the High Commander ordered."

Medik relaxes. "Good, good." He smiles at me and I realize he truly was worried. It is amazing how the lies of our enemies can undermine even the most secure of alliances. "And congratulations, Commander. I did not want to tell you, in case it would have affected your decision, but Frllil said this Tribute is matched to you."

To me.

My tribute.

My armor flashes bright gold and Medik's smile broadens. I can see the relief in his expression. Clapping me on the shoulder, he nods and then exits my room, leaving me standing there with my universe turned upside down for the second time in my life.

Immediately, I spring into action, calling into the bridge and ordering a War Ship fueled and prepared to retrieve the Tribute—*my* Tribute—from Frllil's waystation. A War Ship that I will be on. The High Commander will understand my absence, when he is informed of it, given such momentous tidings, and my presence is unnecessary anyway.

It won't be long now. Anticipation rushes through me as I hurry through the corridors. Soon, I will possess her. My Tribute. My Future. My Mate.

She is waiting for me.

I am coming, my heart.

～

THANK you for reading Alien Tribute! We're grateful to all who read Alien Captive, demanded Bogdan & Pareena's book and waited patiently—or not so patiently—until we wrote it. Now you have to wait for Arkdhem & Marta's book. (*evil cackle*)

Thank you also to Miranda and Jane for editing and proofreading, and our lovely beta readers—Katherine, Nick, Karen, Marie, Annie, Marta, and Jessica. We couldn't do this without you!!!!

Check out Dawn & Gavrill's story in Alien Captive (if you haven't yet) if you want more alien goodness. -- Golden Angel & Lee

ABOUT LEE SAVINO

Lee Savino is a USA today bestselling author, mom and choco-holic.

Warning: Do not read her Berserker series, or you will be addicted to the huge, dominant warriors who will stop at nothing to claim their mates.

I repeat: Do. Not. Read. The Berserker Saga. Especially not the hot excerpt on the next page...

Download a free book from www.leesavino.com (don't read that, either. Too much hot sexy lovin').

EXCERPT: SOLD TO THE BERSERKERS

A MÉNAGE SHIFTER ROMANCE

By Lee Savino

I woke tied to a tree.

The light was lower, heralding dusk. I struggled silently, frantic gasps escaping from my scarred throat. My stepfather stepped into view and I felt a second of relief at a familiar face, before remembering the evil this man had wrought on my body. Whatever he was planning, it would bode ill for me, and my younger sisters. If I didn't survive, they would eventually share the same fate as mine.

"You're awake," he said. "Just in time for the sale."

I strained but my bonds held fast. As my stepfather approached, I realized that the scarf that I wrapped around my neck to hide my scars had fallen, exposing them. Out of habit, I twitched my head to the side, tucking my bad side towards my shoulder.

My stepfather smirked.

"So ugly," he sneered. "I could never find a husband for you, but I found someone to take you. A group of warriors passing through who saw you, and want to slake their lust on your body. Who knows, if you please them, they may let you live. But I doubt you'll survive these men. They're foreigners, mercenaries, come to fight for the king. Berserkers. If you're lucky your death will be swift when they tear you apart."

I'd heard the tales of berserker warriors, fearsome warriors of old. Ageless, timeless, they'd sailed over the seas to the land, plundering, killing, taking slaves, they fought for our kings, and their own. Nothing could stand in their path when they went into a killing rage.

I fought to keep my fear off my face. Berserker's were a myth, so my stepfather had probably sold me to a band of passing soldiers who would take their pleasure from my flesh before leaving me for dead, or selling me on.

"I could've sold you long ago, if I stripped you bare and put a bag over you head to hide those scars."

His hands pawed at me, and I shied away from his disgusting breath. He slapped me, then tore at my braid, letting my hair spill over my face and shoulders.

Bound as I was, I still could glare at him. I could do nothing to stop the sale, but I hoped my fierce expression told him I'd fight to the death if he tried to force himself on me.

His hand started to wander down towards my breast when a shadow moved on the edge of the clearing. It caught my eye and I startled. My stepfather stepped back as the warriors poured from the trees.

My first thought was that they were not men, but beasts. They prowled forward, dark shapes almost one with the shadows. A few wore animal pelts and held back, lurking on the edge of the woods. Two came forward, wearing the garb of warriors, bristling with weapons. One had dark hair, and the other long, dirty blond with a beard to match.

Their eyes glowed with a terrifying light.

As they approached, the smell of raw meat and blood wafted over us, and my stomach twisted. I was glad my stepfather hadn't fed me all day, or I would've emptied my guts on the ground.

My stepfather's face and tone took on the wheedling expression I'd seen when he was selling in the market.

"Good evening, sirs," he cringed before the largest, the blond with hair streaming down his chest.

They were perfectly silent, but the blond approached, fixing me with strange golden eyes.

Their faces were fair enough, but their hulking forms and the quick, light way they moved made me catch my breath. I had never seen such massive men. Beside them, my stepfather looked like an ugly dwarf.

"This is the one you wanted," my stepfather continued. "She's healthy and strong. She will be a good slave for you."

My body would've shaken with terror, if I were not bound so tightly.

A dark haired warrior stepped up beside the blond and the two exchanged a look.

"You asked for the one with scars." My stepfather took my hair and jerked my head back, exposing the horrible, silvery mass. I shut my eyes, tears squeezing out at the sudden pain and humiliation.

The next thing I knew, my stepfather's grip loosened. A grunt, and I opened my eyes to see the dark haired warrior standing at my side. My stepfather sprawled on the ground as if he'd been pushed.

The blond leader prodded a boot into my stepfather's side.

"Get up," the blond said, in a voice that was more a

growl than a human sound. It curdled my blood. My stepfather scrambled to his feet.

The black haired man cut away the last of my bonds, and I sagged forward. I would've fallen but he caught me easily and set me on my feet, keeping his arms around me. I was not the smallest woman, but he was a giant. Muscles bulged in his arms and chest, but he held me carefully. I stared at him, taking in his raven dark hair and strange gold eyes.

He tucked me closer to his muscled body.

Meanwhile, my stepfather whined. "I just wanted to show you the scars—"

Again that frightening growl from the blond. "You don't touch what is ours."

"I don't want to touch her." My stepfather spat.

Despite myself, I cowered against the man who held me. A stranger I had never met, he was still a safer haven than my stepfather.

"I only wish to make sure you are satisfied, milords. Do you want to sample her?" my stepfather asked in an evil tone. He wanted to see me torn apart.

A growl rumbled under my ear and I lifted my head. Who were these men, these great warriors who had bought and paid for me? The arms around my body were strong and solid, inescapable, but the gold eyes looking down at me were kind. The warrior ran his thumb across the pad of my lips, and his fingers were gentle for such a large, violent looking warrior. Under the scent of blood, he smelled of snow and sharp cold, a clean scent.

He pressed his face against my head, breathing in a deep breath.

The blond was looking at us.

"It's her," the black haired man growled, his voice so guttural. "This is the one."

One of his hands came to cover the side of my face and throat, holding my face to his chest in a protective gesture.

I closed my eyes, relaxing in the solid warmth of the warrior's body.

A clink of gold, and the deed was done. I'd been sold.

～

SOLD TO THE BERSERKERS

When Brenna's father sells her to a band of passing warriors, her only thought is to survive. She doesn't expect to be claimed by the two fearsome warriors who lead the Berserker clan. Kept in captivity, she is coddled and cared for, treated more like a savior than a slave. Can captivity lead to love? And when she discovers the truth behind the myth of the fearsome warriors, can she accept her place as the Berserkers' true mate?

~

Sold to the Berserkers is a standalone, short, MFM ménage romance starring two huge, dominant warriors who make it all about the woman. Read now in the Berserker Saga (on sale now).

ALSO BY LEE SAVINO

Sci Fi Romance

Draekons (Dragons in Exile) with Lili Zander (menage alien dragons)

Crashed spaceship. Prison planet. Two big, hulking, bronzed aliens who turn into dragons. The best part? The dragons insist I'm their mate.

Paranormal romance

The Berserker Saga and Berserker Brides (menage werewolves)

These fierce warriors will stop at nothing to claim their mates.

Bad Boy Alphas with Renee Rose (bad boy werewolves)

Never ever date a werewolf.

Contemporary Romance

Royal Bad Boy

I'm not falling in love with my arrogant, annoying, sex god boss. Nope. No way.

Royally Fake Fiancé

The Duke of New Arcadia has an image problem only a fiancé can fix. And I'm the lucky lady he's chosen to play Cinderella.

Beauty & The Lumberjacks

After this logging season, I'm giving up sex. For...reasons.

Her Marine Daddy

My hot Marine hero wants me to call him daddy...

Her Dueling Daddies

Two daddies are better than one.

Innocence: dark mafia romance with Stasia Black

I'm the king of the criminal underworld. I always get what I want. And she is my obsession.

Beauty's Beast: a dark romance with Stasia Black

Years ago, Daphne's father stole from me. Now it's time for her to pay her family's debt...with her body.

ABOUT GOLDEN ANGEL

Angel is an international best-selling BDSM and interracial romance author and self-described bibliophile with a "kinky" bent who loves to write stories for the characters in her head. If she didn't get them out, she's pretty sure she'd go just a little crazy.

She is happily married, old enough to know better but still too young to care, and a big fan of happily-ever-afters, strong heroes and heroines, and sizzling chemistry.

She believes the world is a better place when there's a little magic in it.

Sign up for the Angel Legion newsletter here - https://mailchi.mp/9eb82a414844/angelnewsletter - and grab several FREE sexy stories immediately in a welcome message!

Read on for an excerpt from her alien romance, Mated on Hades...

EXCERPT: MATED ON HADES

"Welcome to your new home for the next four twenty-cycles," he said, stepping aside so she could enter the cabin behind him, his tone dryly sarcastic. "As you can see, you would have been better off with my parents."

Rather than telling him that the room was about the size of her entire living space back on Earth—and unlike her home there, this room wasn't crammed with equipment—Jules just looked around as she walked past him. Sparsely furnished, the massive bed on the far wall dominated the whole area. It was even bigger than the bed in her room at Tobik and Sirilla's, and she'd thought *that* was huge.

Turning around, she enjoyed the disgruntled look on Tarrik's face as he set her bag down next to the open closet door. Since his clothing seemed to consist mostly of pants and a kind of tunic vest that she'd seen on a lot of winged Hadesians, there was plenty of space for her meager belongings.

"This looks great," she said. "As long as you keep to your side of the bed."

Now his expression was almost infuriated. "Of course I will. I'm not the one who can't keep her hands to herself."

"Excuse me?" Jules' hands slammed onto her hips as she glared back at him. "Since when have I not kept my hands to myself?"

"Uh, that would be last night when you kissed me."

She gaped. "You kissed me!"

"I sure as hell did not," he snapped back. "I'm not even attracted to you."

"Is that why your cock was digging a hole in my stomach last night when *you kissed me*?"

"Look, just stay on whichever side of the bed you pick, keep your hands to yourself, and this trip will be over before you know it."

Jules was still sputtering and trying to find a good retort as he swept out of the room. *Jerk!* She couldn't believe she'd let him have the last word.

"Stupid butt monkey," she muttered, flopping back onto the bed just to see how it felt. It was ridiculously comfortable of course. Which only made her more irritated with him for some reason, even though he had nothing to do with it.

He'd definitely kissed her first.

At the very least, they'd kissed each other.

Her lips pursed as a wicked idea occurred to her. It would be playing with fire a little bit... but on the other hand, he definitely deserved it. And it would be even more amusing than keeping his ship grounded until her say so.

Just as that thought flickered through her mind, she felt the reverberations of the ship as it began to blast off. Excitement surged. She, Jules, who had never even thought she would see planet other than Earth, was now on her second spaceship this week and off to see a whole *bunch* of planets.

While part of her couldn't help but wonder what was happening back on Earth, if anyone was helping those in need, another part of her was thrilled to be on an adventure. New places, new beings, new things to see and do... If this was how traveling made Tarrik feel, no wonder he didn't want to give it up.

As soon as she thought it, she scowled. She didn't want to feel sympathy for him dammit.

Pushing any thoughts of the alien male aside, Jules made herself get up from the bed and start unpacking. The sooner she was done, the sooner she could explore the ship.

THE SYSTEMS WERE RUNNING PERFECTLY, the entire crew was happy, and Tarrik was feeling a lot better than he'd expected. The only thing that would make this trip better was if Juliette wasn't on board.

Not that she was in the way. No, she was entirely helpful, going out of her way to make herself useful.

Tarrik told himself he wasn't jealous over the way she and Mrik had obviously bonded. They definitely weren't behaving as though they were sexually attracted to each other—Tarrik knew that Mrik would never move on Tarrik's female regardless—but he still got a gnawing feeling in his stomach when he saw them laughing together. It might be more envy than jealousy though... she definitely didn't smile at him that way or laugh with him...

Not that he'd given her any reason to.

Because I don't want to, he reminded himself for the umpteenth time. The problem was that saying it wasn't making it true.

She was beautiful when she smiled. Engaging when she

laughed. The rest of the crew definitely liked her, she'd already made fast friends with his maintenance engineers, Lessys and Sasslys, who were both Vloss and mated to each other. When they asked if Juliette had ever seen anything like them before, she said they looked like miniature Godzillas, without the back plates. The whole crew found this hysterical when Myrik looked up what she was speaking of.

So he wasn't in the best mood by bedtime.

His mood got a hell of a lot worse when he laid down and Juliette announced she was going to take a shower.

"Great," he said. And then nearly choked when she started undressing right in the middle of the bedroom. She pulled her shirt over her head, revealing tanned skin, soft mounds of her breasts filling out her feminine support, a gently rounded stomach that he suddenly ached to draw his tongue over... When she began tugging down her pants, he finally managed to find his voice again even if it did sound like he was being strangled when he spoke. "What the gark are you doing?"

Juliette glanced at him and he bit back a groan as her pants slid to the ground, revealing muscled legs and tight-fitting panties. The white underwear wasn't the sexiest he'd ever seen, it was more utilitarian than anything else, and yet he found he couldn't look away. The temperature in the room seemed to have risen by a few degrees and his tail was lashing back and forth furiously as his cock started to swell.

"I'm taking a shower," she said, blinking at him like he'd said something incomprehensible.

"The shower is in there." Pointing to the facilities, he shifted slightly to hopefully cover up his growing erection.

"Why do you care?" she asked, pulling off her support garment. Tarrik almost whimpered as her rounded, full breasts were revealed, perfectly sized to fit in his palm, with tightly ruched brown nipples just begging for attention. His erection swelled to fullness and his tail had taken on a mind of its own—any attempt to control it was useless. "You're not attracted to me, remember?"

Turning, she bent at the waist to pull her undergarments down, giving him a glorious view of her ass before she sauntered into the bathroom.

Closing his eyes didn't help in the least. The image of her naked body was burned into his retinas. Gark it, he didn't even *want* to forget.

When he heard the water turn on, he did groan, because now all he could think about was the hot water sluicing over her body, caressing her skin the way he wanted to.

Garking...

Laying back in the bed, Tarrik jerked off the tunic he was going to sleep in out of respect for her. Immediately he fisted his hand around his shaft and groaned as he began to pump, closing his eyes and picturing her rounded bottom and the little smirk on her lips... the way the water would slide over her breasts and stomach and down between her legs... he hadn't gotten nearly as close a look of *that* as he'd wanted to.

He'd seen images of nude human females though, and his feverish brain extrapolated for him.

Wet flesh, ripe and ready for him.

He pumped his cock harder, faster as he imagined her bent over for him, the way she had taken off her underwear, his hand slapping against her ass as he pounded into her from behind, his tail twining around her breasts...

He wanted her *bad*.

Pleasure surged and his *jimen* spurted, sticky and hot onto his stomach, leaving him only slightly less wound up.

WAS HE... WAS HE MASTURBATING? JULES' paused as she washed her hair, her body flushing as she heard another low masculine groan, just barely audible to her. Yeah, so much for not being attracted to her.

Of course, she was very much in the same boat. Just stripping down in front of him had given her a little thrill. She'd never known she had a little bit of exhibitionist in her, but she'd definitely gotten turned on feeling his eyes sliding over her naked skin with every article of clothing she'd peeled off. It had made her feel freaking sexy.

Knowing he was out there jerking off after the little show she'd put on...

Well that just made her feel even sexier.

It didn't help that she hadn't gotten laid in... geez, it had been months since her last encounter with the male kind. So she also had a lot of pent-up sexual energy to work off.

Her hands moved over her body, slick and soapy, touching her hard nipples and massaging her breasts before moving down her stomach. Leaning back against the cool wall, she kept one hand on her breast while the other slipped between her pussy lips. Biting her lip to keep her own moans quiet, she closed her eyes and pictured him coming into the bathroom, watching her touch herself...

Then he wouldn't be able to stay back. He'd step in, crowding her in the shower, his body hot and hard against hers as he lifted her up, and she'd wrap her legs around his waist as she slid down his body and right onto his hard cock.

Shuddering, Jules managed to keep her noises to heavy breathing as she rubbed out a hard, fast orgasm that took the edge off but didn't completely satisfy her. She didn't want to take too long in the shower though; she definitely didn't want him to think she was in here getting off to him... the same way she was pretty sure he was getting off to her.

Stepping out of the shower, Jules quickly dried off and went into the main cabin. The lights were already dim and Tarrik was on his side of the bed, the sheets pulled up to his waist and he'd built a wall of cushions down the center of the bed. His muscled chest and arms were clearly visible— he'd taken off his tunic and it lay in a crumpled heap on the floor. Had he been wearing anything else? Or was he naked under the sheet?

Don't think about that!

In the dark, her body thrumming with sexual frustration, Jules was no closer to sleep than she had been when the lights had been turned on. Despite the wall of cushions between them, she was far, far too aware of the insanely sexy alien on the bed with her, less than a foot of distance separating them. How much body heat did a Hadesian emanate? Because she swore she could feel him.

Then she really did feel something, touching her ankle between the sheets, and she shrieked, kicking.

"Sorry, sorry!" Tarrik's deep voice actually sounded sincere. "That was my tail, sorry."

Jules' heart pounded so hard it felt like it was going to go right out of her chest as her fear of the unknown settled.

"Well get your tail under control," she hissed at him, pulling her legs up slightly, closer to her body and telling herself that she definitely was not going to think about the possibilities of a tail that had a mind of its own.

"It's not exactly easy," he hissed back. "I can *smell* your arousal. So don't bother lying and telling me that you aren't."

Heat flushed her cheeks and she was very glad the room was dark enough that he wouldn't be able to see her blush.

"That's just a physical response—and you were the one who started jerking off while I was in the shower!"

"You stripped down in front of me!"

"*You* said you weren't attracted to me!"

"I lied, alright?!" There was a strange ominous red glow in the darkness and suddenly cushions went flying. Tarrik loomed over her, wings spread slightly in his agitation. Holy fracking radiation. He freaking glowed in the dark. "I'm attracted to you, okay? That doesn't mean I want to mate you."

"I don't want to mate you either, you overgrown ignoramus."

"But you want to *fuck* me, right?" From the way he said 'fuck', she could tell he'd looked up the human word at some point but that it wasn't terminology he was used to. The glow of his skin brightened a little more, illuminating her body as he taunted her, his own sexual frustration clear on his face. It was eerie and sexy all at the same time and this time when his tail curled around her ankle, the heat of his flesh warming her skin, she didn't jump or kick.

"Oh shut up and do something useful with your mouth," she snarled back, reaching up to grab his face and pull his lips down to meet hers.

MATED ON HADES

The Celestial Mates agency always knows what - or who - you need.

TARRIK WOULD DO anything to avoid breaking his mother's heart, so he begrudgingly signs up for Celestial Mates and agrees to come home and settle down once the agency finds his match. There's just one catch: he's not ready to give up his free and easy life traveling the galaxy. And he's doing exactly as his mother asked, so what will it hurt if he makes himself as unappealing as possible on his mate application?

JULIETTE IS a woman on the run. Her attitude, and more importantly her hacking skills, have pissed off all the wrong people. Now the target of a contract hit, she's decided the solution to her problems is to leave the planet as fast as she can. The Celestial Mates program is exactly what she needs. By the time her "mate" realizes she's impossible to live with, hopefully it will be safe for her to return to earth. She wasn't counting on a seriously hot alien who looked like the devil and could do the most sinful things with his tail...

THE SPARKS FLY at first meeting when their chemistry ignites. But they can barely stand to be in the same room with each other.

THEY SHOULDN'T WORK AT ALL.

BUT CELESTIAL MATES always knows best.

ALSO BY GOLDEN ANGEL

Free stories on her website

Stronghold Doms and Venus Rising (Contemporary Bdsm)

Bridal Discipline and the Domestic Discipline Quartet
(Victorian Domestic Discipline- this is Lee Savino's favorite!!!!! :)

Big Bad Bunnies (paranormal romance)

Dark erotic romance under the pen name Sinistre Ange

Standalone novels - including a sci fi romance involving an alien who has a naughty tail...

www.ingramcontent.com/pod-product-compliance
Lightning Source LLC
Chambersburg PA
CBHW050515110726
47899CB00005B/1462